LOST WORLDS
SHADOW CREATURES

To Ben,

ANDREW
LANE

Thanks for everything,

MACMILLAN CHILDREN'S BOOKS

First published 2014 by Macmillan Children's Books
a division of Macmillan Publishers Limited
20 New Wharf Road, London N1 9RR
Basingstoke and Oxford
Associated companies throughout the world
www.panmacmillan.com

ISBN 978-1-4472-2800-4

A CIP catalogue record for this book is available from
the British Library.

Typeset by Ellipses Digital Limited, Glasgow
Printed and bound by CPI Group (UK) Ltd, Croydon CR0 4YY

prologue

'Rhino' Gillis jumped aboard the Hong Kong MTR train at Sham Shui Po station. He quickly looked around. Lots of people, most of them with shopping bags or rucksacks, but no sign of the creature he was chasing. He swore quietly to himself. It had to be there *somewhere*.

He glanced at his mobile. Surprisingly, he was still getting a signal below ground, and the map showed that he and the glowing dot that was the creature were nearly in the same place.

When he'd been up on the surface, the tracker had clearly shown the creature travelling in a straight line, crossing roads and passing buildings, much faster than he knew it could travel. Every now and then it would stop for a few minutes, then start moving again. The only possible explanation was that it was below ground, travelling on the Mass Transit Rail system. That was why he'd hailed a taxi, tracked the creature above ground, got the driver to overtake the underground train by slipping him a few Hong Kong dollars to speed through the streets and jump some red lights, then leaped out and rushed down the escalators, pushing Chinese travellers out of his way, until he got to the platform. This was the next train in, and he was reasonably sure that the creature was on it somewhere.

Or on top of it.

Or below it.

In fact, thinking about it, Rhino wasn't sure that he had any clear way of determining *where* the creature was. He just had to hope it would make itself obvious without actually killing anyone.

As the doors slid closed and the train set off, he scanned the inside. It was incredibly clean, as if someone polished it at the end of every run. The carriages joined seamlessly on to one another so that he could see all the way down to the far end. Or at least he could have, if there hadn't been so many people in the way.

The train entered a tunnel and he pushed through the crowd, looking for anything out of the ordinary. It stopped at Prince Edward, Mong Kok, Yau Ma Tei and Jordan stations as he made his way along the length of the carriages. Still nothing. You would think that a creature like that would raise *some* interest, if not sheer abject terror, in the passengers.

He was nearly at the end of the train when it started pulling into Tsim Sha Tsui station. He looked at his mobile again, and suddenly the glowing red dot separated from him and made a break sideways. He shoved forward to the doors and slipped through them even before they were fully open. The platform was crowded, but a sudden scream cut through the air from near the exit. The creature *had* been on top of the train! Rhino saw a flash of motion as it ran, and a ripple in the crowd as people jumped out of its way.

This was *not* going the way he wanted.

As he ran towards the escalators, he remembered bitterly how simple this adventure had seemed when he had first heard about it . . .

one

From the roof of the warehouse where he had his apartment, Calum Challenger could see the jets landing and taking off at Heathrow Airport. The sun was setting in the west, and the aircraft were just black geometric shapes as they moved against the red sky. Occasionally one of them would flash as the low sunlight refracted through the cabin windows.

The sounds of London's constant traffic drifted up from the street below: beeping horns, sudden screeches of brakes, the pneumatic hiss of buses arriving at bus stops. The faint purple haze of exhaust fumes hung in the air, giving everything a slightly unreal appearance. Looking round, he could clearly make out the four stacks in the air above the home counties where the arriving aircraft circled for a while in big loops, one above another for thousands and thousands of metres, until they received a runway designation and instructions to land. The stacks were based above Bovingdon, Lambourne, Ockham and Biggin Hill. His father had told him that once, and he had wondered at the time what it would be like, living in one of those four places, and seeing the aircraft circling above all the time like vultures circling a fresh corpse.

Calum's father had spent a lot of time flying into and out of Heathrow. His mother too, usually with his father. They had often spent most of the year away from home, taking part in various archaeological digs or giving papers at international symposia, leaving Calum in the care of his great-aunt. And then one day they had died in a car crash – not in some isolated foreign country, on some remote and dangerous mountainside road, but here in England, on a country road in Hampshire.

There was a chill in the air, along with the haze of exhaust fumes. Calum shivered slightly.

'You OK?' Gecko asked from beside him. The Brazilian boy had been quiet and motionless for so long that Calum had almost forgotten he was there.

Calum nodded. 'Yeah. Just some unwelcome memories popping up.'

'You want to go back down?'

'Not yet. Let's wait until sunset.' He smiled slightly. 'I've not seen a real sunset since the accident, you know – just photographs, and videos. None of the windows in the apartment give me a clear view of the horizon. I suppose I could have ordered up a car and had someone take me out to a vantage point, just so I could see the sun go down, but that seemed too . . . self-indulgent. And the car crash . . . well, it happened at sunset too. Somehow I just couldn't face it for a while.' He paused momentarily. 'What I'm trying to say is: thanks for getting me up here. Thanks for talking me into it.'

Gecko shifted, uneasy at being praised. He was still more used to his own company to than anyone else's, and conversation was not his strong suit. 'It is nothing. I had to get you out of that place before you went mad. Tara was worried that you might suddenly start coming at us with a carving knife in your hand. "Stir crazy" was what she said, but I did not understand the phrase. You do not use a knife to stir something – you use a spoon or a spatula.'

'"Stir" is another word for "prison",' Calum pointed out. 'And Tara should know better. I can only chase people in the apartment if I'm using the straps on the ceiling to move around, and if I'm holding a knife then I can't swing from the straps, can I?'

Gecko shrugged. 'I did not say she had thought it through at all, but that was her concern.'

'I'm fine,' Calum said, but he could hear the edge of wistfulness in his own voice.

'Besides, *I* could do it.'

'You're a free-runner. You could probably hold the knife between your toes while you were swinging from the straps. Or hold the straps in your toes and swing upside down while holding the knife.'

'No,' Gecko said with some finality.

'Why not?'

'No style. No . . .' he hesitated, looking for the right word, ' . . . no *panache*. Free-running is all about the style.'

'I'll remember that next time I try it.'

Calum glanced sideways, to the point on the roof where

the large window that was situated directly above his sofa was located. Well, directly above where his sofa *had* been located, until Gecko had pushed it out of the way an hour or so ago. The window was wide open, and the top of a wooden ladder poked through the gap into the evening air. Calum had used the ladder to get up to the roof earlier, pulling himself up by his arms, rung after painful rung, feeling the sweat prickling on his back and shoulders, dragging his useless legs after him and sensing that they were banging against the ladder. Gecko, meanwhile, had sensitively suddenly decided that he needed to use the bathroom. The boy knew that Calum hated to be watched while he exerted himself like that. He also knew that Calum would have refused any offer of help.

'She will be on one of those aircraft,' Gecko pointed out, nodding in the direction of Heathrow.

'Who will?' Calum asked innocently.

'You know who. Natalie.'

'Natalie?'

'Natalie *Livingstone*, along with her mother.'

'Oh,' he said casually, 'is it tonight that they are arriving?'

'You know it is. You have the date, the time and the flight number written on a Post-it note, which is fastened to your fridge.'

'I wondered where that had gone.' Calum shrugged. 'I doubt that they'll come over tonight. Gillian will want to get to a hotel, unpack and have a long bath. Maybe tomorrow, if they're not busy.'

'Natalie might come over tonight. She knows how to

hail a taxi, surely? She is American. They virtually live in taxis and restaurants.'

'She's more likely to head to Oxford Street for the late-night shopping.'

'Do you know what it is that her mother wants to talk to you about?'

'Not sure.' Calum thought for a moment. 'I haven't bought anything expensive recently, so she's not going to tell me off about my finances, and I've already had my telling off for what happened in Georgia. It's possible she wants to talk about what's going on with the Almasti DNA that you, Natalie, Tara and Rhino recovered. She's certainly keen to get it analysed in one of the laboratories that she has links with.'

'And you are not? I thought you would have been eager to have the DNA analysed as soon as possible.'

'I am, but I want it done properly. What I *don't* want is some company grabbing hold of it, patenting the genes and then hiding them away until they can make a profit from them. I want the genetic information to be as freely available as possible.'

'Without saying where it came from?' Gecko asked.

'Hair samples, maybe. Preserved samples in a bog somewhere. Just as long as we don't give away the location of the Almasti. I don't want them becoming a tourist attraction.' He shrugged. 'Actually, I think Gillian has something else on her mind. She said she was bringing something across from America for me to look at.' He looked over at the Brazilian boy. 'And what about Tara? Where is she tonight?'

'Don't change the subject.'

'It's my roof. I can change the subject if I want to.'

'Tara had a project to finish for college.'

'And you're not there to give her moral support and feed her coffee every ten minutes?'

Gecko shook his head. 'She has given up coffee for a while. She drinks green tea with honey now. She says it calms her down.'

'Ironic.'

'What is?'

Calum smiled. 'She's given up coffee, and you're from Brazil, which is the largest coffee producer in the world. Presumably you could have got her some kind of bulk supply, if she'd wanted.'

'Funny,' Gecko said darkly. 'I suppose you think that every family in Brazil works in the coffee industry, just like every family in France owns a vineyard.'

'Fair point,' Calum admitted. 'What does every family in England do?'

'They talk about the weather and the traffic conditions,' Gecko replied.

'OK, you want me to shut up? I'll shut up.'

The two boys stared at the aircraft for a while, as the sun slipped slowly from the sky.

'I wish I was on one of them,' Calum said, almost whispering to himself. He jumped when Gecko replied.

'Going to where?'

'Anywhere. Everywhere.' He shook his head. 'I've always wanted to travel. My parents travelled all the time, but they left me here. Now I just . . . watch as other people do the travelling.'

'With your money, you could fly anywhere you wanted to,' Gecko pointed out. 'The airline people could get you on to and off an aircraft with a wheelchair, and put you in First Class, where you would have lots of room —' He caught himself. 'Yes, of course. You would not like the fuss.'

'I would need someone babysitting me all the time,' Calum said. 'In a foreign country, in a foreign hotel, I wouldn't be able to do anything for myself apart from go to sleep and wake up again. At least here I can be self-sufficient. The apartment has been organized for me that way.'

'You could charter a private aircraft,' Gecko pointed out. 'And you could buy a house in some exotic foreign location and have it fitted out with straps and labour-saving gadgets and anything else that you need, including specially imported Coca-Cola and coffee beans. You can afford to make a safe nest for yourself anywhere you want. Have lots of them, all around the world.'

'And then just stare out of the window at the other people playing on the beach, and swimming in the sea?' Calum shook his head bleakly. 'If I want to watch other people having fun, I can link in to any webcam that's connected to the World Wide Web, anywhere in the world.' He sighed. 'What you don't understand is—'

'Wait!' Gecko held a hand up. 'Wait for a moment.

Watch where the sun is just going below the horizon.'

'Watch for what?'

'You'll see.'

Calum suddenly realized what Gecko was doing. 'Oh, it's the Green Ray, isn't it? I've heard about that. You know it's just an atmospheric mirage caused by the last rays of the sun refracting through the heated atmosphere? I've seen photographs, and videos, on the Web.'

'But you've never seen it in real life,' Gecko pointed out. 'The sun is just about to dip below the horizon. It is safe to look at. Keep watching.'

Calum did as he was told, knowing that he wouldn't see anything worth the effort. He knew the physics of the situation. It was a visual effect caused by geometry and optics. Nothing special.

The sun was merely a rim of light on the horizon now, set against a watercolour sky of purple, orange and red. A few moments passed and the sun was merely a line of brightness.

And then, for a moment, a green flash seemed to radiate upward from the point where it had slipped beneath the horizon. Calum gasped. Just for a moment it was there, like some beacon being broadcast up into the universe, and then it was gone, leaving an after-image on his retina. Had he really seen it, or had it only been an illusion?

'Was that worth it?' Gecko asked from the gathering darkness.

'I suppose,' Calum said, but his voice was shaky. He hadn't anticipated the effect on him of actually seeing the

Green Ray there in front of him, its light directly shining into his eyes, not as an image on a screen.

Maybe he *was* missing things by staying in his apartment all the time, he mused. Maybe he *ought* to get out sometimes, and see the world.

A cold wind blew across the roof, making him shiver again.

'Have you seen the Green Ray before?' he asked Gecko.

'Many times, in many places,' the boy replied, 'but I never get tired of it. It is a moment of wonder and mystery in a world that seems to be trying to suck the wonder out of everything.' Calum could feel him turn and stare. 'And I know there is a simple physical explanation for it, but I would prefer just to be able to marvel at the fact that the universe can still provide moments like this.' He paused. '*Now* do you want to go back?'

'Yes,' Calum admitted. He looked over at the roof window again. 'I'm just wondering how.'

'Ah,' Gecko said slowly. 'I may not have thought this through fully.'

'Really?' Calum asked. 'You think?'

It was morning, and Tara Fitzgerald was sitting in a coffee shop in the Charing Cross Road, sipping at a green tea (with honey) and checking the internet on her tablet.

The coffee shop was located on the first floor of a bookshop – once upon a time the largest in the world, apparently, with over fifty miles of shelf space. The coffee shop was a recent and very welcome addition, with decent drinks and very good cakes, all in a pleasantly ramshackle environment. She loved it there. It was certainly more relaxing than her room in the college hall of residence. She had also spent a lot of time in the college library, but the fact that a mysterious multinational company had tracked her down and harassed her there a few months before had freaked her out, and she now felt that the stacks of books towered over her like toppling tombstones if she sat among them too long. So she had tried various coffee shops in the area until she'd found this one.

She hadn't quite recovered yet from the few days that she had spent in the former Soviet republic of Georgia, in search of the fabled Almasti. It had all happened so quickly. At the beginning of one week she was a lonely student in London who spent most of her time trawling the internet, and by the end of the week she had a group of new friends and she was in a foreign country being held captive by Neanderthals, or whatever the Almasti were. She still felt breathless.

And her friends. What an odd bunch. There was Calum, with his partial paralysis and his iron will to keep moving and not accept any help; Gecko, with his gymnastic ability to get over, under and around obstacles, usually at height; Natalie, whose flashes of honesty and decency shone through her normally prickly and spoilt demeanour like rays of sunshine through rainclouds; and the solid, dependable but slightly distant Rhino.

Natalie was flying in with her mother tonight. Tara

wasn't sure whether or not to head over to Calum's apartment. She liked hanging out there, but she didn't want to overstay her welcome. She'd done that before, with groups of people that she thought were friends but who turned out just to be tolerating her. One of the most hurtful things that had ever happened to her had been when she had been at a sleepover and overheard two supposed 'friends' talking privately about her. One of them had said, 'Well, we only let her come in because she's your friend,' to which the other one replied, '*My* friend? I thought she came here with *you*?'

Tara had left then, and never gone back.

Would Rhino be there at Calum's? That was the big question. He had turned up a couple of times over the past few weeks, mainly to finish up some paperwork and give Calum an invoice for 'services rendered', but he wasn't really part of the group. He wasn't really *integrating*. Maybe he was feeling isolated, left out. Maybe it was because he was older than the rest of them.

Maybe she should just keep herself to herself and let him make his own decisions.

She took another sip of green tea, and grimaced. The idea of giving up caffeine was great, but the taste didn't match the smell, even sweetened with honey. It didn't do much to keep her awake either. Maybe she should just cave in and go back to the coffees she used to drink, and put up with the trembling and the heart palpitations.

Calum managed to put away a fair amount of that special Mexican Coca-Cola that he drank, she noticed. That had a lot of caffeine in it. How did he manage to process it all without showing any symptoms?

Her tablet beeped. Putting down her green tea, she tapped the screen to bring it back to life. The 'Notifications' tab indicated that she'd had an email. She quickly checked it, and found that it was actually an automated notification from one of the many software search-bots she had created and sent roaming around the World Wide Web like little scavengers, looking for particular things. One of them had found something.

She booted up the search-bot controller app that she'd written, and selected the particular bot that had sent her a successful *ping*. The other search-bots were looking for phrases in emails or on websites that might match things that Calum Challenger was interested in – cryptids, Neanderthals, monsters and so on – but this one was particularly interested in images. It scanned through thousands of JPEGs, GIFs or whatever every second, looking for particular shapes. A few years ago Tara would have been lucky if a search-bot could locate a shape like a dog in a photograph labelled 'dog', but they were now so sophisticated that they could not only identify a whole range of animate or inanimate things in a single photograph but could also decide how large or small they were, based on the things that were around them.

Which is why Tara was now looking at a photograph of a giant rat.

One of the many images that the search-bot had been looking for was that of a rat – facing left, facing right, dead, alive, it didn't matter. It was just looking for a rat. That was one of the search terms that Calum had specified – Tara wasn't sure why. Having found a rat, the bot would then check its size. If it seemed unusually large, then it would send Tara an email with a copy of the image. Nine times out of ten the images were of rats in situations where perspective made them look larger than they really were, but, on examining this particular image, the rat in it was huge. Not elephant-sized, but still pretty impressive: about the size of a fully grown Alsatian, but bulkier. The bot had sent Tara a photograph of a grinning Asian man holding a turtle. The rat was in a cage in the background. The man gave the rat its scale.

Tara found that she'd stopped breathing, and took a sudden gulp of air. The rat looked completely ordinary until you realized its unusual size. It was side-on to the camera, and Tara could clearly see its beady black eye and its blossom-like ear.

Calum would want to see this. He'd told Tara that there had been intermittent reports from locals in Indonesia of colonies of giant rats living in the jungles, but nobody had ever taken a photograph or brought a body back for examination. And now here was one, sitting meekly in a cage somewhere.

Actually, maybe not 'meekly'. Its mouth was open slightly, and Tara could see the glint of large incisors inside.

She checked the metadata that the search-bot had thoughtfully included in the email, just in case the image had been taken from a horror movie and was just a rather good special effect rather than something real. Interestingly, the website from which it had come was part of the 'shadow' internet – the massive collection of web pages that deliberately stopped themselves from being indexed by search engines, keeping themselves hidden so that you actually had to know the web address to find them – or have a set of sophisticated search-bots like Tara did. They didn't want to be found by casual browsers because they were either borderline illegal or, frankly, *completely* illegal. This particular website was hosted in China, which was interesting too. She used her tablet web-browser to navigate to the site, and moved up until she hit the home page.

She gasped.

The banner on top of the website proudly proclaimed, in English: *Xi Lang's Emporium of Unusual Pets!* The main space was taken up by several images of lions, crocodiles, a sullen-looking gorilla and a really big snake. All were in strangely inappropriate settings like landscaped lawns, outside swimming pools and flagstone patios. A message underneath the photographs read: *You have a desire for some strange or exotic animal, and we can supply it, direct to your door! Come inside and take a look!*

Interesting. Interesting and rather creepy. Tara had known of course that some people with more money than sense kept pets that you wouldn't or couldn't fit into a normal house – Michael Jackson had kept a chimpanzee, for instance – but she had never thought to wonder where they got them. Of course, it made sense that there would be a middleman, a facilitator who could offer these animals for sale the way a normal pet shop would offer kittens or puppies.

It was almost certainly illegal. There were international laws against trafficking in endangered or dangerous animals, but that didn't stop some people from wanting them. They were status symbols.

She scanned through several pages, grateful that she had hacked her tablet's settings so that anyone else – like the owners of the website she was currently looking at – would think that she was based somewhere in Russia. After Nemor Incorporated had managed to track her location within a few seconds of her hacking their website from a desk in her college library, she had invested in some seriously hardcore security apps. Or, rather, Calum had invested in them for her. He had his own sophisticated computer set-up, but he knew that she was better than him at digital technology. That was the thing about Calum – he could be arrogant and selfish, but he did recognize talent when he saw it.

There were no other obvious cryptids on the site apart from the possible giant rat, and there were no other images showing the rat. The fact that it was in a cage suggested that it was for sale, but the mysterious Xi Lang wasn't advertising it. Maybe it was a special commission. Maybe it had just come into his warehouse, wherever that was, and he was still trying to work out what it was and how much he could charge for it.

That was a point – where *was* this warehouse? Checking all the web pages, Tara couldn't find any details. Just because the website said it was based in China didn't mean anything, of course, despite the obviously Chinese name of the site's supposed owner. She opened a separate browser window and set her search-bots looking for any information on *Xi Lang* and/or his *Emporium of Unusual Pets*. Even if he was trying to disguise his location, they would probably find it.

And they did. Within a few seconds Tara was looking at a scanned image of a receipt from one Xi Lang to a company named Celebrity Services Inc. for the sum of US$100,000. The item purchased was described only as 'Biological Specimen', but Tara was pretty certain that the specimen would have been alive. The address on the invoice was a location in Kowloon, Hong Kong. Which was, technically, in China.

Calum really needed to know about this.

Tara was about to email him when it occurred to her that it would be better to just take a bus across London and pop in to see him. The chances were that he would be in – he rarely left his apartment. He would have questions that were better answered face to face rather than by a string of emails.

She was about to switch her tablet to *hibernate* when it pinged again, indicating another incoming email. She debated whether to check it now or later, but she was a sucker for instant gratification.

This wasn't from one of her search-bots. It appeared to be from a real human being named Tom Karavla. The message read:

Hi,

I hope I've got the right Tara Fitzgerald – apologies if I haven't. If I have, then you don't know me, but I've been a fan of the lostworlds.co.uk website for a while now. I love the whole idea of cryptids, and the fact that there are so many undiscovered creatures and unexplored locations out there in the world. I noticed that you've taken over as the website administrator, and I just wanted to say that you've managed to turn an already excellent site into something superb. Keep up the good work!

Regards,

Tom Karavla

Tara's immediate reaction was that it was a scam of some kind. She'd been expecting Nemor Incorporated to make a move against her, after the way she'd let them down when they'd wanted her to investigate Calum for them, and this might be it. If so, it was a lot more subtle than their last attempt.

She was about to delete the message when a sudden compulsion grabbed hold of her. She ought to check a little bit further, just in case. She put the name *Tom Karavla* into her search-bots and let them loose.

Within thirty seconds she had a potted life history

of Tom Karavla, plus a series of photographs. He was about her age – apparently – and good-looking in the kind of understated muscular way that she liked. He was studying politics at the London School of Economics, and lived in east London. He had a wide circle of friends, but according to his social-media profile he was single. And, yes, he did list one of his interests as *cryptids*, as well as *ice hockey* and *dubstep*, which was a mark against him as far as she was concerned, but one she might be able to forgive. As far as she could see from just a cursory analysis, he was real. She even had the IP address of his computer, which gave her another idea.

She logged into the *lostworlds.co.uk* website as *administrator* and looked at the log of the times and durations of site accesses, along with the IP addresses of the computers that had looked at the site. The log showed that Tom Karavla's IP address had accessed the site forty or fifty times over the past year and a bit. That was well before Nemor Incorporated had contacted her. It might still be them, of course, being very clever, but she didn't think so. Why would they try a clumsy approach a few weeks back if they had a more sophisticated surrogate identity to use? No, the chances were that Tom Karavla was who he said he was.

She ran some quick diagnostics over the website just in case it had been hacked and the logs recently falsified to give the impression that someone with that IP address had been looking at the site for much longer than they had, but everything seemed intact and secure.

She took a last gulp of her green tea and quickly typed a response:

How did you find my email address?

After sending the email, her finger hovered over the *Power Off* button on the side of the tablet, but she hesitated. If Tom was still online, then he might respond immediately. Maybe. That would save her sitting on the bus and wondering if he had got back to her or not.

Five seconds later a new email appeared:

Hi Tara,

I hope you don't think I'm stalking you, but I did a search on your name when I saw it on the website. I was curious, because I'd only ever seen Calum Challenger's name on the website before, and then suddenly you were there. I couldn't find that many Tara Fitzgeralds around, and the ones I did find were older than I expected you to be. I found a likely candidate on the student roll of St Anne's College of Art. For a while I wondered if that really was you – I couldn't imagine an artist being a website administrator as well – but then I noticed that you were studying computer graphics and animation, and it kind of made sense.

Sorry, that was a longer explanation than I

anticipated! You can tell that I know a little bit about computing as well!

Regards,

Tom Karavla

Hesitating for a moment, Tara typed a reply:

Hi Tom,

Thanks for getting in touch – and it was very clever of you to locate me. What started your interest in cryptids? Have you ever seen one?

Best regards,

Tara F.

It wouldn't hurt to do a little customer relations, she thought; and, besides, he might actually have some information that Calum could use. It was worth a go, anyway.

Before she was tempted to stay and see what he said in response, she turned her tablet off and slipped it into her bag. Time to go.

two

Gecko was exercising on the straps that hung from Calum's ceiling: pulling himself up and down first using one hand and then the other.

'This isn't a gymnasium,' Calum pointed out from where he sat in front of his ten-screen octo-core computer set-up. He was scanning numerous websites in parallel, as well as watching some live feeds from various webcams that other people – usually researchers or television-programme makers – had set up in various remote parts of the world, powered by solar panels. It was a long shot, but it was just possible that some previously unknown big cat or deer might wander into shot, and Calum wanted to be there when it happened. 'I should start charging you a membership fee.'

'If you do that I will have to insist on showers and a coffee bar,' Gecko replied, using his left arm to pull himself up to the ceiling. He could feel the burn in his bicep.

'You do use my shower.' Calum's eyes were still fixed on the screens. 'And if I don't make you coffee on a regular basis then you steal cans of cola from the fridge – don't think I haven't seen you.'

'It is a small recompense for the services I offer.'

'Which are?'

Gecko thought for a moment as he lowered himself down to the ground again. 'Conversation, of course, and my activities as bodyguard and thief-deterrent.'

'Bodyguard?' Calum glanced over at Gecko. 'Apart from the time Nemor Incorporated broke in, when you weren't even here, there haven't been any attempted burglaries or attacks.'

'Which only goes to prove how effective I am,' Gecko pointed out.

'I bow to your superior logic.' Calum swivelled his chair round to face Gecko. 'Which reminds me – have you seen or heard anything from those Eastern European gangsters who wanted you to become a thief for them?'

Gecko scowled. 'Nothing. And that is a worry for me.'

'Maybe they've decided to leave you alone.'

He shook his head. 'I doubt it. People like them, they get an idea in their heads and they cannot get it out. If they have decided they want me, then they will keep on trying until I say yes. It is like a matter of honour to them. I am disrespecting them if I say no.'

'Have you been back to your flat?'

'No.' Gecko shrugged. 'Well, only quickly, to get fresh clothes, and I have been very careful to check the flat out from a distance before I go in. I have been staying with friends.'

Calum turned back to the screens. 'You could stay here,' he said casually. 'I have spare bedrooms.' He glanced up to the skylight. 'And you already have a key.'

Gecko felt a sudden wave of gratitude wash over him. 'Would I have to pay rent as well as a membership fee?' he asked.

'Not for as long as your presence here discourages burglars and muggers.' Gecko could see Calum smiling slightly. 'It's like having a guard dog.'

'One who drinks coffee and cola,' Gecko suggested.

'Have you thought about going to the police?'

'What would I tell them? I cannot identify the two men who were in my flat, and I would have to admit that the reason they want me is because I already take part in an activity that is barely legal in the first place.'

'Actively *il*legal, as I think I said the first time I met you,' Calum said. 'Free-running might be fun, but it does involve trespass. But, yes, I take your point. The police wouldn't be interested. Not unless they could get you working as an informant and actively encourage you to join up with a gang so you could be their mole on the inside.'

Gecko shivered. 'The only thing worse than working for a gang like that would be working for a gang like that *and* the Metropolitan Police.'

'The pay might be OK,' Calum pointed out, 'but the pension is lousy.'

'In the unlikely event that I live long enough to collect a pension.'

Before Calum could respond, the doorbell rang. Calum pressed a key on his keyboard, and one of his ten screens shifted to a view from the camera outside his apartment door. Professor Gillian Livingstone and her daughter, Natalie, were standing outside. The professor had a large box with her.

Calum quickly ran a hand through his hair and pressed another key. The security lock on the door clicked to the open position.

'Come in!' he yelled.

Gecko noticed that rather than stay in his seat he levered himself upright and held on to one of the ceiling straps with his right hand, making it look as if he was just casually standing there.

'Calum!' Professor Livingstone exclaimed as she entered the large loft apartment and strode across the floorboards. She was a petite, athletic, blonde American who was old enough to be Gecko's mother but didn't look nearly that old. She obviously kept herself in good condition with exercise, vitamins and probably, Gecko thought, some strange and secret research programmes at one or another of the various laboratories worldwide that she either funded or consulted with. She gave Calum a hug and he responded, one-armed. 'You're looking well. How are you feeling?'

'Fine, as usual,' he said. He glanced past her. 'Hi, Natalie.'

Gillian's daughter entered the room, lugging the large box behind her. It was strapped up with plastic tape and it was on a kind of trolley that Natalie was pulling with some effort.

'Hi, Calum,' she said, and then glanced at Gecko. 'Hi, Gecko.'

'Hello, Eduardo,' Gillian Livingstone said, looking over at him. Apart from Gecko's mother, Gillian Livingstone was the only person who used his real name.

'Professor Livingstone,' Gecko said, nodding. He glanced between the two women. 'Can I get you anything? Tea? Coffee? Water?'

'I'll have a latte, please,' Gillian Livingstone said. 'Semi-skimmed milk if you have it.'

'Grapefruit juice?' Natalie asked, shrugging.

'Coming right up.'

As Gecko headed for the kitchen area, he heard Calum say, 'I got your message about coming across to England, but you didn't say why.'

'Do I need a reason to see my favourite ward?'

'Usually, yes,' Calum replied. 'What's happened? Has Aunt Merrily asked you to check on me? If she did, then it's a long way for you to come, just for that. All she has to do is send a car for me and I'll pop across to see her in Richmond. She knows that.'

'Merrily hasn't been in touch, Calum,' Professor Livingstone reassured him. 'I had to be in London anyway, to sign some official documents, and I thought I'd take the opportunity to catch up. And, besides, there's something I want to show you. Something that came out of a research laboratory I'm associated with.'

'What about you?' Calum asked Natalie. 'Aren't

you still in school, or something?'

'Aren't you?' Natalie countered.

'Special exemption because of the car accident,' he said. 'I'm home-schooled.'

'Oh yeah?' Natalie countered. 'Where's your tutor, then?'

'Actually,' her mother admitted with a tinge of embarrassment in her voice, 'that's me. I had to promise the authorities that I would supervise Calum's education.'

'And do you?'

'Better than I supervise yours, apparently,' Gillian Livingstone said with an edge to her voice. 'I send Calum a list of topics to research every term, and he sends me back proof that he's researched them. Usually within a week.'

'It's a chore,' Calum said, 'but I have to put in the time. I want my allowance to continue.' When Gecko came back into the main area of the apartment with a tray of drinks, he saw his friend was smiling as he asked, 'So what's your story, Natalie?'

'She was asked to leave her college,' Gillian said darkly. 'I wouldn't say it was under a cloud, but there were definitely adverse weather warnings.'

'What did you do?' Gecko asked, handing Natalie her glass of grapefruit juice.

'I bought a dog,' Natalie said, taking the drink.

'What is the problem with that?'

'It's a boarding school.'

He nodded. 'Ah. I see. No, actually, I don't.'

'Apparently they don't allow dogs in lessons. I *told* them it was only a chihuahua, and I could carry it around in my handbag all day without anyone noticing, but apparently handbags aren't allowed in lessons either.' She shrugged. 'They've got rules for everything. Who knew?'

'I blame your father,' Gillian interrupted. 'He should have been looking after you.'

'Someone should,' Natalie muttered. 'At least, that's what the principal said.'

Gecko glanced at the box on the trolley behind Natalie. It was, now he came to look at it, more of a crate than a box. It was heavy-duty plastic with snap-locks holding the two sides together. There was a sticker on the side with a company logo, but Gecko couldn't see what it was.

'It's not my birthday,' Calum said, seeing Gecko looking at the box. He was still hanging nonchalantly from his strap.

'No, I forget birthdays,' Gillian replied, 'but I make up for it at other times with random gifts.' She glanced across at Gecko. 'Could you be a dear, Eduardo, and open it for us. Calum is fixed in place trying to look casual, I don't want to wreck my nails and Natalie's favourite word at the moment is "no". At least, that's when she's not saying "As if!" and "puh-*lease*!"'

'Oh, puh-*lease*!' Natalie said, on cue, and flounced off to the sofa in a huff.

'Of course I can,' Gecko said. He knelt down and shifted the crate on to the floor. The sticker, he saw, said: *Robledo Mountains Technology, Las Cruces, New Mexico*. Their logo was a stylized mountain range with a sunset behind it. The tape surrounding the crate was hard and razor-edged, made of lots of fibres all wound together. The join looked as if it had been heat-sealed. He slipped a folding knife out of his back pocket and sliced through it, and then snapped the plastic catches. He swung the lid upward, revealing the crate's contents.

For a long moment they all looked inside.

'Leg braces,' Calum said in a cold voice. 'Gee, thanks. Just what I always wanted.'

'I knew that's what you would say.' Professor Livingstone crossed over to him and put a hand on his shoulder. 'That's not what they are.'

It was, Gecko thought, what they looked like. There were two objects side by side inside the crate, each one the mirror image of the other. They were made of some black, dull material – not metal, but maybe carbon fibre or something similar. It looked as though they were meant to strap round Calum's legs, running from a thick carbon-fibre belt round his waist, down past the top of his thighs and on down towards his ankles. The hip and knee joints were complicated – not just simple hinges, but arrangements of small pistons and what looked like circular motors. There were wires everywhere, and a box on the belt area that looked to Gecko as if it housed a battery pack.

'These are *bionic* legs,' he said quietly. 'They have power, and they can move your legs for you, Calum.'

'Like I said. Braces.'

'Don't be negative,' Gillian Livingstone said. 'These are a product of the latest research into enabling paraplegics to walk again. It's a spin-off from military work into helping soldiers march for longer and carry heavier loads in hot temperatures. The idea is to give them mechanical exo-skeletons that can take the strain and do some of the work for them.' She indicated the "legs" in the box. 'These things are made of carbon fibre – they are lightweight but extremely strong. There's no chance of them snapping or breaking unless you happen to crash a truck into them. Don't do that, by the way. The motor units in the joints are based on the ones used in satellites and the International Space Station to rotate solar panels. They only draw a low power, but they are exceptionally reliable and they can apply a lot of torque in a hurry. The braking systems are also state of the art – it's not much use rotating a joint if you can't lock it off in the right position.'

'What about the battery?' Natalie asked. She had left the sofa, and her huff, and come over to stand beside Calum. 'How long does the charge last? If it's anything like my mobile phone, it'll die after three hours.'

'That's because you leave your social networking sites on all the time,' Gecko pointed out.

'How else am I going to know what my friends are doing?' Natalie protested.

Gillian interrupted: 'The battery isn't a battery at all. It's a next-generation fuel cell, and it can provide enough power to keep these legs going at a run for a day. At walking pace it's more like a week.'

'And how is it controlled?' Calum asked, his voice not reflecting any emotion. 'Does it come with some kind of game-console controller where I twiddle a joystick to get moving, or does someone else use a remote control to move me around like a puppet?'

'Neither.' Gillian obviously wasn't going to rise to the bait by getting into an argument. 'Although it's funny you should mention game-control consoles, because it's partly a spin-off of that technology. This is the really clever part. I sit on the board of directors of a company that's seeking to develop a way to control computer games using brain waves rather than buttons and joysticks. The brain produces electrical and magnetic signals that can be detected using sensors placed on the scalp. There's been a lot of work recently using functional magnetic resonance imaging to determine which parts of the brain trigger when the mind thinks about an action like moving an arm, or bending a knee, or flexing toes. It's got to the stage where we can take a real-time scan of the brain's electrical activity and *predict* what the person wants to do. Converting that to actual movement is then just child's play.' She smiled. 'It's interesting, but the researchers have found out that the brain displays signals that it's made a decision before the person being scanned consciously knows they have made a decision. Some of the researchers are using this as evidence that there's no such thing as consciousness – that what we *think* of as being consciousness is just the brain catching up with a decision that it's already made and trying to rationalize it after the event.'

'Like I've been saying,' Natalie murmured, 'I don't actually *choose* to spend all that money on shoes – there's something in my head that makes me do it!'

'I didn't say I bought into the theory,' Gillian warned; 'I just said that some people believe it.'

'And this is being done just to play *games*?' Gecko asked.

'It's a multi-billion dollar industry,' she responded. 'Military spending is going down, year on year, while entertainment spending is going the other way. If you want to get anything developed these days, you need to get game- or film-related funding for it.'

Gecko turned to look at Calum, ready to say that this sounded like a good thing, not a bad thing, but the expression on his friend's face made him stop. Instead of the stubborn scowl that he was expecting, what he saw was that Calum looked almost *hungry*.

'So how does it work – technically?' he asked in a quiet voice. 'Do I have to have my head shaved? Do I have to have electrodes implanted in my brain?'

'You're not listening,' Gillian replied. 'This is all done externally. You put on a headband with sensors inside. There's a Bluetooth link to the controller in the waistband. The sensors pick up what your brain wants to do before it has even formulated the thought properly and activates the motors. That way you start moving just at the point when you *want* to start moving – not too early or too late.'

'A headband?' Calum grimaced. 'I don't want to look like a 1980s rock star.'

Natalie glared at him. 'You didn't worry about that when you made us wear those camera and microphone headbands when we went to Georgia!'

'You didn't wear yours most of the time,' Calum countered. 'That's why you got into trouble.'

Gillian Livingstone frowned. 'What trouble?'

'No trouble at all,' her daughter said quickly.

'What do you think?' Gillian asked, turning back to Calum. 'Can you work with it? I'm not saying it'll be the answer to all your problems, but it might help out.' She paused. 'It might help you get out and about a bit more.'

'I'll look like a freak,' he said softly.

It was Natalie who responded. 'No,' she said, 'you won't. Looking at those things, they'll go under a baggy pair of trousers – and frankly you could do with something more fashionable than the chinos you always wear. I can't say what the walking will be like, but you'll look fine.'

'The walking will look perfectly natural,' her mother added. 'It may take a little time to get used to them, a little practice in private, but nobody who doesn't already know will be able to tell.'

Silence fell across the room as they all looked at Calum. He just stared into the box as if it contained all the secrets of the future – which, Gecko considered, it did. At least for Calum.

'All right,' he said quietly. 'I'll give it a go.' He glanced at Gillian Livingstone. 'How do we do this? Do you want me to try them on now? I warn you, if I've got to take my trousers off I'm not going to do it in public.'

'There's a process to go through,' Gillian replied, 'and we can't do it here. It has to be done at Robledo Mountains Technology. They have to calibrate the headband sensors quite carefully to pick up what the brain is doing.'

Gecko pointed at the sticker on the side of the case. 'But they are in Las Cruces, New Mexico. That is in America, I think.'

Gillian raised a hand to reassure him. 'They have a facility in Hampshire, near Farnborough. Calum can go down there some time in the next few days and they will spend a few hours fitting the bionic legs to him, making sure he's comfortable and then tracking what his brainwaves look like whenever he's thinking about various movements of his own legs. I'm told it's a very simple process.'

Calum nodded. 'OK. I'll do it.'

'Wonderful. I'll get the people at Robledo to get in touch. Which reminds me – do you still have that robot – ARLENE?'

Calum nodded. 'It's downstairs in the warehouse area. Rhino dropped it off when he and the others returned from Georgia.'

'That's fine. It was Robledo that originally developed it before it was passed across to the US army at the Aberdeen Proving Ground. They asked me if you could bring it back when you go across to them. I think they want to download the logs from the robot's memory core and assess its performance. There's some invaluable data in there on real-life conditions, they think.'

'Logs?' Calum said carefully. He glanced across at Gecko.

'Geographical locations, speeds across terrain, how bumpy the ground was – that kind of thing. It will tell them a lot about how the robot coped with everything you asked it to do.'

Gecko checked that Gillian wasn't looking his way, and then quickly shook his head. He already knew what Calum was thinking. The robot's memory logs contained the exact location of the Almasti village, and Calum didn't want anyone else knowing where the last Neanderthals were living.

Gecko glanced across at Natalie. She was looking worried, but he suspected it was for a different reason. She clearly hadn't told her mother that she had been kidnapped by mercenary representatives of Nemor Incorporated and had only been rescued when she climbed on to ARLENE's back and raced across the Georgian foothills to safety.

'That sounds fine,' Calum said casually. 'I'll get Tara to give it a quick once-over before Robledo take it back, just to make sure it's in good condition.'

And just to make sure that the robot's memory is wiped of any GPS coordinates before it gets handed across, Gecko thought with a smile. He nodded briefly to Calum. If Calum wasn't around, he would make sure that Tara knew what to do.

'I should be going. Things to do; people to see. Natalie – you'll be OK here for a while, won't you? I'll see you back at the hotel later.' She turned, as if she was about to head to the door, and then turned back. 'Oh, I nearly forgot,' she said casually, 'I need to ask you about that DNA sample that Natalie and the others picked up for you in Georgia. Have you decided what to do with it yet?'

Calum looked over to Gecko again and raised an eyebrow. They had talked about that earlier. Calum was paranoid about anyone getting hold of the Almasti DNA and using it in a way he didn't approve of.

'I'm still making lists of different places that could do the work,' he said.

'Fine.' She shrugged, as if the matter was of no importance, then went on: 'It's just that I also have contacts with a laboratory in Oxford. If you wanted to, you could pop the sample in to them for genetic sequencing. I can highly recommend them – they've done work for several Nobel Laureates, as well as Oxford University.'

'I'll bear that in mind,' Calum said noncommittally.

'They're very discreet. Nothing will leak out.'

'Well, maybe I want it to leak out.'

She stared at him. 'Pardon me?'

'We *have* talked about this before, Gillian. I want the information to be made as widely available as possible. I want the *world* to be able to make use of that DNA.'

'Even if you won't say where it came from?'

'Information shouldn't be owned,' he pointed out. 'It's not like diamonds, or land. It's a resource that should be freely available.'

'I'll remind you of those words the next time you think

someone has got hold of your bank-account details. And knowing where the DNA came from *is* information, isn't it? Shouldn't you make that freely available?'

He smiled. 'OK, I take the point – some information should be kept private, but DNA sequences? If DNA doesn't belong to the person or creature that it's been taken from, then it doesn't belong either to the person who takes it or the researchers they give it to. Genes can't be copyrighted. At least, they *shouldn't* be copyrighted.'

She stared at him sympathetically for a moment. 'You're still hoping, aren't you?'

He looked away. 'Still hoping what?'

'Still hoping that, somewhere out there, some unknown plant or animal has a DNA sequence that will help regenerate nerve cells.'

He shrugged. 'Starfish, newts, salamanders – they can all regenerate lost tails or lost limbs. Who's to say there's not something out there that can do the same with spinal nerve cells?'

'And you think that the more laboratories working on the problem, the better the chance that someone will solve it?'

He nodded. 'Yes. That's exactly what I think.'

'Has it occurred to you, Calum,' she said softly, 'that the laboratories working in the public domain are, by and large, underfunded, underequipped, understaffed and under-resourced? They may have all the bright ideals of public service in the world, but if they have trouble paying for a test-tube cleaner then how are they going to make any big breakthrough in the fields of genetics or medicine? No, it's the private companies that have the resources. They can put millions of dollars into a project to solve a problem—'

'If they see the chance of making *billions* of dollars from marketing the final result,' Calum finished. 'And part of their tactics for doing that is to keep prices high and to control the supply. Only those who can afford the cure will get it.'

'You *can* afford it!' she cried stubbornly. 'And if you can't then there are people in your life who will afford it *for* you.'

He shook his head sadly. 'But I'm not the only paraplegic person in the world, Gillian. What happens to the rest of them? The big pharmaceutical companies are there to make money for their shareholders – that's their *raison d'etre*. They aren't much into philanthropic gestures. You know as well as I do that there are strains of bacteria resistant to almost any antibiotic we can throw at them. The big pharmaceutical companies could solve that problem within a year if they threw money at it, by working on modified versions of the antibiotics we have, but they won't, because all those antibiotics are out of their licence period and won't make them any money. That's the sad truth.' His gaze flickered towards Gecko with a silent apology: he knew that Gecko's father had died from tuberculosis – a disease that could have been cured if the drugs had been available.

'Welcome to capitalism,' Gillian said, shaking her head. 'It may not be an ideal system, but it's the best we've got.' She took a deep breath. 'We're not going to agree on this, are we?'

Calum shook his head. 'I don't think so. I still love you though.'

'And I love you too. Now give me a hug before I leave.'

She moved towards him, and he slipped his free arm round her. 'It's good to see you again. And thanks for the leg braces. I promise I'll give them a go.'

'See that you do. I'll be angry if you don't, and you know what that means.'

'No Ferrari?'

'That's right – no Ferrari.'

Professor Livingstone waved at Gecko, gave Natalie a quick peck on the cheek and walked out.

Natalie huffed. 'She doesn't let me talk to her like that,' she said.

'But you do anyway,' Calum pointed out.

Gecko snorted. 'Not with the same razor-edged logic and the same bright, shining moralistic position.' He moved across and punched Calum gently on the shoulder. 'That was well said.'

Natalie looked at them both. 'You guys really think my mom would do that? I mean, keep a medical treatment under wraps so that a company she was involved in could make more money than they already have?'

'Where do you think the money for those shoes comes from?' Gecko asked gently.

He was saved from Natalie's scathing response by the doorbell.

Before Gecko could move to the computer keyboard to

activate the door lock, the door pushed open.

'Sorry – it was unlocked,' a voice said. 'Can I come in?'

It was Tara. Gecko felt his face suddenly flush, and he quickly brushed a hand over his clothes, aware that they were dirty from the free-running he'd done earlier. Using Calum's shower was one thing, but he really ought to keep a few spare sets of clothes here as well. He smiled to himself. Calum was right – it was almost as if he was moving in!

'Hi, Tara,' Calum called. 'You can always come in here – you know that.'

'Best to check,' she said, entering. 'Oh, hi, Gecko. Hi, Natalie – I saw your mum outside.' She frowned. 'I'm not sure she saw me though.'

'She gets like that,' Natalie pointed out. 'Very driven.' She glanced at Calum. 'Aren't you getting tired, hanging around there? Can't we, like, all go and chill out on the sofa or something?'

'That's a good idea,' Gecko said, before Calum could protest that, no, he was fine where he was, thank you very much. He knew how stubborn the boy could be.

'Ooh, what's this?' Tara said, gazing into the opened crate.

'I'll tell you later,' Calum promised.

'OK.' Tara sat down, brandishing her tablet in the air. 'But I've got something for you! There's a hidden website out there on the shadow internet, and I think they've got a photograph of a cryptid on it! It's one of the things you specifically asked me to look for.'

Calum swung himself over and almost fell into the sofa. 'Let me see!'

Tara powered up her tablet, touched the screen a few times and then passed it across to Calum. Natalie sat down beside him and leaned in to look. Gecko moved round to the back of the sofa and gazed over Calum's shoulder.

'I hate to tell you this,' Gecko said, looking at the photo of the man holding the turtle, 'but that's a Bostami turtle. It's a very rare soft-shelled turtle – there are only supposed to be a hundred and fifty or so of them left, and they all live in a pond of the Tripureswari Temple in Gomati district of Tripura, which is in India. This man certainly shouldn't be offering one for sale, and he ought to be reported, but it's not exactly a cryptid.'

'I'm not talking about the turtle,' Tara said, exasperated, 'I'm talking about the thing in the cage behind it.'

There was silence in the room for a few moments, as they all tried to take in what they were seeing.

'Eeuw!' said Natalie finally.

three

'**W**hat's with the interest in giant rats?' Natalie asked after she had stopped gagging at the photograph. 'Aren't there any *nice* cryptids out there? You know, like ponies?'

Calum shrugged. 'I guess it actually started with Sir Arthur Conan Doyle.'

She recognized the name, but she wasn't sure why. 'The writer?' she ventured.

'Exactly.' Calum seemed impressed that she knew that, which made her smile inwardly. Not outwardly, of course. That wouldn't be cool.

'He invented the character of Sherlock Holmes, the world's greatest detective,' Gecko pointed out helpfully. 'Very popular in Brazil.'

'Doyle had this habit of telling his audience about Sherlock Holmes's more ordinary cases,' Calum went on, 'but mentioning in passing more bizarre ones that he never got around to explaining. It was all a bit of a tease, I suppose. For instance, in one of the Sherlock Holmes stories there's a reference to the affair of the Politician, the Lighthouse and the Trained Cormorant. Fans have wondered for more than a hundred years what that case might have involved.'

'Presumably it involved a politician, a lighthouse and a cormorant that had been trained to do something interesting,' Tara said.

Calum glared at her. 'That's a given, but what was the connection between them?'

Tara shrugged. 'Beats me. I'm not a writer.'

'Anyway, in another of the stories Doyle mentions the case of the Giant Rat of Sumatra, and he goes on to say that it's a case for which the world is not yet prepared. Again, fans of Sherlock Holmes would far rather read about a bizarre giant rat than an ordinary theft or murder.'

'Is there a giant rat in Sumatra?' Gecko asked. 'Oh, and by the way – where *is* Sumatra?'

'Sumatra is an island in western Indonesia, and there *are* large rats on the island, although they're only about the size of a house cat.'

'In South America we have the capybara,' Gecko offered. 'It is also a rodent, and it is about the size of a large dog.' His face fell somewhat. 'The problem is that it looks nothing like a rat. More like a small hippopotamus covered with hair.'

Natalie grimaced at the thought.

'Skeletons and fossils of giant rats have been discovered in places like East Timor,' Calum went on. 'They were about the size of a large dog too, although, judging by the skulls, they looked a lot more like the rats we know about now. The odds are that they only died out about a thousand years ago – if they did die out. They might still be around, in isolated locations.'

'So has anyone actually reported *seeing* giant rats anywhere?' Natalie persisted.

Calum shook his head. 'Not as such. I mean, there's a photograph on the internet of a large dead rat in New York, but it's almost certainly a tropical rat that had probably been smuggled to America as a pet. It's just that if there *are* unknown species out there, it's more likely that they are going to be versions of things we already know about: new kinds of deer, new kinds of spider, and so on. Rats are one of the most successful and widespread species on earth. Next to cockroaches they are nature's best survivors. It seemed to me that looking for some references to giant rats wouldn't be a long shot. And then, of course, there's the naked mole rat.'

'Of course there is,' Natalie said, suppressing a shudder. 'There's always the naked mole rat.' She shook her head. 'Actually – naked? Is that really what it's called?'

'Oh yes,' Calum confirmed.

'And they're called naked because why? People don't dress them up, do they? They don't dress themselves up?'

'I'm guessing it's because they don't have hair,' Tara offered.

'Correct.' Calum leaned back into the comfort of the sofa. 'They're rodents – hence the rat bit – but they live underground – hence the mole bit – and they don't have any hair – hence the naked bit.'

'Biologists are like that, I have noticed,' Gecko said.

'They are very literal-minded.'

Ignoring the bantering interruptions, Calum continued: 'They're about ten centimetres long and they live in Africa. There's a whole raft of interesting things about naked mole rats. For instance, they have a social structure that's more like that of insects than mammals – each colony has a queen, a small number of fertile males and a whole load of sterile "workers" who don't get to breed. Also they've only got a crude heat-regulation system in their bodies, more like that of lizards than mammals. They can run backwards or forwards through their burrows at the same speed and they don't seem to have any nerves on their skin. They can stand levels of carbon dioxide that would kill any other creature, they live for a lot longer than any other species their size and they've got these four incisor teeth that project from their mouths and which they can wiggle around independently . . .' He put his hand in front of his mouth and wiggled his fingers to demonstrate.

'OK, so far, so comedic,' Natalie said. She was trying to imagine an elderly, hairless, pink rat running backwards in its burrow and waggling its teeth, and she wasn't sure whether the resulting image was funny or horrific. 'I think we can all agree that there're some strange creatures in the world. What's the thing about naked mole rats that's attracted your attention?'

'They don't get cancer,' Calum said simply. 'They have this chemical in their bodies – it's a kind of complicated sugary polymer thing – that kills tumour cells. All tumour cells. They're the only creature that's known to have this.'

'What's it for?' Gecko asked, obviously intrigued. 'Is it actually there to stop cancer, or to do something else?'

'It looks,' Calum answered, 'as if they evolved this chemical in their bodies to make them more supple and flexible, to help them move around their burrows, but it has this great and completely unexpected side effect. There's a lot of research going on around the world to try to find out how exactly this chemical works, and replicate its results.' He glanced around the group. 'The point is that rats may seem boring, but that's only because they're everywhere. There's a reason why they are everywhere, and it's because they are survivors. What they can't do by adapting their behaviour they do by adapting their genetic structure and biology.'

'They can't fly,' Natalie pointed out.

'That's not true,' Gecko said. 'Have you ever looked at a pigeon? They are rats with wings.'

Calum was looking away from them, towards the wall. Natalie could tell that he was uncomfortable. 'You just want there to be a giant rat out there because of that stupid Sherlock Holmes story,' she said.

'*It's not a –*' He caught himself. 'Yes,' he said, taking a deep breath, 'I want there to be a giant rat out there because of that Sherlock Holmes story.'

He gestured to Tara to hand her tablet across. She did – reluctantly, Natalie thought – and Calum touched it a couple of times. The nine LCD screens that were clustered around his workstation suddenly swivelled on their articulated arms and came together to form a larger screen facing the sofa. The picture of the man holding the turtle appeared in high definition on it. Calum used his fingers to identify the corners of a box on the image, marking out the creature in the background. That section of image suddenly expanded to fill the screen. Calum made some more gestures and imaging-processing software improved the quality, getting rid of some of the graininess and making the picture sharper. A serial number, stencilled on the side of the crate, came into focus: 119078B.

It still looked like a large rat in a cage. Not a dog, and not a hairy hippopotamus.

'This thing really does look like a giant rat,' Calum conceded. 'Is there any other information about it on the website? Any close-ups, or details of where it was found, or anything?'

Tara shook her head. 'Not that I could find. Actually, getting to the site was difficult enough – there are all sorts of firewalls and protocols protecting it from casual viewing. You can't find it using normal search engines. As far as I can see, you actually need a password to get past the front page, although I didn't let that stop me.' Tara glanced at the screen, and then at Calum. 'What do you want to do about it?'

'I want to buy it,' he said.

'Oh, you should have mentioned that earlier,' Natalie said brightly. 'I've got my credit card with me. Can we order online? Do they deliver?'

Calum glared at her – which was unusual, she thought. Normally, for some reason, he tried to look away from her as much as possible. She didn't think he liked her very much, which didn't actually bother her. Lots of people didn't like her, but then she didn't like lots of people, so that was OK.

'I'm not kidding,' he said. 'I really do want to buy one. And you know as well as I do that someone engaged in the illegal buying and selling of exotic or extremely exotic animals is not just going to take a credit-card order online, put it in a box with some bubble wrap and FedEx it from Hong Kong to here. They are criminals. They are going to be operating very, very carefully. Someone is going to have to travel to Hong Kong and get in touch with this Xi Lang, which almost certainly isn't his real name. Any clumsy or direct approach is going to spook him. He'll assume it's a trap set by the police. We're going to have to be very careful.

They all looked at one another, each thinking the same thought.

Tara was the first one to say it. 'Have you seen Rhino recently?'

Gecko glanced over at Calum. 'Do you want me to text him?'

Calum nodded. 'Please.'

'You're serious, aren't you?' Natalie asked. 'You actually want someone – us! – to go to China –'

'Hong Kong,' Calum corrected mildly.

'Which was, the last time I checked, in China –'

'It's actually a Special Administrative Region of China, rather than being part of the mainland. It used to belong to England, but it was handed back in 1997.'

'Whatever. The point is, it's not England and it's not America. It's a foreign country controlled by a government that does not have a good record on human rights. And once we're there you want us to go undercover and actually make a deal with these people. It's not a good idea, Calum. It's really not.'

'Hong Kong has some very good shopping areas.'

'That joke got old some time ago,' she hissed. 'Nice shops don't work like catnip on me. Not any more.' She shook her head for a moment, dismissing Calum's attempts to get her off topic. 'Look, these guys are committing felonies. Firstly, that makes them very dangerous. This is almost certainly something to do with the Triads! Haven't you ever heard of them? They're criminal gangs who are heavily into extortion, money laundering, people trafficking, smuggling and counterfeiting.'

'How is it that you know so much about the Triads?' Gecko asked.

'I saw a documentary once,' she said, without looking at him. 'Calum, they kill people who get in their way! We need to tell the authorities about this, not go out there and actually give them more money!'

'I understand what you're saying,' he pointed out, 'and I agree with you – in theory. The trouble is that if we report them then there'll be a raid on the warehouse and all the exotic animals will be taken away. Most of them will probably die, because the authorities will have no idea how to look after them. The rest will be released back into the wild wherever they were taken from, where they'll probably die anyway because they'll be undernourished and under-exercised. Our only chance is to go and buy that giant rat now.'

'*Our* only chance?'

He gazed at her. 'I thought we were all part of *thelostworlds.co.uk*, Natalie.'

'Don't try and guilt me out, Calum. I was there when you were arguing with my mom, remember? You want that DNA. *I* don't want it. *Tara* doesn't want it. *Gecko*—'

'All right.' He held up a hand. 'I get the message. Yes, I have an ulterior motive, but if you really listened to the argument that your mother and I were having then you'd know it's not just about me – it's about everyone who is paralysed, or has cancer, or suffers from some sort of genetic problem that could be treated using gene therapy, if only the right genes could be found. That rat might have them.'

'"That *dirty* rat",' Tara murmured. She was quoting some film, Natalie knew, but Natalie wasn't sure which one. Neither did she care. Rats *were* dirty.

'You're not helping,' she snapped.

'I'm not trying to help.'

Natalie turned to Calum. 'So what happens when we do buy it? Do you want us to pretend it's a dog and have it shipped back here in a pet carrier in the hold of an aircraft? I'm pretty sure that customs will have something to say about that. Just getting a valid rabies certificate is going to be impossible.'

'Xi Lang can probably fake one for you.' Calum shrugged. 'I'm sure he has this problem with all his exotic specimens.' He shook his head, letting out a deep breath. 'No, you're right to raise these objections. The best thing to do would be to take a DNA sample and then hand the creature over to the Hong Kong authorities, along with the location of the warehouse. I don't need the giant rat *per se* – I just need its genetic material.'

'So you will let us notify the authorities?' she pushed.

'*We?*' he questioned. 'So you *are* part of the team, then?'

'I guess I am.' She smiled ruefully. 'Besides, I can always sell it to Mom as an educational visit. If Rhino is going with us, then she'll be content. She trusts him. And it's not like it's the back end of nowhere – Hong Kong is a major city, with five-star hotels and good restaurants and everything.'

Calum glanced over at Gecko, who was just finishing typing a message into his mobile. 'What about you, Gecko – are you in?'

He nodded enthusiastically. 'For sure. I have never been to Hong Kong, but from what I have seen in movies the opportunities for free-running will be incredible!'

Tara put her hand up. 'What about me? Can I go?'

Calum shook his head. 'Actually,' he said, 'there's something technology-related that I need your help and advice on.'

Tara glanced at the bionic legs in the plastic crate. 'Would it be those things?'

'It would,' he confirmed. 'Controlled using brain waves.'

'Ooh!' she said, brightening up. 'That sounds like fun!'

Gecko put his mobile back into his pocket. 'I've texted Rhino and asked him to get in touch. I haven't mentioned anything about giant rats or Chinese criminal gangs.'

Calum nodded. 'OK, thanks.' He glanced from Gecko to Natalie. 'I suggest that the two of you make sure your passports are in order, and that you've had whatever inoculations you'll need for a trip to Hong Kong . . .'

'Hepatitis A is recommended,' Tara said, looking at the screen of her tablet, 'and Hep B, typhoid, diphtheria and tuberculosis are suggested.'

Natalie looked confused. Is "recommended" one of those understated British ways of saying, "you'd be stupid not to"? Like "we *recommend* you wear a sun hat if you're going to spend several hours on Laguna Beach"? or "we *recommend* that you don't put your entire arm inside a crocodile's mouth"?'

Tara shook her head. 'No,' she said, 'that's "*strongly* recommended". Different category entirely. There are no "*strongly* recommended" inoculations for Hong Kong.'

'Great,' Calum said, clapping his hands together. 'Go and start packing. Let's meet back here tomorrow, and hopefully Rhino can be here as well.'

The coffee shop was on the edge of a small unfenced area of trees and grass – more of a village green than a park, Rhino Gillis thought to himself. He was moving around casually, as if looking for something in particular. There was a pet shop on one side and an extreme sports shop on the other. There were also a lot of restaurants and wine bars – more than one might expect for an area like this.

He was in Poole – a seaside town a stone's throw away from Bournemouth. He was on business, and hadn't chosen the location, but he was familiar with the area. The Royal Marines and the Special Boat Service – the SAS's aquatic sibling – were both based in Hamworthy Barracks, just a walk away.

That knowledge was going to give him an edge, and often having an edge was what saved his life.

He could smell the distant sea, and more closely the bitter odour of roasting coffee beans. Seagulls wheeled overhead in a bright blue sky. Men and women were lying out on the grass, soaking up the sunshine, probably realizing that this was likely to be the only summer's day that year. Dogs were being walked by relaxed owners in shorts or cargo pants. One of the dogs – a big black Labrador – was playing in the fountain in the centre of the park.

With a practised gaze he checked out the various people around him. None of them seemed to be paying him undue attention. None of them looked as though they were poised to spring into action if anything suddenly happened. To all intents and purposes, everyone was what they seemed: local people relaxing in the hot weather.

He walked into the cafe. It was small, wood-floored, with hand-painted cartoons on the walls.

Rhino scanned the tables. Only two of them were occupied: one by an elderly woman and the other by two blond surfer types who were talking in low voices. His contact had not yet arrived.

He put his jacket down on a chair close to the door and went up to the counter. A small blonde girl with a tattooed arm smiled at him. 'What can I get you?'

'A double espresso,' he replied, smiling back.

'Anything to eat?'

'Too hot,' he said. 'I completely lose my appetite in the summer.'

'I know what you mean. Take a seat and I'll bring the coffee over.'

He sat at the table he had already reserved with his jacket, making sure that his back was against the wall and that he could see the entire cafe.

He checked his watch. One minute to go.

The blonde girl brought his coffee across and placed it in front of him. He smiled a 'thank you' and took a sip of the bitter liquid.

On the dot of one o'clock a man walked into the cafe. He was tall, black, with close-cropped black hair. He was wearing suit trousers, but had the jacket slung over his arm. His white shirt was crisp despite the heat. He had the sleeves rolled up. His tie was pulled loose.

He saw Rhino, nodded, and came across to stand over the table.

'Mr Gillis?'

Rhino nodded.

'My name is Tzuke.' His voice was deep and almost theatrical. 'Forgive me, but given the circumstances I won't shake hands.'

'Worried that I might be able to trace you through DNA transfer?' Rhino asked, smiling.

Tzuke smiled back, but didn't say anything.

'Can I get you a drink?' Rhino asked.

'Let me pay for *your* drink, and get one for myself.' He smiled, revealing perfect white teeth. 'It's the least I can do.'

He turned and went up to the counter. Rhino glanced outside the cafe. Nobody else was standing there. Either Tzuke had come alone or his bodyguards were being exceptionally discreet.

The man returned with a glass of cloudy lemonade, placed his jacket on the back of a chair and sat down. He glanced at Rhino's chest. 'Thank you for leaving your jacket off. I can see no evidence of any recording device on you.' He ran his hands beneath the table, leaning forward to cover the area nearer Rhino. The floral smell of his aftershave was almost overpowering. 'And nothing hidden beneath the table either. Well done.'

'Your instructions were clear,' Rhino said calmly. He nodded his head towards the coffee roaster. 'And, besides, I presume you chose the location and the time so that there would be enough background noise to prevent any eavesdropping.'

'Indeed,' Tzuke said casually, 'but technology has come a long way; it's best to take all precautions possible. Speaking of which, may I see your mobile phone?'

Rhino took it out of his jacket and placed it on the table. While Tzuke checked it over with economical, practised movements he took another sip of his espresso, nearly finishing it.

'Already switched off,' Tzuke said. 'Thank you. I am carrying a mobile-phone jammer in my suit, of course, but I always believe in a "belt and braces" approach.'

'You've done this before,' Rhino murmured.

Tzuke raised an eyebrow. 'You need to be aware that I am just a facilitator,' he said, 'a go-between. I am not a criminal.'

'You just work for criminals,' Rhino said.

'I make no moral judgements. I am a solicitor. I am hired to do a job by a client. The job is entirely legal.'

'Two people were kidnapped by Somali pirates while they were sailing off the coast of Africa,' Rhino pointed out, 'and you are here collecting the ransom. That doesn't sound legal to me.'

'I don't know what the money is for,' Tzuke said, smiling cheerfully, 'and I don't know where it is going. I have merely been hired to collect a payment and pass it on.'

'While taking a cut yourself.'

'I am providing a business service. That does not come free.'

'Speaking of the "service" you provide, I believe you have to give me proof of life,' Rhino countered. 'I need to know that Peter and Sarah Wilkerson are still alive and in good health; otherwise the ransom does not get paid and you do not get your cut.'

Tzuke reached into his jacket and removed a brown A4

envelope, which had been folded in half. He handed it across to Rhino. 'I do not know what is in the envelope. I was just told to give it to you.'

Rhino pulled the flap open and removed a single sheet of paper. It was a photograph, printed by a laser printer. It showed a couple who looked as if they were in their thirties. It also looked as if they had been wearing the same clothes for several weeks, and had spent most of that time either worrying or crying. There were shadows beneath their eyes, and the man – definitely Peter Wilkerson, based on other photographs Rhino had seen, provided by his family – was unshaven. They both looked as if they were at the end of their tether. Peter Wilkerson had his arm protectively around his wife's shoulders. She was holding up an African newspaper so that the front page was clearly visible. Rhino presumed that it was yesterday's newspaper, proving at least that they had been alive and in relatively good health twenty-four hours ago. He would make sure later, from his laptop.

'Is that sufficient?' Tzuke asked.

'It is.'

'Thankfully, the days when the envelope would have contained a severed finger or an ear are long gone. Digital cameras and emails are a boon.'

'By the way,' Rhino said, 'if we checked, I presume we wouldn't find out that this image had been printed on your *own* home or office printer?' He folded the page back up and put it back into the envelope.

'Of course not.' Tzuke smiled his easy smile again. 'I am

not that stupid, and neither are my clients.'

'Of course.' Rhino smiled back at him. 'You *are* Somali though, aren't you?'

'As are several million other people, most of whom are neither engaged in acts of piracy nor working for or with the pirates. I am, as I said, just a solicitor.' He indicated the envelope. 'Are you satisfied?'

'Very little about this business satisfies me, but that's a cross I have to bear. You seem to have fulfilled your side of the agreement.'

'Then I believe you have an envelope for me.'

'For *you*?'

'To transfer to my clients,' he continued smoothly. 'Unopened.'

Rhino removed a smaller white envelope from his own pocket. He slid it across the table. 'This is a banker's draft for half a million pounds. Being a banker's draft, it cannot be rescinded or cancelled. It is as good as cash.'

'With the advantage,' Tzuke said, taking the envelope, 'of being a lot easier to carry. I would not want to be carrying around a briefcase with half a million pounds in it. Not in this heat.'

Rhino indicated the envelope. 'Don't lose it. Mr and Mrs Wilkerson are depending on that money to free them. It would be tragic if it was carried away by a freak gust of wind.'

'Worry not. I will take all possible precautions with this envelope before passing it to my clients.'

Tzuke held the envelope up and stared at it for a

moment. He ran his fingers along it, looking for the tell-tale bulge of an electronic tracking device, Rhino presumed. Finding nothing, he slid the envelope into an inside jacket pocket.

'As I said,' Rhino murmured, 'you *have* done this before.'

Tzuke ignored the taunt. 'Was it their family or their employers who provided the money?' he asked.

'Does it matter?'

The solicitor shrugged. 'I suppose not. I am merely interested in the generosity of people in the Western world towards relatives, friends and work colleagues.'

'I take it your . . . clients . . . wouldn't do the same for you?'

Tzuke glanced sharply at Rhino. 'You and I both know what the penalty for failure, carelessness and bad luck is in our respective professions,' he said quietly.

Rhino smiled. 'You're just a solicitor,' he said, 'and I'm just a postman.' He paused. 'What are the arrangements for the handover?'

'I understand from my clients that the . . . goods . . . will be released in the port of Mogadishu, close to the British embassy. Then they will be on their own.'

'And you know, of course, that if you *don't* release them then nobody will ever pay a ransom again?'

Tzuke nodded.

'Then I think our business is complete.'

Tzuke picked up his lemonade and drained it in one go. He reached into a jacket and pulled out a plastic bottle with a spray top. He sprayed the empty glass with some colourless fluid, and then, using one napkin to pick up the glass, he used a second napkin to wipe the glass dry, then very carefully wiped down any part of the table that he might have touched, including the underneath.

'More DNA and fingerprint paranoia?' Rhino inquired.

Tzuke shook his head. 'Call it a pathological desire to leave everything neat and tidy.' Placing the glass down on the table, he stood up and retrieved his jacket from the back of the chair. 'I have taken the liberty of paying for another coffee for you. I suggest you stay here for at least twenty minutes before you leave. Do not try to follow me. Mr and Mrs Wilkerson would not be happy if you did that.'

Rhino watched the man leave. As he sat there, draining the last bitter dregs of his espresso, he turned his mobile phone back on. Immediately it told him that he had a text message. He checked it curiously, and was surprised to find that it was from Eduardo Ortiz – or Gecko, as Rhino had learned to call him. The message was terse, but informative. *Strange animal seen in Hong Kong. Need your help to travel out and find it. Are you interested and free?*

A strange animal? Presumably it wasn't going to be anything the size of an Almasti. Maybe it would just be a snake, or a beetle, or something.

A few days away in a place he liked with a bunch of kids whose company he enjoyed? And presumably paid as well? What could go wrong?

four

The car was arriving at seven o'clock in the morning to pick up Calum and Tara.

Tara had slept in one of Calum's spare rooms, and she had stayed up late working on ARLENE at Calum's request: deleting all information from the robot's memory on where they had used it. Seven o'clock in the morning was a lot earlier than she normally got up. When she came out of the bathroom ten minutes before the car was due, she was rubbing her eyes – smearing her heavy eyeliner – and yawning.

'Sleep OK?' Calum asked, sipping at the breakfast smoothie he had made himself. He had been awake for a while.

'Uh, I guess,' she slurred. 'I kinda stayed up, checking stuff out on the internet. I've got a lot of background material on Hong Kong and the Triads that I can give to Rhino, Gecko and Natalie before they go.' She winced. 'I think I lost track of time.'

'What time did you *actually* go to sleep?'

'About an hour ago.'

He raised an eyebrow and slid another smoothie across to her. 'A couple of times I thought I heard you laughing. I guess that research must have been pretty funny, huh?'

She blushed, and wouldn't meet his gaze. 'OK, I also got emailing with this guy I know. He was awake as well.'

'A guy? You mean you were laughing and joking with an actual male person?' He stopped and thought for a minute. 'In *my* apartment?'

'It's not like he was actually *here*.'

'That's not the point.'

'It's exactly the point.' She glanced at him suspiciously. 'Besides, what were *you* doing awake so late?'

He wouldn't look at her. 'I kept waking up.'

'Worried about today?'

He shrugged, not really wanting to talk about it.

'It'll be OK, you know?' she said.

He nodded. 'I suppose it will. I just don't want to get my hopes up.'

She nodded. 'I can understand that.' She hesitated, putting her head to one side and staring at him. 'The problem is, I think, that you want success to be all or nothing.'

Her words stung him, because he'd come to the same conclusion himself, lying awake in bed, but he just scowled and said, 'I don't know what you mean.'

'I mean that you either want to be completely cured of your paralysis or not cured at all. You don't want to have to compromise with a half-solution that still leaves you with problems.'

'And you're a psychologist now, as well as being a computer programmer?'

'Hey,' she said, smiling, 'if the brain is just an advanced computer, then the two are essentially the same thing, aren't they?'

'No,' he said firmly, 'they aren't, and you know it. Computer programmers deal in hard facts and testable algorithms, while psychologists just make good guesses based on what people tell them and then try to pretend they have some big theory that backs it all up.'

'Actually, I think that's "psych*iatrists*, rather than psych*ologists*, but I know what you mean.' She bit her lip briefly. 'Did you ever . . . you know . . . see a psychiatrist after the . . . the crash?'

He laughed bitterly. '"I keep seeing purple cows. Am I going mad?" "Tell me, have you seen a psychiatrist?" "No, only purple cows".'

'Look, if you don't want to answer the question . . .'

He shook his head. 'Sorry. I have a bad habit of getting sarcastic when someone asks me something personal. It's a defence mechanism.'

'You don't say!' she murmured innocently.

He glared at her, and then had to smile. She was just trying to help, he knew that. 'Yes, I saw a psychiatrist for a while. Gillian arranged it. "Trauma counselling", she called it.'

'Did it help?'

He shook his head, remembering the sessions he'd had

in a small front room in an old three-storey house in north London. He'd still been in a wheelchair then. 'He told me that I was failing to acknowledge the truth of my injuries because, if I did, it would mean actually admitting that my parents were dead. I told him that I *knew* my parents were dead, and he was just wasting Gillian's money.' Calum laughed briefly: a harsh sound. 'If I could have walked out, I would have done. Instead we had to wait half an hour until the session was over and Mr Macfarlane came to get me.' The thought of Macfarlane made him glance at his watch reflexively. 'Speaking of which, you'd better get that drink down your throat. He'll be here in a minute or two.'

Tara eyed the smoothie suspiciously. 'What exactly *is* that thing?'

'Goat's yogurt, Manuka honey, kiwi fruit, bran and banana, all expertly blended together. It's the best thing for you in the morning.' He indicated the kettle. 'The water's just boiled as well, and I got in some of those green-tea teabags that Gecko says you like.'

Tara glanced around and reached out for the sealed container of ground coffee that Calum kept on the counter. Opening it, she poured a large spoonful into a mug and then poured hot water from the kettle into the mug. She swilled it back and forth for a bit, and then put it down. Looking around, she saw a large bowl in the sink. Retrieving it, she poured the breakfast smoothie into it, then added the coffee, straining it through a tea strainer to remove the coffee grounds. Finally she whisked the whole lot together with a spoon, then raised the bowl to her lips and drained it in one go.

'That's better,' she said, yogurt still on her upper lip.

Calum watched with morbid fascination. 'That was disgusting. And I thought Gecko said you'd given up coffee.'

'I had, but it hadn't given up on me.' She gazed up at him through her black-encrusted eyelashes. 'Look, I *need* the caffeine to keep me going, OK?'

He raised his hands in surrender. 'OK, that's fine, but you know that coffee isn't actually a stimulant if you drink it regularly, don't you? The apparent stimulant effect is only due to the fact that your body gets used to it and gets withdrawal symptoms if it doesn't get a regular dose, and what you *think* is a stimulant effect is actually just your body avoiding the withdrawal symptoms.'

'Whatever,' she growled. 'At least it makes me feel better.'

Calum frowned. 'And by the way – that's a very expensive coffee to be mixing with fruit and goat's yogurt. If you're going to do that again, then I'll get some instant coffee for you. I wouldn't touch the stuff myself, but at least you won't be depleting my special supply.'

Tara glanced at the container of coffee suspiciously. 'Do you get that stuff imported?'

'I do.'

'Is it a special gourmet coffee?'

'It is.'

She winced. 'Please tell me it's not that special coffee

that I've heard about – the one where the ripe coffee berries fall off coffee bushes growing wild in the jungle, and they get eaten by jungle cats, and by the time the seeds inside the berries have passed through the digestive system of the cats they've been softened by the stomach acids, so if they're collected from the droppings, and cleaned and roasted, then the resulting coffee is really sweet and not bitter at all. Please tell me it's not *that* coffee.'

'It's *not* that coffee,' he said reassuringly. After a pause, he added: 'Although that particular coffee, which is called kopi luwak, by the way, is exceptionally good.'

'You've drunk it?'

'I have.'

'And this isn't it?'

'It isn't.

'You're sure?'

'I would have remembered.'

'OK,' she said dubiously.

'This is an organic nkempte from Ethiopia. It hasn't been near – or through – any cats. Trust me on that.' Calum took the bowl from her with one hand and put it in the sink. He paused, thinking, then turned back to Tara. 'It's civet cats in Indonesia that eat the coffee berries,' he said seriously. 'And, yes, the enzymes and acids in their stomachs do soften and sweeten the seeds – the bits that we call the coffee beans. The trouble is that the local Indonesians, knowing how much the coffee sells for in the West, have taken to capturing the civet cats, keeping them in battery cages in their thousands, and feeding them any old coffee berries that they can find. They've turned something special in nature into something grotesque in farming. I stopped drinking the stuff when I found out.'

'Good for you,' Tara said as the door buzzer sounded.

Calum called out, 'Come in, Mr Macfarlane!'

The door opened. Standing there was Mr Macfarlane, the chauffeur and handyman of Calum's Great-Aunt Merrily. He was small – smaller than Tara – with close-cropped hair that was barely distinguishable from the stubble that spread across his cheeks and chin. He wore a pinstripe suit with a waistcoat and a spotted tie. He had always reminded Calum of a cross between a garden gnome and an East End gangster.

'Mornin', sir,' he said in a husky voice. He nodded towards Tara. 'Ma'am.'

'We're heading off towards Farnborough,' Calum told him. 'I can give you the exact address when we get closer.'

'You've got a satnav?' Tara asked. 'If not, we can use my tablet. I've got a 4G connection and a GPS chip, so it's always receiving.'

Macfarlane tapped his forehead. 'Don't need a satnav, ma'am. It's all up 'ere.' He glanced back at Calum. 'You got a box for me, sir?'

Calum indicated the crate containing the bionic leg braces. 'We've got to take that with us. Can you manage?'

'I can manage stuff bigger than that, sir, with respect.' He frowned. 'But what about . . . ?'

Calum felt his muscles tense, and forced himself to

relax. Macfarlane was talking – or, rather, *not* talking – about the wheelchair. It was use the wheelchair to get down to the limousine or be carried. Calum didn't particularly fancy either option, but of the two the wheelchair was the least objectionable. Marginally.

He turned his head to look at Tara. 'Would you . . . ?' he started, unexpectedly tongue-tied, 'I mean, could you . . . ?'

'Yes,' she said simply, 'of course I could.'

Calum was about to ask her how she knew what he meant, but she was already going to the cupboard near the door where he kept his wheelchair.

'Don't worry,' Tara murmured. 'I won't tell anyone about it. At least, I won't if you keep quiet about me falling off the coffee wagon.'

'It's a fair trade,' Calum said. He swung himself across the room towards the door. Macfarlane moved inside, out of his way, and walked across to the crate. 'Come on, then. Let's get this out of the way so we can concentrate on the big rat.'

'I saw a big rat once,' Macfarlane said conversationally to Tara. 'In a warehouse by the side of the Thames. Big thing, it was, 'bout the size of a cat.'

'This one is larger,' Tara confided.

'Right.' He was quiet for a moment. 'You'll probably need a shotgun, then. I just used a revolver.'

Calum swung himself into the wheelchair, while Tara went out into the corridor and held the lift doors open. Macfarlane emerged from the apartment with the crate held in his arms like a dancing partner. He swung the door closed with his foot, and Calum activated the security systems with a remote control on his key ring.

Tara hadn't used the warehouse goods lift to go downstairs before. She'd always used the stairs. It was old, wooden and creaky, and it shuddered so much that she was worried they might not make it to the ground floor.

Outside, the limousine was a symphony in polished black metal and chrome. 'Ready to go?' Tara asked.

'As ready as I'll ever be,' Calum replied.

By the time Rhino had read and considered the text message from Gecko, the solicitor representing the Somali kidnappers – Tzuke – had left the cafe.

Moments later, the elderly woman who had been sitting in the corner of the cafe got up and walked out without catching Rhino's eye. She turned the same way that Tzuke did as she left.

The blonde waitress watched her go with a frown. She seemed to be just about to run after her when Rhino caught her eye.

'It's all right,' he said, 'I'll pay for her coffee. I . . . know her.'

The blonde smiled uncertainly. 'OK – thanks!'

Rhino sat there for a few moments, imagining the elderly woman following Tzuke discretely from a distance. Her age made her almost invisible. Anyone looking for a follower would be expecting someone younger, stronger, more military-looking.

One of the surfers at the other table got up and went to the counter to pay for his coffee. As he handed the money across, he half turned and, without looking at Rhino, said: 'What's our next move?'

'When Liz reports back on where his office and home are located, I want both of them bugged. Surreptitiously, of course. Landlines and mobiles bugged as well,' replied Rhino.

'Of course. "Surreptitious" is my middle name."

"Your middle name is Franklin. I've seen your personnel file.'

'You want him followed after that?'

Rhino shook his head. 'He'll pay the banker's draft into a bank as quickly as he can. Unless we've got someone actually looking over his shoulder we won't know what account it gets paid into. He'll let his clients know that he's paid it in though, and that the handover went smoothly. If we can trace the call, we might have a shot at identifying them and where their base is.'

The surfer nodded. 'Probably won't help these particular hostages,' he said grimly.

'They'll be free, if the pirates fulfil their side of the bargain. Knowing who and where they are might help us when the next hostages are taken for ransom.'

'Or,' the surfer said quietly, 'we could just go in mob-handed and take them all out in whatever rat-infested corner of Somalia they have their base. Stop any more piracy.'

'But who would pay us to recover hostages if there are no more pirates?' Rhino asked.

The surfer frowned. 'Doesn't that make us—'

'Don't go there,' Rhino interrupted harshly. 'Just be content that we're on the side of the angels.'

The surfer smiled. 'As long as someone has told the angels that, I'll be happy.' He gestured to his friend, who got up and collected their possessions from the table. 'Good working with you again, Rhino.'

'Likewise. I'll have your fee paid across via bank transfer.'

'Appreciated.' He slid some money across the counter towards the waitress and left, along with his companion.

The girl looked curiously at Rhino. 'Do you know *everyone* in here?'

'I've got a lot of friends in the area. It's nice to see them from time to time.'

She smiled sunnily. 'Fair enough. It's good to have friends.' She paused. 'Did you want that other coffee now?'

'Yes, please.'

He sat there until he had finished his second coffee and until Tzuke was a good distance away, and presumably unaware that he was being followed by a little old lady who had been one of the first women in Special Forces. Everyone called her 'Grandma', but Rhino knew some of the missions she had been involved in over the years, some of the things she had done, and she was about as far away from the popular conception of a cuddly grandmother as a lion was from a Siamese cat.

He thought for a moment about Gecko's text message. Hong Kong. He hadn't been there for a good few years, but he remembered its bustle, its life and its vibrant energy with great affection. He'd still been in the British army then, and was on a highly sensitive mission close to the Chinese border, but he'd managed to take a week's leave afterwards, and spent it enjoying Hong Kong's nightlife. It was the island, just a little way off the mainland, that was officially Hong Kong, of course, but the former British dependency expanded to the area of Kowloon on the mainland and back into the New Territories.

After waiting long enough for Tzuke to clear the area, Rhino walked the couple of miles to the station. The sun beat down on him, bringing out a light sweat, but there was a cooling breeze coming in from the sea, and Rhino comforted himself with the thought that he had been in places a lot hotter than this while wearing body armour and a helmet at the same time.

From Poole station he caught a train to London. He had a netbook with him, so he was able to catch up on work – responding to emails and bringing his accounts up to date. The netbook was fully encrypted, of course, and virus-protected too. It had to be. It would be embarrassing at the very least if his contacts list, his mission reports and the contents of some of his emails were obtained by someone like Tzuke, or the people for whom he worked.

As the thought crossed his mind, he glanced around casually, as if trying to work out where the train was on its journey. Nobody in the carriage was paying him any interest. Three of the other passengers had got on at Poole with him, and so theoretically could have been following him in the same way that his people were following Tzuke, but he wasn't detecting any interest from them. He would just have to keep an eye on them when he got out at Waterloo station and, of course, make sure that if he got up to go to the toilet that he took his netbook with him.

The journey took just over two hours. By the time he looked up from his screen again he was approaching London Waterloo station. Calum's warehouse apartment was a reasonable walk or a short taxi ride away. He decided to go on foot – the route would take him along the Thames, past a number of historic sites, and Tower Bridge. He always enjoyed walking around London.

As he walked off the train and on to the concourse at Waterloo station, he kept an eye on the three people who had got on with him at Poole. He made sure that he was last off the carriage, following them rather than the other way round. None of them looked back to see where he was, and as soon as they got through the ticket barrier they headed off in the direction of the Underground. Either nobody was following him or, he thought with a prickle of unease, whoever *was* following him was exceptionally good. Unlikely, but possible.

As he headed for the exit, his invisible mental antennae pricked up. Something had caught the attention of his subconscious mind – something important. Was it a watcher – a follower? Instead of glancing around to see what or who it was, Rhino let his mind and gaze wander. He knew how his subconscious operated. It would either bring the anomalous element to his attention, or it wouldn't find it again.

His gaze drifted to the coffee shop on the far side of the station, and his conscious mind suddenly realized that his subconscious had identified two people there. They were sitting at a table talking, heads close together. The reason his conscious mind had ignored the information was that he'd never seen them together before, and he hadn't known that they knew one another. In fact, there were very good reasons why they *shouldn't* know one another.

One of them was named Craig Roxton. He was tall and thin, with a face that was all angles and planes. His hair was blond and fine, and in high winds it would whip back off his face into a short comet's tail. Rhino knew that because he knew Craig Roxton. The man had once been in Special Forces, fighting alongside Rhino in some of the most unpleasant places in the world. They had both left the British army at more or less the same time, and for more or less the same reasons, but they had gone in different directions. Rhino had ended up in hostage rescue and bodyguard work – things that made him feel as if he was doing some good in the world. Roxton had become a mercenary, hiring himself out to anyone who could pay, and willing to do anything they wanted. And the last employer that Rhino had heard about, the last set of people whose money Roxton had been taking, was Nemor Incorporated.

Nemor Incorporated – the secretive, mysterious company that had tried to use Tara to spy on Calum, and then had kidnapped Natalie and threatened to torture her. Not a nice bunch of people, which meant, as far as Rhino was concerned, that they and Craig Roxton deserved one another.

If it had just been Roxton there by himself, sipping a cappuccino, or if Roxton had been sitting with a total stranger, then Rhino would have slipped back into the crowd and gone on his way. He had no desire ever to encounter Roxton again. The problem was that he was sitting at a table with someone Rhino knew.

It was Professor Gillian Livingstone – Natalie's mother.

Rhino moved into the shadow of a row of ticket machines. He let his body and head point across the concourse, towards the main exit, but allowed his gaze to drift sideways so that he could see the two of them without them being aware that he was looking in their direction. The fragmentary hope he'd nurtured that the two of them had accidentally ended up on the same table – two travellers heading in different directions whose lives had momentarily crossed – was dashed when he saw Gillian pass Roxton a sheet of paper. He picked it up and read through it, then nodded and said something to her. She shook her head.

This, Rhino decided, was bad. The possibility that there was a link between Gillian Livingstone and Nemor Incorporated meant that Calum's team potentially had a spy in its midst. Rhino didn't believe that Natalie was involved as well – he had seen how terrified she had been when she had escaped from Roxton's clutches – but her mother was privy to all Calum's secrets.

The question was, what was he going to tell Calum?

And what was he going to tell Natalie?

'Comfortable?' Tara asked Calum as they set off in the car towards Farnborough.

'Not so's you would notice,' he said. He and Tara were sitting in the back of the limousine and Tara could see that Calum's knuckles were white as they clutched at his knees. 'Cars make me nervous, for obvious reasons.'

'I understand.'

The limousine joined one of the main arterial roads that linked the beating heart of London to the rest of the country.

'Can I put some music on for you, sir?' Mr Macfarlane's gruff voice asked from the front.

'What are you listening to at the moment?' Calum asked.

'Dubstep,' the voice came back straight away.

'Definitely not!' Calum and Tara chorused together.

Calum glanced at Tara and raised an eyebrow. 'I'd go for post-rock,' he said, 'and I think Tara here would go for emo. What have you got that's in the middle?'

'Dark Wave, I fink,' Macfarlane said judiciously. 'Perhaps some Dead Can Dance?'

Tara nodded. 'I'm willing to give it a go,' she said.

Within a few moments the car was filled with a throbbing soundscape that had elements of African rhythms, Celtic pipes and Eastern European plucked strings. Tara hadn't heard anything quite like it before, but she approved immediately.

'Good choice,' Calum said.

'Thank you, sir.'

The car drove on and Calum seemed wrapped up in his own thoughts, his forehead lowered broodingly as he stared at something that only he could see, and so Tara busied herself on her tablet computer. She checked her emails, and immediately saw one from the *lostworlds.co.uk* fan who had emailed her before – Tom Karavla.

Hi Tara,

You asked how I got interested in cryptids. I guess I've always been interested, ever since I was a kid. It started off with dinosaurs, and then I started getting obsessed with the possibility that dinosaurs might still exist, somewhere in the world. Not like the Loch Ness Monster actually being a plesiosaur – that's much more likely to be a collection of branches and twigs that just happens to look like something with a long neck and a small head – but more that there might be a small area somewhere unexplored, maybe in South America or Africa, where dinosaurs still exist. What do you think?

Regards,

Tom

So, it was 'Tom' now, and not 'Tom Karavla' she noted. He was getting less formal, more friendly. She felt a little shiver of pleasure at the thought: she had a new friend. *Another* new friend, to go along with Calum, Gecko, Natalie and Rhino.

Calum glanced up from whatever dark realm his thoughts had taken him to. 'Something interesting?' he asked.

'Just someone wanting to talk about cryptids,' she said.

Calum's lowered eyebrows raised in interest. 'Have they seen one?'

'No – they just want to talk about dinosaurs.'

'Dinosaurs!' Calum snorted dismissively. 'I don't think anyone seriously thinks there are any dinosaurs out there in the wild. Not any more.'

Calum sank back into his thoughts, and Tara started typing a response into her tablet.

Hi Tom,

I think if there were any dinosaurs out there any more they would have evolved into something new and different by now. Isn't it strange that any films and TV programmes about dinosaurs still living these days assume that they stopped evolving several million years ago, and still look exactly the same now as they did then?

Funny you should mention the Loch Ness Monster. The best explanation I ever saw for it was that circuses driving up and down the road that runs alongside Loch

Ness used to stop and let their elephants swim in the water, to cool them down and to let them get a drink. An elephant, swimming just beneath the water looks a lot like some kind of plesiosaur – there's the hump made by its back, another hump made by the tops of its head and then the trunk looking like a neck with a small head at the end. Someone seeing the elephant swimming might mistake it for a monster. Strange, but true!

Regards,

Tara

She reread it, just to check that she wasn't sounding stupid, and then pressed *Send*.

She browsed the internet for a while, and did some administrative stuff on *thelostworlds.co.uk*. She kept checking her emails, but there was no response from Tom. She wondered why. Maybe he'd gone offline, or maybe she *had* said something stupid and he'd decided to stop talking to her. She wanted to send another message straight away to apologize, but she stopped herself. That would just make her seem needy. She had to wait for him to respond.

When she looked up from her screen, the car was travelling along a country lane. They must have come off the motorway without her realizing.

Macfarlane swung the car left, off the road, and up to

a set of gates. They were closed, but there was a security box just where the driver's window would be when the car stopped. As Macfarlane lowered the window, Tara gazed around. The security gates were in a double fence, both stretches of which were topped with barbed wire. The inside fence was electrified as well, if the signs hanging on it were to be believed. If there was a building inside the wire, then it was hidden by trees and some expert landscaping.

'Yes?' a voice said from the security box. It might have been human, or it might have been computer-generated.

'Oi 'ave Mr Calum Challenger,' Mr Macfarlane said gruffly. 'Oi believe you are expectin' 'im.'

Tara heard a loud electronic buzz, and the gates began to swing open. 'Please follow the road,' the voice said, 'and park in a designated visitor spot. Someone will be there to meet you in reception.'

'Their customer relations leave a lot to be desired,' Calum murmured as they drove through the gap and the gates swung shut behind them. 'I'm beginning to regret this already.'

five

'**T**his is the mobility lab,' Dr Kircher said as he gestured Calum and Tara through yet another security door and into a large, over-illuminated space. There were tables along the walls, something that looked like a medical scanner off to one side and a harness hanging from the ceiling that, Calum suspected, was there for him to be strapped into like a puppet. It was attached to a set of tracks that ran from one side of the lab to the other.

He was not enjoying this. Not one bit.

Dr Kircher had met Calum and Tara in reception. He had obviously been expecting Calum, but Tara came as a surprise to him. It was also obviously the bionic legs that he really wanted to see. Calum was just a means to an end.

Tara walked beside Calum as he manoeuvred his wheelchair into the lab. He suspected that the next couple of hours were going to be painful and emotional, and the fewer people who saw him like that the better.

Across on the other side of the lab, two assistants were carefully unpacking the mechanical legs from their crate and laying them on a table, spreading the wires out so they didn't become entangled.

'So what kind of things do you do here?' Tara asked politely to break the tension.

'We study the ways in which biological organisms walk, and we try to replicate those ways as closely as we can using technology,' Dr Kircher answered. He was a thin man, with black hair brushed straight back from his prominent forehead. He had a way of walking fast and with long strides that, Calum thought ironically, would be a challenge to replicate with technology.

'Why?' Tara asked simply. Calum smiled inwardly. She was very good at asking apparently innocent but actually quite pointed questions like that.

'A whole variety of reasons,' Dr Kircher answered. 'For one, we can calculate the likely weight and speed of dinosaurs by looking at their fossilized bones, looking at the grooves where the tendons would have attached and then simulating it all on a computer. That's useful not only for palaeontologists, but also for film and TV special-effects companies, so they can make their CGI creatures look as realistic as possible.'

Strange, Calum thought — *we were only talking about dinosaurs half an hour ago in the car.* Out loud, he said, 'That's great, but it's not going to help me much.'

'True,' Dr Kircher said with a tight smile. 'We do a lot of work with athletes as well, helping them optimize their running, or jumping, or swimming, or whatever it is that they do. Sometimes a small change in gait can achieve a big reduction in energy expenditure for a given result.' Before Calum could interrupt, Kircher raised a hand and said: 'And that also applies to paralympic athletes. We design prosthetic running blades for sprinters, and prosthetic fins for swimmers, all based on computer-aided designs.'

'And that's where I come in,' Calum said.

'Exactly.' The doctor gestured at Calum's lower half. 'Your legs are still present, with all the joints and muscles, but the nerve impulses aren't getting through. With the right mechanical exoskeleton we can provide the power in the right place at the right time to get your legs moving in the same way that they would if your spine was intact. In effect, we provide the nervous impulses.' He frowned. 'One day, of course,' he went on, 'we hope to be able to regenerate nerve tissue, but that's a while away yet.'

Not if I have anything to do with it, Calum thought.

'But you are going to use Calum's brain impulses to control the legs, aren't you?' Tara said. 'Did I get that right?'

'That's exactly right. Another part of what we do here is to analyse the electrical activity in the brain when decisions are taken to do various things, like walking, or picking an object up off a table. Once we've characterized Calum's brain processes, we can programme the controller on the legs to react to his thoughts.' He grinned, and clapped his hands together. 'It's like telepathy!'

Calum winced. 'OK, then,' he said. 'Where do we start? Do you want me in that harness while you strap the legs on?'

Kircher frowned. 'Oh no, that won't be necessary. Not yet, anyway. What we need to do first is take a look inside your brain.' He gestured towards the medical scanner.

'That's an MRI scanner, isn't it?' Tara asked.

'It is,' Kircher said.

'It uses a strong magnetic field to invert all the neurons in your brain,' Tara said, patting Calum on the shoulder. 'When the field is turned off, the neurons return to their previous orientation and give out a radio impulse. The machine picks up the radio impulses and uses them to draw up a three-dimensional map of your mind.'

Calum stared at the machine balefully. 'Are you seriously trying to tell me that every single atom in my brain gets rearranged by that thing and then *pings* back like a rubber band?'

'Pretty much,' said Kircher, eyebrow raised as he stared at Tara. 'We then inject a radioactive contrast medium into your bloodstream and take some more readings while you're thinking about various actions – moving your lower left leg, moving your upper left leg, and so on. The contrast medium will tell us which parts of your brain are active when you're thinking about those things. We can then target those areas with a net of electrodes across your scalp specifically tuned to pick up electrical triggers in those areas.'

'You make it sound so easy,' Calum murmured.

Kircher turned to Tara. 'This is going to take a while,' he said in a suddenly businesslike tone of voice. 'You'll be bored. I'll arrange to have you driven back to London.'

'That's not necessary,' she said brightly. 'Technology fascinates me. I'm happy to stay and watch.'

Kircher looked apologetic, but firm. 'Trade secrets, I'm afraid. We're willing to extend some latitude to Mr Challenger here, but you are . . . an unknown quantity, I'm afraid. We didn't know you were coming. You will have to go.'

Tara started to protest, but Calum raised a hand. 'If that's what Dr Kircher wants,' he said, 'then it's for the best. I'll get Mr Macfarlane to take you back. He can come back for me afterwards.'

He could tell that Tara wanted to stay, but he also didn't want to annoy Dr Kircher. These legs were his way out of paralysis, and now that he had come this far he fully intended to take advantage of them.

'Sorry,' he added.

Tara just looked at him. 'If that's what you want,' she said eventually, in a small and very controlled voice, 'then that's what I'll do. Have fun.'

Calum watched her go, feeling guilt washing through him. He half wanted to call her back, but Dr Kircher seemed so sure that she couldn't be there, and Calum didn't want Dr Kircher to pull the plug on the tests and the fitting session.

Kircher handed him a tablet computer and an electronic pen. 'If you can just sign this form . . .' he said casually. 'It's a standard waiver, in case anything goes wrong.'

Calum scribbled his signature in the box on the tablet. He was eager to find out what happened next . . .

*

Calum felt like an idiot. He also felt as if he should never have agreed to come along to the Robledo Mountains Technology laboratories in the first place.

He was suspended in the cradle that he had seen earlier – the one that ran along a track attached to the ceiling of the lab. The waistcoat-like corset was strapped round his chest so tightly that he couldn't breathe properly, and his legs hung uselessly down, dangling a few centimetres above the floor. He had a skullcap of thin wires wound through his hair, close to his scalp, and thicker ones that ran round his forehead. A small box had been stuck to the nape of his neck with some kind of biological glue, which, they had promised him, wouldn't be permanent.

Worse than that, he'd had to take his trousers off, and was hanging there in his boxer shorts and a T-shirt.

'I feel like the fairy in a cheap pantomime,' he said. He raised a hand to the wires that ran round his forehead. 'If I just move this thing up a few centimetres, it could be a halo.'

Everyone ignored him. The various technicians bustled around the laboratory, taking readings and typing into computers. The big display on the wall showed various coloured graphs in three dimensions, updating every second with new readings.

'No, seriously,' he said, 'how much longer am I going to have to hang around here?'

He was glad that Tara wasn't there to see his humiliation. He could feel the skin of his face radiating heat as he blushed.

Dr Kircher looked up from what he was doing. 'Just a

few more minutes,' he said. 'We're just making sure that the data we downloaded from your brain during the MRI scan has transmitted to the processor unit in the legs properly. It would be a tragedy if the files had been corrupted somewhere along the way, and you ended up doing a goose-step march across the lab when all you wanted to do was take a small step forward.'

'Yes,' Calum admitted, 'that *would* be a bad thing.'

Dr Kircher watched his team until one by one they looked over and gave him a thumbs-up signal.

'I think,' he said, 'we're ready to go.'

A group of technicians came over with one of the bionic legs – the left one. They carefully fitted it round Calum's own leg and strapped it tight to his calf and to his thigh. He couldn't feel it, but then he couldn't feel anything from his legs anyway. They were dead to him. Once they had the leg fitted, they added a separate section that Calum hadn't noticed before – one that cradled his foot and connected to the leg via a rotating joint. It was, he supposed, a bit like being a medieval knight getting strapped into armour by his squire.

More technicians came across with the right leg. They strapped that to him as well, and then added the foot. Once they had both legs attached, they connected the two legs together at the level of Calum's hips with a kind of brace. He wasn't entirely sure how the bits all connected together: it was difficult for him to see what they were doing down there, and he couldn't feel a thing.

He felt like a side of beef hanging in an abattoir on which butchers were working, trimming the fat and removing the tendons.

Eventually the technicians stood back, checking over their work. One of them held a bunch of wires in her hands, which she plugged into a box that she clipped to Calum's belt.

'Is everyone happy?' Dr Kircher asked.

The technicians nodded.

Dr Kircher gestured to another of the technicians across the lab. This one, a young man with black hair, was standing beside the controls for the wires that had hoisted Calum in the air half an hour before. 'Can you lower Mr Challenger down gradually to the floor, please, until you get feedback from the legs that his full weight has been taken off the wires.'

The technician nodded and pressed a series of buttons, and with a whining sound the motor above Calum's head lowered him smoothly down. He couldn't feel the point where his heels touched the floor, but he could tell when it happened because he stopped going down any further and the wires holding him began to sag. The bionic legs were now taking his weight.

'Keep the wires attached,' Kircher warned. 'Just in case something goes wrong and the legs buckle.'

Yes, Calum thought in a heartfelt way, *please do keep the wires attached!*

'Now,' Kircher went on, but talking specifically to Calum

at last, 'what I want you to do is to think, very carefully, about bending your right knee. Don't shift your weight at all – just try to flex your right knee.'

'OK.'

Calum tried to do consciously what he had been dreaming about ever since the accident: tell his leg to move. In dreams, it worked. In reality, up until now, it hadn't, but even as he formulated the thought of moving his leg in his mind he was amazed to actually see it shifting. The knee was bending – moving forward and upward! His right foot was lifting off the ground! He could hardly hear the motors operating – just a faint hum, like a bee flying past in the distance.

'It's working!' he breathed.

'There is a cut-out to stop the motors moving the knee beyond its structural limit,' Dr Kircher warned, 'but I want you to think about stopping bending your knee now.'

Calum did so, and his knee stopped moving. The motors stopped humming as well.

'Now lower your knee and put your right foot on the ground again.'

Breathless with amazement, he did so. He could feel the *thud* of his foot hitting the ground as it was transmitted up through his leg to his chest.

'Now your left knee.'

He raised his left knee, just the same way in which he had raised the right one.

'That's fine.' Dr Kircher glanced at the technicians,

who were watching the fluctuating graphs on their computer screens intently. 'Everything OK with you people?'

A chorus of 'Yes, sirs!' echoed around the lab.

'Let's spend a while consolidating what we've achieved, shall we?' Dr Kircher patted Calum on the shoulder. 'You're doing fine, Calum. I know this is an emotional moment for you, and I know you want to rush through it and try walking by yourself, but we have to take it literally one step at a time. You really do have to learn to walk before you can run, and you need to learn how to step before you can walk.'

For the next half-hour, Dr Kircher took Calum through a series of movements: bending his knees again; flexing his feet; raising his right leg and left leg up without bending his knees, like a clockwork soldier; moving his legs away from each other, out to the sides; moving them backwards as well as forwards . . . all the movements that ordinary people took for granted. Calum felt a bit like a ballet dancer doing stretching exercises, except that he wasn't holding a barre or standing next to a mirror. All the time Kircher made sure that his technicians were getting the feedback they expected from the sensors embedded all over the bionic leg braces. Where the movements were too fast, or too extreme, the technicians fine-tuned the electronics and the computerized "brain" until the movements that Calum imagined were the movements that occurred. And then they started adding movements together into sequences – bend the right knee, shift the weight of the body forward by bending slightly at the hips, extend the right leg and so on. Calum was having to deconstruct the whole intuitive process of walking into single logical steps, and then follow them one after the other in a smooth set of actions.

'The thing to remember,' Dr Kircher said, 'is that walking for bipeds such as us is really just a form of controlled falling. You lift one leg off the ground, start falling forward, and then stop yourself from falling with the same leg. That's the way it works.'

Three hours from the point at which Calum had been lowered to the ground, he took five steps in a row, supported by the wires but not needing them. The feeling of actually being able to walk was . . . incredible. Calum couldn't really equate it to anything else in his life. An hour later, Dr Kircher ordered the wires and the corset to be removed, and Calum stood, unsupported, and walked by himself for the first time since the accident. He could feel tears running down his face, but he didn't care. The technicians applauded.

'I think,' Dr Kircher said, 'that we can judiciously consider this a success.'

They took a break, with coffee and cake. Calum sat down carefully on one of the stools that were placed around the lab. 'I can't thank you enough –' he said haltingly.

Kircher raised a hand to stop him. 'Say no more. We're learning just as much from you as you are learning from us. This is a process of discovery for all concerned.'

'Can I ask a question?'

'Of course.'

'The legs are operated by my thoughts, yes? What's to

stop them suddenly moving if I happen to randomly think about moving my legs without actually intending to do so? Maybe if I was remembering something, or imagining it?'

'Good question.' He thought for a moment. 'The brain is quite an incredible thing, and we're really only now beginning to appreciate the way it works. There are thoughts, which, as you indicate, are really just imaginary rehearsals for things that *might* happen – little daydreams, if you like. They activate the same regions in the brain that are activated when you actually *intend* to move. The difference is that when you *intend* to move, there's another part of your brain that also activates – a part that has to do with decision-making. That activity is necessary in order for the signal to actually be sent to your legs. The sensors on your scalp have to detect both sets of activity before they will activate the motors on the leg braces. That way we can screen out all those daydreams, memories, odd ideas about moving, and so on.' He smiled. 'Have you ever sat in a chair and thought about reaching out for something – maybe a cup of tea – but not actually done it? And then, a few minutes later, you find your hand is actually reaching out without you consciously thinking about it? That's the difference between a stray thought and a thought with intention behind it.'

Calum nodded. 'OK – I understand that.'

Kircher frowned. 'I know that Gillian Livingstone broached the subject of heading to our parent laboratory in the USA to have some more detailed tests run. How do you feel about that?'

'I'd rather not; not now, anyway. There's a lot going on in my life.'

'So I can't talk you into it?'

'I'm afraid not.'

'In that case, I think that the best thing is for you to stay here for a few days while we run a comprehensive battery of tests. They won't be as detailed as the tests we can run in America, but it will give us some extra data. I'll have your chauffeur fetch some clothes for you and bring them here.'

Somewhere in the back of Calum's mind, a little alarm bell started to ring. It was muffled, almost inaudible, but it was definitely there.

'Actually,' he said, 'I would rather go back to my apartment. I feel safer there.'

'I don't think that's a good idea . . .' Kircher started to say.

'It's what's going to happen,' Calum insisted. 'I can always get Mr Macfarlane to drive me here tomorrow, and the day after, and whenever you want, but I'm not going to stay.'

Kircher grimaced, but said nothing.

'The only question,' Calum went on, 'is whether I take the legs with me and bring them back, or whether they stay here.'

Kircher stared at Calum for a few moments, and then said, 'It *would* be best if you got as much practice with the legs as possible, and they are perfectly safe now that your brain patterns have been properly characterized. The charge in the fuel cells will last for a week or more of normal use. Is there anyone who can check on you regularly, to make sure you're all right?'

'My friend Tara. She can stay with me for a few days.'

Kircher shrugged. 'OK, then. Home it is. I'll call you tomorrow to arrange our next session.' He reached inside his white lab coat and pulled a card from an inside pocket. Handing it over to Calum, he said, 'My office number and mobile numbers are both on the card. If you have any problems – day or night – give me a call immediately. Some of the technicians here are on twenty-four-hour call-out. We have a number of clients who require mobility in their daily lives, and need to be back on their feet immediately if they have a problem. Call us if you need us.'

He handed the card to Calum. Calum took it, and turned it over to see the front.

DR THEO KIRCHER
HEAD OF MOBILITY
ROBLEDO MOUNTAINS TECHNOLOGY

There was also an address and several phone numbers, but Calum noticed that a line of small text underneath the 'Robledo Mountains Technology' had been blacked out with a felt-tip pen.

'What did that say?' he asked, intrigued.

Dr Kircher looked away. 'Just some corporate stuff,' he said. 'You know the kind of thing – companies get taken over, sold, bought or traded all the time. It's greener to keep the same business cards and just cross out the stuff that doesn't apply any more.' He raised a finger warningly, looking back at Calum. 'No running though. And don't climb any stairs – we need to rehearse those movements thoroughly with you in our next session.'

'I promise,' Calum said, 'no running or climbing stairs.' He hoped that Dr Kircher couldn't see his fingers, crossed beneath the table.

Natalie had spent the long flight to Hong Kong partly reading a trashy novel on her e-reader, partly looking at the pictures of duty-free items she could buy on-board, partly watching a vacuous comedy about rich Californian girls who spent every day shopping and bitching about boys, and partly asleep. Between this journey and the one she'd only just done from New York to London, she was fed up with long-haul.

Rhino had had his head buried in a book – a *real* book, not an electronic one – for most of the flight. Gecko had slept a lot, and eaten whenever any food was going. Natalie supposed his free-running activities meant that he needed all the nutrition and all the rest that he could get. It must be nice not to put on weight just by *looking* at food.

At least they were in First Class, which meant that the seats had little barriers around them to make them more private, and they could be laid flat to turn into small but functional beds. That was a boon. Calum had booked the tickets without complaint, saying that there was no point in them getting to Hong Kong and needing three days to recover from the flight. There were even sets of pyjamas in cotton bags in the overhead lockers that people could wear, if they chose, along with a neat little blindfold to block out the aircraft's interior lights. Natalie decided not to take advantage of them. The toilets were still small, despite the fact that it was First Class, and she didn't want to have to bash her elbows and knees while struggling to get changed into the pyjamas, only to have to do the same thing in reverse a few hours later. Sleeping in her own clothes was *icky*, but she could manage. She had slummed it before.

The captain came on the tannoy to say that they were preparing to land, and everyone should go back to their seats and fasten their seatbelts. Natalie glanced across to see that Rhino had looked up from his book.

'Have you ever flown into Hong Kong before?' he asked.

'No. What about you?'

He nodded. 'When I was in the military, I came in and out a few times. That was when Hong Kong was owned by the British, of course. They've built a new airport since I was here, Chek Lap Kok Airport, which has to be an improvement.'

Natalie was intrigued. 'Why's that? Was the old one not very good?'

He shook his head. 'It's not that, it's just that the approach to landing at the old one – Kai Tak Airport – was quite –' he hesitated for a moment, trying to choose the appropriate word – 'dramatic. Especially on runway thirteen.

It was ranked by some TV programme a few years back as the sixth most dangerous airport in the world for landings.'

'So what was so bad about runway thirteen?'

Rhino smiled, obviously remembering. 'The problem was that there was no direct line in. Pilots had to come in over the harbour and the populated area of Kowloon, descending all the time, and watch out for a particular hill with an orange-and-white checkerboard-pattern sign on the top. The moment they saw that hill they had to make a sudden forty-seven-degree turn to the right and lose height rapidly while lining up on the runway, and they had to make that line-up visually, rather than using instruments. The plane would enter the final right turn at a height of about two hundred metres and come out of it at about forty-three metres. At that stage the plane would be flying with tower blocks just a few hundred metres to either side, and I distinctly remember looking out of the window on one occasion and staring straight into someone's kitchen, watching them drain some noodles in a sieve – we were that close. And then seconds later we were hitting the ground – hard – and braking really sharply so we didn't go off the end of the runway and into the waters of the harbour.' He thought for a moment. 'And that was on a good day. On a bad day the winds coming down off the mountains would try to push the aircraft sideways, into the tower blocks. That was fun.'

'Yeah,' Natalie said slowly, 'it sounds like fun. But this new airport – nothing like as bad as the old one, right?'

'Right.' He nodded. 'Except that they did build it on

reclaimed marshland, but I'm sure it's stable.'

'Great – thanks for that.' Natalie settled back in her seat, grabbed the blindfold and slipped it over her eyes. She was only going to take it off once they had actually, definitively landed.

Calum phoned Tara as soon as Macfarlane dropped him back home. It sounded as if she was in a coffee shop, but she said she would come straight over.

When she arrived, she stood in the doorway of his apartment, looking at him as he stood, without using the overhead straps, in the centre of the room, looking back at her.

'Wow,' she said.

He held his arms out to either side and shrugged. 'Look, Ma – no hands!'

'Are you actually wearing the bionic legs now?'

He tapped his jeans. He could feel the metal braces beneath the denim. 'I actually am.'

She glanced up at the straps that hung from the ceiling. 'Are you going to take those things down, then?'

'Not just yet.' He gently touched the metal frame that encased his right leg. 'I want to be absolutely sure that these things work properly and won't suddenly fail on me before I start doing something drastic. Which is why you're here.'

She put her hands on her hips and tilted her head to one side. 'You mean this isn't just a social visit?'

'You know I'm always glad to see you, and the others,'

he said, suddenly aware that he might have been a little too . . . *honest*.

'Yeah, I remember how grateful you were that Gecko and I had drunk all of that Mexican cola that you have imported.'

'But that's my special cola!' he protested, aware even as he said the words of how petty they sounded.

'Calum, there's no point having really tasty drinks around, and then *boasting* to your friends that you have really tasty drinks around, and then not letting your friends actually *drink* those really tasty drinks.'

'Point taken,' he said. 'Anyway – back to me.'

She smiled tolerantly.

Calum took a deep breath. 'I want to go outside,' he said.

A long pause, then: 'Are you sure about that? Shouldn't you test those bionic things around the apartment for a while, just to iron out any glitches? Because if there's one thing I know about complicated electronics and computerized systems, it's that there're always glitches.'

He shook his head. 'Look, apart from being up on the roof with Gecko a few days ago, I haven't felt the sun on my face or the breeze on my skin for . . . for as long as I can remember.'

'You went for a drive only this morning,' she pointed out with the kind of remorseless logic that Calum usually used on people. 'You could feel the sun and the breeze then.'

'It wasn't the same.' He took a breath. This was

important to him. '*Then*, I was out in the open for about ten seconds between the door to the apartment and the car, and I was in a wheelchair. The same at the other end. I want to be able to walk there, in the open air, somewhere with grass around me, and just . . . soak it in. Be in the moment.'

Tara stared at him for a few seconds. 'OK, then – let's go and get an ice cream. There's a community park a little way down the road.'

'I didn't know that,' Calum said in a small voice, and it was true – he hadn't known. He'd moved in here after his parents died. He didn't know the area. He'd chosen it because the warehouse had belonged to his great-grandfather. In fact, his great-grandfather's stuff was still stored in the basement, along with ARLENE. But he would have known that if he'd been able to go out.

Shutting the apartment door behind him and activating the security systems, Calum turned and headed for the stairs.

'Don't you want to use the lift?' Tara asked, standing by the lift doors.

'I've got legs and I'm going to use them,' he said stubbornly.

Tara frowned. 'That sounds like an old ZZ Top song,' she mused. She looked up at him. 'Are you sure you're allowed to use those legs on stairs? Have they been cleared as safe?'

He nodded. 'I'm meant to use them whenever and however I can,' he said, fingers crossed behind his back again.

She looked dubious. 'OK, then.

He took the stairs carefully, with Tara in front of him

in case he fell forward. The steps were concrete, and had eroded edges, and cracks running through them. They dated from the time the warehouse was built, back when his great-grandfather was exploring the world. He moved gingerly, but the legs coped well with the challenge. He was amazed at how natural it felt to be walking again.

Outside, he luxuriated in the feel of the sun on his skin. He looked left and right along the narrow road where the warehouse and apartment were located. 'Which way now?'

Tara pointed left. 'That way.'

They walked along the road, to all intents and purposes like a couple of ordinary teenagers wandering around London. Tara led Calum to the park, and while he stood there and watched the pigeons pecking for food, the grey squirrels eyeing up the sunbathers cautiously and the dogs jumping in the fountains she bought two ice-cream cones from the cafe.

They sat on a park bench and ate their ice creams. Calum couldn't remember anything ever tasting as delicious.

'This,' he said quietly, 'is paradise.'

Tara was distracted. 'Sorry?'

'I said, this is paradise.'

'Oh.'

He glanced at her. She was looking off to one side. He followed her gaze, to see two men with close-cropped hair wearing leather jackets leaving the park through a different gate to the one he and Tara had used. 'Seen someone you recognize?' he asked.

'Kind of,' she said, frowning. 'I think I've seen those two men before. I just can't remember where or when.'

Calum felt a sudden chill run through him. 'Nemor Incorporated?' he asked quietly.

'It could be,' she said, just as quietly, 'but which one of us are they interested in?'

With Rhino, Gecko and Natalie on their way to Hong Kong, and Calum in his apartment resting after the strain of trying out his new legs, Tara found herself at a loose end once she'd seen him home. She drifted from coffee shop to bookshop and bookshop to coffee shop, wasting time. She realized now that she had thought that suddenly having so many friends would mean she'd never be lonely again, but that wasn't the case. Ultimately, she was still by herself.

It occurred to her, somewhere between one latte and the next, that she could easily go and get her passport from her room, head for Heathrow, stand in front of the ticket desk and say, 'I'd like to buy a return ticket to Hong Kong, please.' Nobody would miss her. The dream lasted while she got up and left the coffee shop she was in at the time, but after a few steps she stopped. The tickets for Rhino, Gecko and Natalie had been paid for by Calum, from his own seemingly inexhaustible funds, just like the flights to Georgia a few months back. Tara didn't have the money to jet off around the world. She was a poor student.

She felt that familiar crushing sense of loneliness falling over her again like a dark blanket. The more things changed in her life, the more they stayed the same.

She headed for yet another small coffee shop that she knew, where they made cheap ham-and-cheese bagels and would let her sit for several hours nibbling at her food without disturbing her. Passing so many laughing families and groups of friends on the way made her loneliness feel more acute.

Once she got to the coffee shop, she ordered a bagel and a drink and curled up in a corner seat, taking her tablet out of her bag. While she was waiting for her order, she thought she'd see if Rhino or anyone had mailed from Hong Kong. They hadn't, but there was one from Tom Karavla waiting for her. Suddenly Tara didn't feel quite so alone.

Hi Tara!

I was thinking about what you said – you know, about people making modern-day films and TV programmes with dinosaurs in them and assuming that no evolution had taken place in the meantime, and you're right. The creatures would have changed quite a bit in the intervening time. For instance, there's a biological law that says that animals living on an island or in an isolated area like a plateau tend to get smaller over thousands of years, because smaller animals need less food and tend not to starve. Well, it occurred to me that if any diplodocus had survived from the prehistoric era then they might have naturally grown smaller so they were the size of a dog now, or a triceratops that had shrunk to the size of a large horse. Wouldn't that be great? You probably know about the dwarf elephant fossils that have been found in various places around the world – elephants that had naturally reduced in size over many generations until they were smaller than a person (well, smaller than some people, anyway). There's supposed to be a group of these dwarf elephants still living in the rainforests of the Kerala region of southern India. The locals called them 'kallana', and they say they avoid associating with the 'normal-sized' Indian elephants (well, you would if you were less than a quarter of their size, wouldn't you?). I keep hoping that thelostworlds.com will put up a photograph by some tourist or researcher showing that the kallana actually exist, but that hasn't happened yet. (I don't suppose that Calum Challenger has some images tucked away in a drawer somewhere that he hasn't got around to using yet? That would be awesome!)

Thinking about it, the other thing that gets me about dinosaur movies is that they only use the dinosaurs we know about. Given the infrequent way that bones get changed into fossils, and the difficulty in actually finding those fossils in the rocks, there's no way we've found all the dinosaurs that ever existed yet. In fact, I saw a statistic recently that suggested we've only identified 30% of the types of dinosaur that ever existed. And yet whenever a dinosaur appears on film or TV, it's one we already know about, rather than a new one that the special-effects guys could have come up with themselves. In fact, if you remember the film *Jurassic Park III*, the film-makers there used a type of dinosaur called a spinosaurus that had only recently been characterized. Funny, that.

Sorry – I'm going on a bit. I tend to do that when I get excited about something. I'll go now, but I just wanted to say that I live in London, so if you're ever in the area let me know and I'll buy you a coffee and talk about extinct animals that might not be extinct . . .

Cheers,

Tom

He was in London? Instinctively, Tara looked around to see if there was anyone watching her, but of course there wasn't. Everyone was minding their own business. He wasn't there.

London? She shook herself. Wow. Yes, they *could* meet up for coffee. Tom sounded as if he had a very similar kind of mind to hers, and it would be nice to deal with someone like that on an equal level. Now she came to think about it, she still felt like a bit of an outsider with Calum and his friends. Every now and then, in her darker moments, she wondered if they were just using her for her computing skills – in a nice way, of course. Having a new friend who wasn't part of that group would be great.

Except that he would *want* to be part of that group. He had already made it clear that he loved thelostworlds.com and the kinds of things that Calum was into. Well, she would just have to manage that as and when it happened. It was a risk.

There was another risk, of course – the risk that Tom wasn't what he seemed to be. Everybody had heard terrible stories of girls arranging to meet in real life people they'd previously just met online, only for them to disappear or turn up dead. Tara didn't want to become another statistic.

Maybe she could subtly find out where he was going to be at a particular time – maybe say she *might* be able to meet up, but no promises. She could go along and watch out for him. If he was the guy from his photo, she could head over and introduce herself. If not, she could leave and never communicate with him again.

Before she could have second thoughts about the dangers of this plan, she typed a response:

Hi Tom,

Thanks for emailing. I agree with everything you say about dinosaurs. It's kind of interesting the way that they've been portrayed in films over the years – in those old 1950s and 1960s stop-motion films the T-rexes all stood upright, and the triceratops all had their legs sticking out to the side like crocodiles, which is the way the Victorian palaeontologists put the skeletons together, but more recently the tyrannosaurs have been horizontal, with their tails balancing their extended necks, and the triceratops have their legs beneath them like cows. Latest research indicates that some dinosaurs might have been covered with hair, or things like early feathers. I mean, we don't even know what colour they were! Tyrannosaurs might have had bright red and yellow stripes, for all we know!

I'm in London quite a lot. Let me know where you tend to hang out, and if I'm passing I might be able to pop in and introduce myself!

Regards,

Tara

She felt a bit guilty, misleading him like that, but it was necessary. She needed to check him out without him knowing she was there.

Who knew? If he was real, and if they got on together, maybe the relationship would lead to something on a different level. Which, she thought ruefully, would be a first for her.

Calum stood in the middle of his apartment, wondering what to do now with his new-found mobility.

The walk out to the park and back had been incredible; he'd crashed out as soon as he'd got home, and Tara wasn't there when he woke up. He'd tried to check in with Rhino, Gecko and Natalie, but it looked as if they were still travelling. Desperate for someone to talk to, he'd even tried to call Gillian Livingstone so he could tell her how wonderful it was to be able to walk again, and how grateful he was, but her number went straight to voicemail. Knowing her, she had meetings stacked up with various scientists, technicians and potential investors.

He looked around. There was always the website – thelostworlds.com. He hadn't spent much time on it recently, not now that Tara had been given administrator privileges, but it was always possible that someone had emailed in with a new report of some cryptid somewhere in the world.

He was just kidding himself. He wanted to keep walking. He wanted to revel in the unexpected luxury of actually being able to move around without hanging from straps or using crutches.

He glanced over at the window. The sun was low in the sky, but the weather was good. He could always go out for another walk. The moment the thought crossed his mind, he recoiled from it. He'd spent so long cooped up in his apartment since the accident that the idea of actually talking to strangers, or being somewhere unfamiliar alone, was scary.

Briefly he wondered about heading over to see his Great-Aunt Merrily and showing off the new bionic legs to her, but he knew he'd have to stay for hours while she chatted, and he wanted to be sure that the legs were going to be a full-time solution before he went public with them.

So, what could he do?

His mind flicked back to the moment earlier that

afternoon when he and Tara had walked – *walked!* – down the stairs and left the warehouse. They had passed the door to the bottom floor of the warehouse, where his great-grandfather's possessions and artefacts were stored. There were crates of them, all labelled, from the many expeditions that Professor George Challenger had made between the years 1899 and 1933. Calum had always wanted to take a look around. Before the crash he'd never found the time; since the crash he'd not had the mobility – and he certainly wasn't going to send anyone else down there on his behalf. But now . . . now he could simply wander down there and take a look for himself.

Part of his mind tried to point out that wandering around by himself with a new and relatively untested pair of bionic legs was not a good idea, but another part responded that there might well be crates containing stuffed or preserved cryptids, found in various remote locations, and what was the point of going to Hong Kong in search of one when there might be an example of it less than a hundred metres away? Would the DNA still be viable? Well, he wouldn't know until he checked.

He left his apartment, setting the security system behind him, and headed cautiously down the stairs. At the bottom he turned right instead of heading straight on to the front door. There was another door there, in the shadow cast by the stairs. It was made of riveted metal, like the door to Calum's apartment, and it had a similar alarm system connected to it. He typed in the security code. Fortunately he'd had it changed to match the upstairs one when he'd moved in and upgraded the whole system. The door clicked, and opened an inch.

He pushed it further open and entered the room beyond.

It was less of a room and more of a cavern. This was the original warehouse space, unmodified: a huge area filled with piled-up wooden crates of various sizes. Aisles had been left between the stacks: a winding maze of narrow canyons running between wooden cliff-faces. The windows were boarded up, but stray beams of sunshine penetrated through chinks in the boards and formed a diagonal lattice of light across the entire area. Motes of dust drifted through the glowing lattice and glittered for a few seconds before they vanished again.

Just to one side of the door, tucked out of the way, was the metal bulk of the ARLENE robot that Gillian Livingstone had provided the team for their trip to Georgia. It was about the size of a horse, with six legs instead of four, but its 'head' was a collection of cameras, sensors and lights, and its 'skin' was metal plating. He shuffled past it, patting it on the side as he went.

In the light trickling in from outside, Calum could just about read the words that had been stencilled in big black letters on to the sides of the nearest crate.

PROFESSOR GEORGE EDWARD CHALLENGER

SOUTH AMERICA EXPEDITION

APRIL 1912

CRATE #233

CONTENTS: ASSORTED PTERODACTYL EGGS (BROKEN)

Pterodactyls? This had to be some kind of mistake, surely. Professor Challenger might have found some fossils that he *thought* might be pterodactyl eggs, but they wouldn't be *real* eggs. That would be . . . insane.

He looked at the stencilled sign again. *Crate #233* of Professor George Challenger's April 1912 South American expedition. That meant there were at least 232 other crates, and that was only in the unlikely event that he'd accidentally stumbled across the last box.

He moved further down the row. The next crate in line also had a label stencilled on it, but this one was slightly different.

Professor George Edward Challenger
South America Expedition
April 1912
Crate #232
Contents: Assorted Pterodactyl Eggs (intact)
DANGER! Do not store at temperatures above 30˚ c!

Why not? What were they going to do – hatch?

Smiling to himself, Calum walked along the aisle. Many of the crates were from the 1912 South American expedition, but there were other expeditions there as well: a 1909 Siberian expedition, a 1915 Arctic expedition, a 1925 expedition to the South China Seas. His great-grandfather had obviously spent an awful lot of time away from home. Pity his poor family.

He came to a junction, and on a whim turned left. The

crates along that aisle didn't seem to be associated with any expeditions. One was labelled:

PROFESSOR GEORGE EDWARD CHALLENGER
CONTENTS: SAMPLES FROM DRILLING THROUGH EARTH'S CRUST
DECEMBER 1927
CRATE #5

Another, a little further along, said:

PROFESSOR GEORGE EDWARD CHALLENGER
CONTENTS: SAMPLES OF SOPORIFIC ETHERIC GAS BELT
JANUARY 1913
DANGER! DO NOT OPEN WITHOUT
RESPIRATORS/OXYGEN SUPPLY

Next to it was a much larger crate labelled:

PROFESSOR GEORGE EDWARD CHALLENGER
JANUARY 1929
CONTENTS: DISINTEGRATION MACHINE
EXTREME DANGER!!
DO NOT CONNECT TO ANY ELECTRICAL SUPPLY!

A disintegration machine? That had to be a joke, surely.

All he could see ahead of him were more and more crates. He could spend hours down here, but he was beginning to realize that doing any serious inventory of the warehouse's contents was going to take time. At least he'd scoped the problem out, he consoled himself. And done it on his own terms.

He turned round and headed back to the crossroads where he'd turned left, but instead of turning right, back towards the lobby, he headed straight on, down the right-hand arm. His curiosity was engaged, and he was still revelling in his ability to walk.

For the first hundred metres or so it was just more and more obscurely labelled crates, but then he came to an area that had been left clear. Well, clear apart from an object about the size of a bus that was covered in a dusty old tarpaulin.

What the hell? he thought. It wasn't as if there was a sign saying: Keep Off! Or even: Danger! Keep off if you value your life! So he pulled the tarpaulin away.

And froze in shock.

It was a dinosaur. Fortunately it wasn't moving.

It was stuffed – that much was obvious from a second's examination. It had a lumpy look to it, and Calum could see a line of stitching running underneath its belly where two skin seams had been secured together. It was also covered with cobwebs that had been built over the course of probably a hundred years by generation upon generation of spiders. The cobwebs filled the area underneath it with a hazy mass of dusty strands, and gave its head a strange and inappropriate beard. It had been mounted on a wooden base that had to be six metres long and three metres across, and which was barely large enough to take the creature.

Except that this was a dinosaur like Calum had never seen before. He would have recognized a stegosaurus, a triceratops, a T-rex, a diplodocus and probably seventy or eighty other different types of dinosaur. This particular one had four legs and a long, muscular tail, but its body seemed to be covered with thick armoured plates, and around its neck area was a frill of sharp spines, all pointing backwards. Its head was small and wide and snake-like, and covered with smaller spines. Spiders had built cobwebs between the spines as well.

By its front right foot was a label that read:

SPECIMEN OF **PREVIOUSLY UNDISCOVERED** DINOSAUR STUFFED BY **PROFESSOR GEORGE EDWARD CHALLENGER** DURING THIRD SOUTH AMERICAN EXPEDITION, APRIL 1917. PROVISIONALLY NAMED <u>MULTICERATOPS CHALLENGERII</u> (AWAITING CONFIRMATION)

Incredible. Absolutely incredible.

Calum reached out to touch the skin of the creature. It was dry and leathery, and covered with dust, just the way he thought it would be, but the idea that he was actually *touching* the skin of a real dinosaur was mind-blowing. Especially if it was one that had been missed, apparently, from all the catalogues and textbooks.

He stared at the creature for a while, marvelling at it, and then covered it up again with the tarpaulin, leaving it the way he had found it. There would be time later for a full examination of the warehouse and its contents – preferably with his friends there to help. For now, he was content in the knowledge that he had a storehouse of wonders located just below his apartment.

He turned to head back to the lobby.

Something clattered against wood. It sounded as if it was about thirty metres behind him.

As he turned, Calum thought he saw something move at the far end of the aisle. It looked as if someone had been watching him, and had ducked into one of the side aisles as soon as they'd realized they'd been seen.

'Hello?' he called. 'Tara, is that you?'

No reply. He took a couple of steps towards where the sound had come from. 'Mr Macfarlane?'

Still no answer, but Calum thought he could see a shadow cast by one of the diagonal beams of sunlight. It looked as if someone was standing just round the corner of an aisle, hidden by a crate.

The shadow suddenly shifted. Now that he was listening, Calum thought he could hear footsteps moving away. A sudden flush of anger ran through him like a hot wave. This was his warehouse, and someone was in it!

He couldn't run – at least, he didn't *think* he could run, not with the bionic leg braces – but he moved as fast as he dared along the aisle back to the crossroads.

He could see nothing. No movement, no people, nothing. The dust on the floor was disturbed, but Calum had come from there, so he was probably just looking at his own footprints.

He sighed. Whatever the situation was, he ought to head back to his apartment. If there had been someone here and they had left, then he could set the security lock again to stop them from getting back in. If there had been someone here and they were still hiding, then he would lock them in, and the motion sensors would tell him if they moved. Then he could call the police.

Heading down the aisle, back towards the door to the lobby, Calum noticed that ARLENE was almost blocking his way. He slowed down, momentarily confused. He was sure that the six-legged robot had been tucked to one side when he'd entered the warehouse, neatly out of the way. Maybe it had something to do with the angle he was coming at it from, but he could swear that it had . . . moved.

He took a couple of steps closer. He had a strange urge to call out and ask ARLENE what it thought it was doing, but that would just be stupid. It was an inanimate collection of circuits, wires, pistons and metal struts. It responded to commands and it sometimes made its own decisions based on a mission-list and local conditions, but it couldn't initiate movement on its own account. It couldn't just wander around.

Could it?

This was stupid. He was letting the shadows and the noises freak him out. He needed to get back to his apartment and settle down with a can of cola.

He walked towards ARLENE, aiming to squeeze past it and head for the lobby.

The robot's head suddenly spun round to stare at Calum.

The lamps on either side of its camera 'eyes' flared to life, almost blinding him. He threw a hand up in front of his eyes, but his immediate instinct to step away was translated into a command for the bionic legs to start walking backwards. Taken by surprise, Calum overbalanced and fell.

The impact drove the breath from his body. His head hit the floor with a sickening thud. For a moment he just stared at the ceiling, wondering what had happened, and then he raised his head to look around.

ARLENE was walking towards him.

The whirr of the motors that powered the robot's legs – similar to his, now he came to think about it – was a repetitive and menacing sound that echoed around the warehouse as it came closer and closer to him.

He raised himself up on his elbows and tried to scrabble backwards, but the bionic braces weren't responding properly. His heels just rapped against the floor. His elbows wouldn't pull the entire weight of his body, not backwards anyway, so he was effectively trapped.

ARLENE stepped closer. Its head swung down so that it could see Calum's face.

And then its front right leg came down on his knee.

He shouldn't have been able to feel the pain, not with his legs the way they were, but the shock was incredible. He screamed – at least, he thought he did. Maybe it was just in his head. But, wherever the sound was – in his mind or out loud – he was definitely screaming.

*

Tara stood outside the small coffee shop, not sure whether to go in or to turn round and head away.

The message had come in from Tom half an hour ago:

Hi Tara!

You asked where I tend to hang out. Most evenings
I end up in a coffee shop near Covent Garden –
Monmouth Street. It's a funny place – really small,
and the seats and tables are quite tiny, but the coffee
is to die for. They have varieties of coffee beans there
that I've actually never heard of before. I'm gradually
working my way through them – alphabetically, of
course. I've got up to 'H' already. It's a really good place
to chill out and read the paper or a book, or do some
work. It would be great to see you there. It's also really
handy for the West End, if you fancied going to see a
film, or a play, or something (as long as it's not clubbing.
I don't do clubbing – not under any circumstances). Or
we could just hang out and talk about cryptids – I've
collected quite a lot of information over the past few
years, some of which isn't on thelostworlds.com. I'd be
happy to share it with you . . .

Hopefully see you around!

Regards,

Tom

Tara felt a little shiver of anticipation as she remembered the message. Somewhere in there she thought Tom had asked her out, without *actually* directly asking her out. He'd certainly mentioned going to see a film or a play together. If that wasn't asking her out, what was?

But they'd not actually met yet. The thought gave her some concerns. What if he wasn't what he said, despite everything she'd managed to discover about him on the internet? What if he was really old, or really strange, or really creepy?

There was only one way to find out, and it involved meeting him. At least it would be at a coffee shop, with other people there, and she could make sure she was closest to the door so she could run out in a hurry if there was any trouble.

A part of her, a guilty part, knew that she should tell someone about the meeting, just so there was a record somewhere of where she was going and what she was doing. The problem was that most of her new friends were away, and the only one left – Calum – would stop her going, telling her she was crazy, it was too big a risk.

And she didn't want to tell him that she had a date – not until after it had gone well and she and Tom were good friends. She wanted to keep this to herself for a while.

Just in case, she had created an event on her personal calendar and uploaded it to the internet cloud, where she kept things that she wanted to be able to access from any computer or phone, anywhere there was Wi-Fi or mobile-phone-signal access. She had also made sure there was a link to a photograph of Tom that she'd found on the internet. At least now there would be some independent record that the police could use as the basis for an investigation.

If anything went wrong.

She knew that she was deliberately delaying going in, but even now that the thought was out in the open she still couldn't quite bring herself to enter the coffee shop. She looked up and down the street. It was lined with shops selling vintage clothes, art prints, film posters and odd little gifts. There was even a Chinese music shop, with bamboo flutes and strange stringed instruments in the window.

This was stupid.

Taking a deep breath, she entered the coffee shop.

It was, as Tom had said, small, but it was interesting, and it smelt strongly of roasted coffee beans. There were six customers already there – four of them alone and two who were obviously a couple. She didn't make it obvious that she was looking around, but instead slid into a high-sided booth.

Tom had been right about the seating as well – it was like sitting on a park bench.

A youth approached her, smiling. 'What can I get you?' he asked brightly.

'A . . . flat white,' Tara said, desperately trying to read all the way through the menu board behind the till.

'Any particular coffee bean?' the boy asked.

'Is there a "house" bean?'

'There is.'

'Then I'll go for that.'

'Anything to eat?'

'Not yet, but I might go for a croissant later.'

'OK. I'll bring your drink over in a moment.'

The boy walked away, and Tara took the opportunity to look around.

Tom was there. He was one of the four customers who were there alone. He was sitting perpendicular to Tara, so she could see the right-hand side of his face. He looked just like his photograph. He was typing something into his own computer tablet.

She could feel herself relaxing, now she had established that he was real, and that he was who he'd said he was. And that he was alone.

Her coffee arrived and she sipped at it, not really thinking about the taste but more interested in watching Tom. He was, she decided, even more attractive in real life than in his photograph. He was wearing a T-shirt, and his arms were really muscular, and quite tanned. His hair was slightly longer than it had been in the photograph.

Her tablet *beeped* with an incoming email. She checked it out.

Hi Tara!

You want to join me? I'm not scary, honest!

Regards,

Tom

He didn't look round at her, but she knew that he knew she was there. She felt herself blushing. What was the phrase they used in police shows when an undercover agent had been identified? She'd been 'made'.

Tara pushed down against the almost overwhelming desire to run out of the coffee shop. Instead she tucked her tablet beneath one arm, picked up her coffee and walked across to Tom's table. She slipped in opposite him.

'Hi!' she said. 'What are the odds I should bump into you here?'

He looked straight at her, but he wasn't smiling. Instead he looked worried, and guilty. Tara felt a small bud of fear begin to blossom in her heart.

'I'm really sorry about this,' Tom said. 'I really am. This wasn't my idea.' He had a slight accent that she hadn't been expecting. She opened her mouth to ask him what was wrong, but he was already sliding out of the booth, his tablet computer in his hand.

Before Tara could slide out too, a man slipped into the booth on her side of the table, blocking her exit. She felt her heart rate suddenly accelerate. As Tom walked away, head low, another man slid in to replace him. They both had short hair and heavy features. She had seen them before, at the park.

She was trapped!

'Before you say anything,' the man opposite her said, 'my brother here has a knife held beneath table level. Keep quiet, and don't move.'

'What . . . what do you want?' she asked, a sick panic sweeping through her. This couldn't be happening! 'Money? Or my computer? Just take them.'

The man beside her opened his mouth. 'Why is it that they always say something when you specifically tell them not to?' he asked.

His colleague shook his head. 'I don't know,' he replied. 'But at least she isn't screaming. If she looks as if she might scream, or call out, then do what you need to. He gazed at Tara. 'We don't want your money, or your computer,' he said. 'Although we might take them anyway.'

'Then what *do* you want?' she asked, her voice shaking uncontrollably.

'We want you.'

She shivered, and wrapped her arms round herself. 'Oh God. Is this about Nemor Incorporated?'

The man looked at his companion in puzzlement. 'Who?' he asked.

seven

Calum couldn't feel the pain of his leg breaking, but he felt the bone snap, and that was bad enough. If he *had* felt the pain, then he would probably have passed out. He knew it was serious, but things were going to get a lot more serious in the next few minutes if he didn't do something fast.

He turned half over, grabbed hold of the edge of a crate with his left hand and pulled himself away from ARLENE. The concrete was gritty beneath him, and he could feel it rasping against the skin of his side as he moved.

Part of him was wondering why ARLENE had suddenly gone mad – was the robot being controlled, was it responding to its own decision-making in an unexpected way or had the short-range radio signals controlling his legs been misinterpreted by ARLENE as some kind of random instructions? Only part of him was wondering that though. The rest of him was wondering how he was going to get away without being trampled or crushed to death.

He desperately reached out with his right hand, grabbed

another crate and hoisted himself forward again. He half heard, half felt the thud from behind as ARLENE pursued him.

He glanced over his shoulder, and winced at the sight of his twisted leg. ARLENE loomed up behind him like some metal analogue of the prehistoric creatures that his great-grandfather had spent his life searching for. Its head scanned back and forth, triangulating on Calum. It looked ready to lunge.

As he hoisted himself forward over the rough concrete, Calum's brain raced, calculating the possibilities. If ARLENE was being controlled from outside, then he was dead. He couldn't get away from the robot fast enough. If it was responding to its own internal programming, then he was probably also dead, depending on what instructions it thought it was following. It might just lose interest and stop – if he was lucky. He didn't feel lucky.

His best bet would be if the robot's control systems had been activated by the transmissions that were going from Calum's brain to his bionic leg braces. The radio waves were short range – if he could move far enough away then ARLENE would lose the signals. But how far was far enough?

Again he pulled against the crates, gaining another metre, but when he looked over his shoulder he saw ARLENE still moving forward. It was staying in range! He couldn't get away fast enough! Desperately he pulled off the headband with the sensors for his legs, but the robot kept coming!

He looked around, hoping against hope that there was

something nearby that he could use, but the aisles were clear. He was, however, almost at a junction of two of them, and that gave him an idea. Instead of laboriously pulling himself, hand over hand, away from the robot, he stretched himself out, pulled his arms into his sides and *rolled*. His body was angled towards the cross-aisle, and he managed to get across the open space in a few seconds. For a split second he bizarrely flashed back to a trip he and his mum and dad had taken to Greenwich Park once, when he was six, and the way he had rolled down the hill there, laughing all the way, with his dad chasing him. But now it was a robot chasing him, and it was concrete rather than grass that he was rolling over.

He rolled faster, trying to increase the gap between him and ARLENE. He tensed, expecting another metal foot to come crashing down on his other leg, but nothing happened. He couldn't hear the thuds of ARLENE walking either, but that might just have been because his blood was roaring in his ears like a waterfall. He stopped rolling and risked a glance backwards.

ARLENE stood there, as still as a statue.

Cautiously, Calum flipped on to his back and sat up, bracing himself with his hands. His breath rasped in his throat, and the skin of his side burned where he had pulled it across the concrete. Still there was no movement from the robot.

It looked as if he was right – it *had* been the transmissions from his brain, routed through the electronic processor and radio transmitter of the bionic legs, that had set the robot off. That was . . . unfortunate . . . but it couldn't have been predicted. And at least he was intact and relatively unscathed.

Apart from his leg. He looked at it ruefully. It was twisted round, and there was blood on his jeans around the knee where ARLENE's foot had smashed it. For the first time ever he thanked his lucky stars that he had no feeling in his legs.

He reached into his trouser pocket, hoping against hope that his mobile hadn't fallen out while he was rolling, and hadn't been smashed by his exertions. It seemed to be OK. He pressed the memory button for Tara's number.

It went to voicemail.

He grimaced. Just his luck that Tara was off somewhere enjoying herself.

Who else? Gecko and Natalie were in Hong Kong. What about Mr Macfarlane? Could he come and rescue Calum?

A small piece of cardboard had fallen out of Calum's pocket when he'd pulled the mobile out. He picked it up curiously and glanced at it. It was the business card that Dr Kircher had given him.

He sighed in relief. This whole fiasco had been caused by the bionic legs – it was only right that the Robledo Mountains Technology team came out and put it right. And Dr Kircher *had* said that Calum could phone him, any time, day or night. And they had access to medical facilities.

He typed the number in and listened to the tone as the phone connected.

This was *not*, he thought desperately, one of his better days.

The call connected, and a voice – a *human* voice, not an answerphone – said: 'Robledo Mountains Technology, emergency helpline. What's the problem?'

'This is Calum Challenger,' Calum said breathlessly. 'I can't move.'

'OK, don't worry. Just hold on a moment while I retrieve your information.' Calum heard a clicking sound as keys were pressed on a keyboard, then: 'Yes, Mr Challenger. You were in earlier today. What's happened?'

'Difficult to explain, but one of the legs has been twisted and crushed. I'm lying on the floor, and I can't get up.'

'OK.' A moment's pause. 'I have an address here in London Docklands. Is that still valid?'

'Yes. I'm on the ground floor.'

'OK, I'm alerting the immediate response team now. They'll be on their way within a few moments.' A pause. 'Are you injured?'

Calum raised his head and looked along his body, quickly evaluating his condition, and his heart sank as he realized how bad things were. 'There's little bleeding, as far as I can tell, but I think my leg is broken. It looks broken – at least, it's twisted in a way that it really shouldn't twist.'

'Are you in pain?'

Calum swallowed, not liking even to say the words. 'I can't feel my legs on a good day – the spinal nerves are damaged. Looking at it, though, I think I would be in quite a lot of pain if the nerves were working properly.' He felt like laughing, and realized how close to panic he was. 'Of course, if the nerves were working properly, then I wouldn't be in this position in the first place.'

'Understood. There's a chance that your injuries are sending your body into shock, even though you can't feel any pain. We'll get to you as soon as possible. Can the team get access to you, or are there any locked doors?'

'I'm on the ground floor. The door to the street is closed but unlocked. The door to the area where I am is open and unlocked, although it usually has an electronic lock on it.' Calum mentally thanked heaven that he had left the security door open when he'd entered the warehouse.

'That's good.'

'Look, should I call for an ambulance?' Calum asked. 'They can get here quicker and they can treat me for the shock until your people turn up.'

'Don't do that!' the voice on the end of the phone said quickly. 'Our people are fully medically trained, and they will get to you soon. We've got a paramedic on a motorbike who can get there faster – he'll make you comfortable and treat any immediate problems. The ambulance van won't be far behind. Just keep talking to me.'

'OK,' Calum said dubiously. 'Are you sure?'

'I'm sure. Leave it to us. If there's a need for a hospital ambulance, then I'll call for one myself. Now, tell me exactly how the accident occurred. Don't leave anything out.'

With some embarrassment, Calum explained about

going downstairs from his apartment and checking out the storage area in the warehouse. He explained about ARLENE, and the way it had reacted – attacking him, or at least lashing out at him. The voice on the end of the phone was very interested in ARLENE, and wanted to know all kinds of details about what the robot had been used for and where it had been. Calum told the voice as much as he knew – more than he normally would have done, given the fact that ARLENE was nominally a military piece of equipment – but by now it was as if he was sitting in the back of his own head watching himself talk but not actually controlling the words. This was probably what shock felt like, he thought. While part of him continued with the conversation, the rest of him relaxed back into a soft black cloud. He found himself thinking about the accident, remembering the impact and the chaos that had followed, but the emotion had been drained away, and he found he could see it as if it was a film being played in his head. The car, sliding across the road towards them. The way the airbags had deployed. The sudden flash of heat.

No driver. The car sliding towards them had no driver. Why hadn't he noticed that before?

'Calum? *Calum!*'

'Wha–?'

'You stopped talking.'

'Sorry. I think I was falling asleep.'

'The tech and medical team is almost there with you. Keep talking. Keep yourself awake.'

'OK.' Calum tried to reach for the lost memory that he'd recovered during his dream – his hallucination? – but it had gone again. He knew that there had been something there, something important, but it had drifted away from him.

He caught a movement in his peripheral vision. He shied away, thinking that it was ARLENE again, attacking him, but a reassuring hand came down on his shoulder.

'Mr Challenger? My name is Bob. I'm here to help. Don't worry.'

Calum glanced upward, and saw a pink and brown blur that he assumed was a face.

'I'm not worried –' he started to say, but he suddenly felt a sting in his arm. 'What's that?'

'I'm sedating you,' Bob said. 'Ready for transporting.'

'I don't need sedating,' he said, then added, 'Transporting *where?*'

'Don't worry about a thing,' Bob replied. His voice was coming from a long way away. 'We're taking you somewhere we can look after you properly.'

Calum wanted to protest that this hadn't been part of the plan, but the soft black cloud that he had sunk into earlier was all around him now, holding him firm, and it closed over his eyes.

The last thing he heard before he fell into unconsciousness was Bob's voice saying to someone else, 'Get the aircraft prepped for take-off. Tell them we'll be there in thirty minutes. And dismantle that robot while you're at it.'

The last coherent thought Calum had was: *Aircraft? What aircraft?*

Tara sat against the wall in the bare room where she had been stashed, and shivered.

It wasn't that she was cold. In fact, the flat the men had taken her to was warmer than she normally liked – not that she thought she had any choice in the ambient temperature.

No, she was shivering because she was terrified. She didn't know what the men wanted with her.

They had hustled her out of the coffee shop. She had felt something sharp pressing into her side and she was too scared to cry out or say anything. One of the men had thrown some money on the counter as they'd passed to pay for her coffee. The other man carried her computer tablet in his hand. They had a car outside – one of them got into the driver's seat while the other slid into the back with her. Within a few moments, the car was gliding away into the London traffic – a kidnapping occurring in broad daylight without anyone realizing.

Tara thought she saw Tom Karavla standing across the road as they pulled away. He was clutching his laptop, and looking desperately unhappy. She wanted to scream at him, make him realize what he had done, but the car pulled away before she could do anything.

The car had driven east, through Aldwych and Mile

End, stopping in an area of cheap flats somewhere around Bow. The two men had pulled her out of the car – not roughly, but making it obvious that she had no choice – and taken her up to the third floor of an old apartment block. They pushed her into what was probably a bedroom, except that there was no bed, just a mattress on the floor. They took her mobile phone from her, and locked the door behind them as they left.

Tara immediately went to the window. It was screwed shut and barred. Through the grimy glass she could see a road, some trees and a handful of people walking. She supposed she could smash the window and call out to them, but how could she break the glass without cutting herself?

This was a disaster, and the worst thing was that she didn't even know why she was there. If the men weren't working for Nemor Incorporated, then who *were* they working for? She couldn't bargain with them if she didn't know what they wanted.

The door abruptly opened behind her. She whirled round, pressing herself against the wall.

One of the men stood in the doorway. He was holding a sandwich in a cellophane package. He threw it into the room.

'Here. Cheese and ham. You need to eat to keep your strength up.'

'What do you want with me?' she asked, hearing the trembling in her voice.

He frowned. 'You? This isn't about you.'

She frowned too. 'Then what *is* it about?'

'You know a boy named Eduardo Ortiz?'

She had to think for a moment. 'You mean *Gecko*?'

He nodded. 'Yes, he is the one. This is about him. We need him to do something for us, and he has said no. So, we ask again, and this time we have you. If he likes you, then he will do what we ask.'

Tara felt a strange whirling feeling in her chest, a mixture of relief at the fact that it wasn't actually *her* that they wanted, combined with a sudden flush of worry for her friend. He'd mentioned the Eastern European gangsters who had wanted him to use his free-running skills to steal things for them. That was why he was spending so much time at Calum's apartment. Obviously the gangsters weren't going to give up that easily.

'He's not in England at the moment,' she said. She wasn't sure why she was giving them information, except that she had heard somewhere that the best thing to do in a hostage or kidnap situation is to try to establish a relationship with your captors. 'He's . . .' she paused, wondering if she should give away his current location, ' . . . in China.'

The man shrugged. 'He has mobile phone, yes? They have service providers in China. Most mobiles are made there anyway. You will phone him and tell him that he must come back and work for us.' He paused. 'We will give him three days to come back. Every day past that, we will cut off one of your fingers. I think he will come back.' He smiled at Tara, but the smile looked like something that would fit better on the face of a shark. Her heart felt as if it was filled with lead. Taking a breath required effort. 'Every day you will talk to him on the phone again, but after a few days we will have to hold the phone for you, I think.'

The arrivals hall at Kai Tak Airport was a marvel of curved glass roofs and walls and white space. People moved across its floor and up and down its escalators like little black ants scurrying around the inside of a refrigerator. As Rhino, Natalie and Gecko walked through its wide corridors towards customs, immigration and their luggage, Gecko found himself mentally planning how he might free-run around the vast space. The possibilities were almost endless.

The three of them cleared customs in less than twenty minutes. Rhino had already reserved a car. The air outside the airport building was heavy with humidity, and the heat was enough to make Gecko break out in a sweat. It reminded him of being back in Brazil. He could smell a combination of flowers, salt water and rotting vegetables.

'We won't necessarily need a car in the centre of Kowloon,' Rhino said as they pulled away from the airport. 'But one of the first rules of covert operations is that you always need to control your own means of transport.'

Covert operations. Gecko rather liked the sound of that.

'So what are the other rules?' Natalie asked.

'Eat whenever you can, sleep whenever you can and know your cover story,' Rhino responded. 'Which reminds me – our own cover story, if anyone asks, is that Natalie is a rich Californian heiress who loves to upstage her friends.'

Gecko smiled. 'So our cover story is the truth?' he said. 'That makes things easier.'

'Bite me,' Natalie retorted.

Rhino drove the hire car out of the airport and along a wide road that was edged on the left by low green hills and on the right by a stretch of water. On the other side of the water was a landmass that rose up gradually to a series of low peaks.

'That's mainland China over there,' Rhino said. 'The largest peak you can see is Tai Mo Shan mountain.'

As they drove over a series of suspension bridges and into Kowloon Peninsula, Gecko saw that there were all kinds of vehicles on the road, from large black limousines to small battered three-wheeled vans.

'Although the whole area is referred to as Hong Kong,' Rhino said, 'Hong Kong Island itself is actually only one of about two hundred separate islands in the area, and it's not even the largest. Lantau Island is ten times as large. Hong Kong Island is, however, the most densely inhabited.'

'Are we staying on Hong Kong Island or on the mainland?' Gecko asked.

'I've booked us rooms in a hotel on the mainland, in Kowloon itself.'

As they drove, Gecko stared, amazed, out of the window. The contrasts that he was seeing were stark and amazing. On the one hand, wherever he turned he could see skyscrapers that were sculpted and designed so that they looked like something from a science-fiction film. On the other, there were also residential tower blocks that were surrounded by scaffolding made not from metal pipes, like in any other country he'd been to, but from bamboo rods tied together with rope, while along the edge of the waterline there seemed to be an alternative city made not from buildings but from rafts and small boats all lashed together to form a continuous platform running for miles. And everywhere there were signs – directions, adverts, neon lights, all jostling together with no evidence of planning. It was as if there was an entire novel's worth of information out there, spread across the landscape in little chunks.

Rhino manoeuvred the car down increasingly narrow roads, avoiding carts and stalls that seemed to spring up out of nowhere, slowly nosing his way through throngs of pedestrians who crowded across the road without worrying about green or red lights. Eventually he pulled off and down a ramp into a car park.

'We're here,' he said. 'Let's unpack and rest for a while, then we can plan what happens next.'

Calum's return to consciousness was gradual and intermittent. Eventually he became aware that he was lying on his back in a crisply starched bed with his arms outside the covers and straight down by his side. He was wearing pyjamas. He lay there for a while, listening for any noise, but there was nothing apart from his own breathing and the faint roar of an air-conditioning system.

He knew that he wasn't in his apartment. The sheets

felt wrong, and there was a smell in the air that he didn't recognize – something sharp, like disinfectant.

He must be at the Robledo premises near Farnborough, the place where he had been trained to use the bionic legs. He was safe.

Except that someone had mentioned an aircraft.

Calum opened his eyes. The ceiling above him was white and tiled, and he could see various items of medical equipment attached to the wall behind his head. Something was pressing against his right arm. Raising his head and looking down the bed, he could see that it was a band round his bicep. Lights flashed intermittently on it as it presumably fed information about his vital signs wirelessly to some central monitoring station.

He pushed himself into a sitting position. The room he was in was empty apart from his bed, the medical equipment attached to the wall behind it, a chair and a flat-screen TV mounted to the wall. A sign on the wall behind his head read *Bed 1*. There were two doors – one open, through which he could see a bathroom, and one closed that presumably led outside to a corridor. There was also a large window through which he could see blue sky. He couldn't see a phone, or anywhere his clothes could have been stored.

He shuffled to the edge of the bed, pulled the sheets back and tried to turn himself round. There were metal rails, like ladders, running along the side of the bed, presumably to stop him falling out, but they were hinged and he managed to lie one flat and turn so that his legs were dangling off the bed and nearly touching the carpeted floor. One of them, he noticed, was in a snazzy-looking plastic cast.

He turned his attention to the window. From his raised position he could now look down through it. He had been expecting a car park, perhaps, or a walkway, or some flowerbeds.

Not desert.

He blinked a couple of times, wondering if his brain was still suffering the lingering after-effects of the sedative, but the view outside steadfastly refused to change. He could see a fence topped with razor wire, a lot of white sand, some scrubby bushes and something that looked like a cactus. And, come to think of it, that sky was bluer than anything he remembered seeing in England.

'Ah,' a familiar voice said, 'you're awake. There was a change in your blood pressure, so I thought I'd better check to see you were OK.'

Calum turned his head and saw Dr Kircher in the doorway. He was wearing a white coat, and had a stethoscope round his neck.

'Where am I?' Calum asked.

'You're safe.'

'I'm not in England, am I?'

'No. You're in Las Cruces.'

Calum's mind raced. 'Las Cruces, New Mexico? Las Cruces, USA?'

'That's right. This is where the main Robledo Mountains Technology facility is located.' Kircher smiled. 'It seemed to make sense to bring you out here so we could conduct some detailed investigations into what went wrong with the bionic legs.' He paused. 'We brought the ARLENE robot back with us as well. It's in a hangar nearby. There may well have been some unfortunate cross-interference between your legs and the robot.'

'You kidnapped me!' Calum exclaimed. His brain was filled with whirling thoughts, the most important of which was that he was thousands of miles from home, and completely isolated.

'Not at all,' Dr Kircher said calmly, smiling. 'We merely took a decision to relocate you in your own best interests.'

'I didn't agree to it.'

'You did,' Kircher continued, still smiling. 'The form you signed when you were fitted with the legs explicitly gives us permission to treat you wherever we feel best.' He shrugged. 'To be fair, it was a small sub-paragraph, buried deep in the text, and you were distracted. I'm not surprised you missed it.'

Calum felt a rising tide of panic lapping against the shores of his mind. 'I want to leave. I want to go back to England.'

'Let's sort out these legs first, eh, and then we'll see. Can you get back into bed properly, by the way?'

'Then I want to make a phone call.'

'Of course. I'll get a phone brought in.' He paused. 'If

I can find one. We don't have that many around.' He cocked his head to one side, considering Calum. 'But, before I do that, I want to get a full psychological profile run on you. I can't help but feel that you are acting a little . . . paranoid. It might just be the lingering effects of the sedative, of course, but it might be that there was some feedback through the headset from ARLENE's circuitry. There might be some damage to your brain. I hope not, but before I let you talk to anyone I do need to check that out.'

His voice was calm and reasonable, but there was something about the way the light from the window reflected off his glasses that made his words seem menacing. More like a threat.

Calum examined his options. He was helpless. He couldn't do anything without the help of the Robledo staff.

'How long have I been unconscious?' he asked, trying to make his voice calm.

'Oh, eight hours or so. We have a private jet at Farnborough airfield, and our own landing strip here. I came with you.'

'You kept me sedated for that long?'

'You were injured, and we were worried about the possibility of brain damage caused by feedback from ARLENE's processor, as I said, so we kept the sedative topped up. Now, that's enough talking. I suggest that you rest for a while, let that sedation run its course. We'll run some tests later.'

He backed into the corridor, and the door closed behind him.

Calum couldn't help but notice that there was no door knob or door handle on his side.

Whichever way he looked at it, he was a prisoner.

eight

The team – Rhino thought of them as the team, even though it was really just him and two kids – was staying at the Marco Polo Hotel, just a few minutes' walk from the harbour in the Tsim Sha Tsui area of Kowloon. It was an exclusive, expensive hotel, but Calum had seemed willing to pay the price for the three rooms. As Rhino had pointed out to him – firstly they needed somewhere comfortable where they could sleep after their long journey and recover from their jet lag, and secondly they needed to have an address in Hong Kong that made them seem as if they had a lot of money, so it wouldn't be unusual for them to be shopping around for exotic animals if anyone checked. And someone *would* check; Rhino was sure of it.

He slept for eight solid hours after they got to the hotel. Waking up naturally, and feeling good, he showered, dressed and grabbed some breakfast in the hotel restaurant. The others were still asleep, so after that he wandered out into the open air. The heat and the humidity – just like walking into a sauna – fell on him like a sodden blanket. He smiled, despite himself. This was Hong Kong, and he loved it.

The harbour was only a hundred metres or so from the hotel, and he wandered down towards it. One of the Star ferries was just docking at its jetty. The sight of the familiar boat, with its green lower deck and white upper deck, sent a shiver of recognition through him.

He wandered to the barrier that separated the jetty from the waters of the harbour and stared across at the incredible sight that was Hong Kong Island. Boats of many different kinds crossed in front of him: from bamboo junks steered with a single long oar up to the most modern of yachts. At night, he knew, the skyscrapers on the other side of the channel would be lit up with garish neon purples, blues, greens, yellows and reds of a thousand different advertising hoardings, with the choppy waters reflecting them like a fractured, shifting mirror. Behind the buildings rose the lush dark green of the hills that sat in the centre of the island, with Victoria Peak the highest.

He shivered as he remembered running through the foliage of the Peak in the dark once, some years ago, desperately trying to get to the tram station and the safety of a crowd of tourists, knowing that an agent of the Guójiā Ānquánbù, the Chinese Secret Service, was somewhere behind him, armed with a silenced automatic pistol and a knife. Rhino's past was littered with such moments – moments where his life depended on something as simple as whether or not a twig cracked beneath his feet, or whether a gate was locked or open. He was happy to have left those days behind. Well, he thought, kind of happy. And only kind of behind as well, considering what he was now getting himself into with Calum Challenger.

He wondered where that agent was now. Was he dead, or was he perhaps leaning on a barrier somewhere nearby and looking out at the same waters as Rhino?

He shook himself. This kind of introspection would not help the mission. He turned and headed back to the Marco Polo.

The hotel was attached to an exclusive shopping mall of the kind in which Natalie would love to spend her time and her mother's money, and Rhino wandered across the hotel lobby and into the heavily air-conditioned mall, looking for places that sold high-quality clothes. Within an hour he had suits in his and Gecko's sizes, plus several shirts for both of them, and a silk dress for Natalie that matched the shoes she was already wearing – all charged to the credit card that Calum had given him. He supposed he could have waited until they'd both woken up and gone shopping *with* him instead of having to shop *for* them, but trailing Natalie around a shopping mall while she tried on all the clothes would have driven him mad. Better that he just presented her with a fait accompli. The problem was that they hadn't had the time to get suitable clothes in London before they left, and the way they dressed, like the place they were staying, would be part of their cover.

He also bought three mobile phones with pay-as-you-go SIMs, and spent a few minutes setting them up and making sure that each phone had the numbers of the others in its memory. Better to be safe than sorry.

Back at the hotel, he found Natalie and Gecko having brunch. He joined them and showed them what he had bought.

'Seriously?' Natalie said when she saw the dress. 'Green? I have blue eyes. It'll clash.'

'So will we if you don't put it on,' Rhino said. 'Besides, you'll be wearing sunglasses. All rich celebrities wear sunglasses all the time, don't they?'

Gecko was running his fingers over the cloth of his suit. 'Not much flexibility of movement here,' he pointed out.

'And you won't be wearing trainers either.' Rhino raised up another bag with a shoebox in it. 'I had to guess your size, but I have a good eye. Fortunately I'm not expecting any trouble that might require your particular skills.'

'So apart from the fun of dressing up,' Natalie said, 'what exactly *is* the plan? I mean, do we have a full cover story and everything?'

'You are a rich American named Jayne-Anne Richmond,' Rhino replied. 'Your father works in oil. You can be as vague as you like about what he does – the vaguer the better, actually. You have a trust fund, and you're interested in buying something cute and cuddly – but, specifically, something that your friends don't have. It's like a competition with you and your friends, to see who can get the rarest, most exotic animal.'

'I guess that we are her bodyguards,' Gecko said. 'The

suits give it away. Do we get sunglasses too?'

'We do. Our job is to stand behind her and look as if we're ready to spring into action at a moment's notice.

Natalie frowned. 'Giant rats aren't cuddly or cute,' she pointed out. 'How am I going to convince them that I have my heart set on one?'

'The point when negotiating and in gathering intelligence is that you don't barrel in and ask for the thing you actually want. If you do, the price goes up rapidly. You play it carefully, not giving away your interests. Let the seller mention the thing you're interested in first, and don't react to it. Be dismissive at first.'

Natalie stared at him. 'You expect this Xi Lang to mention giant rats first? He's going to have to get through a lot of cute and cuddly animals before he gets to that.'

'Not,' Rhino pointed out patiently, 'if you mention that you used to have a pet white rat when you were a child, and you loved it.'

'Like that's going to come up in conversation.'

'Trust me, it will. He's a salesman. He'll ask you about your pets when you were younger so that he can work out what your likes and dislikes are.'

'But I'll have already told him I want something cute and cuddly!' Natalie protested.

'Again, it's the art of the deal. Sellers know that buyers rarely end up buying what they say they want. They almost always buy something else, something that's been at the back of their mind, or that means something special to them.'

'OK!' She shrugged in a way that said 'what*ever*' without actually uttering the word. 'You're the boss.'

'No,' Gecko said, '*you're* the boss. We're just the bodyguards.'

'And remember,' Rhino pointed out seriously, 'that these people are criminals. Gangsters. If we stick to the cover story, we'll be OK, but we're walking a fine line here. I want you to leave anything with your name on it at the hotel. I've got fake IDs that I brought with us from England, and replacement mobile phones for us that can't be traced back to our real identities. Things could get ugly, and if they do it's my job to get you out fast.'

Rhino coached them for a while longer, making sure that they were comfortable in their personas, and then the three of them went back to their rooms and got changed. When Natalie and Gecko reappeared in the hotel lobby, he hardly recognized them. Natalie was the absolute picture of a reality-TV star, complete with sunglasses and high heels and baseball cap, while Gecko was hovering somewhere between inconspicuous and dangerous in his dark suit and sunglasses. He had even gelled his usually unruly hair and brushed it back neatly. Natalie, to give her her due, didn't even glance at Gecko or Rhino as she walked towards the lift that would take them to the cavernous underground car park. Of course she didn't – celebrities never notice their bodyguards.

Before they got into the car, Rhino used his new mobile to dial the number that had been on the receipt that Tara had pulled off the internet – the one from Xi Lang to some unnamed buyer. It was, presumably, the phone number for Xi Lang's Emporium of Unusual Animals. As he dialled, he glanced from Natalie to Gecko, silently warning them that this was it. There was no going back now.

'Hello?' a Chinese voice said in English. Rhino noticed that nothing was given away: not the name of the establishment or the name of the person answering the phone.

'Hello,' he said. 'Is that Mr Xi Lang?'

'Maybe,' the voice conceded. 'What do you want?'

'I want to buy something – or, rather, my employer wants to buy something.'

'What kind of something?'

'Something unusual.'

A slight pause, and then: 'Where you get this number from?'

'From a previous customer of yours – a customer who is a close friend of my employer. She was very happy with the service you provided.'

'You have name?' the voice demanded.

'I do, but I don't really want to say it on the phone.'

'OK.' The voice sounded slightly happier, and Rhino guessed that if he had actually named some celebrity that he thought might have bought an exotic animal from Xi Lang then the phone call would have ended rapidly. Xi Lang only wanted customers who would be careful about giving out too much information.

'You know where we are?' the voice said.

'I do.'

'Then you come over now.' A slight relaxation in the voice. 'We give you good service. You get what you want from us.'

'We will be there in half an hour,' Rhino said, and cut the call off.

The drive out to the Sham Shui Po district of Kowloon took about twenty minutes, and in that time they seemed to cross from affluence to poverty and back several times. The younger Chinese people buzzed around on scooters, dressed expensively in designer jeans and T-shirts, with sunglasses over their eyes and iPods in their ears, but their elders rode around on bicycles, wearing loose, plain shirts and trousers and wide straw hats. As they got closer to Sham Shui Po, the buildings became older and uglier. The majority of them were still high-rise blocks of mixed design and variable height, but they were plainer now, made of water-stained concrete, and they had balconies and air-conditioning units stuck randomly all over them. Clotheslines were stretched from balcony to balcony, and clothes fluttered from them like drab flags.

After a while, they left the residential area behind and entered an area of long, old warehouses made of crumbling breeze blocks and rusty corrugated iron roofs set at shallow angles. Thin, mangy cats with hungry eyes slunk in the shadows. Rhino drove carefully up to a particular warehouse and stopped.

He got out, motioning for Gecko to join him. Stepping

out of the air-conditioned interior of the car was like stepping into an oven. The two of them stood there, looking around, feeling the sweat prickle down their backs and across their foreheads.

A side door in an anonymous warehouse opened and a large Chinese man in a suit emerged into the sunlight. His eyes were hidden behind black sunglasses. There was a bulge beneath his jacket that suggested he was armed. Without saying anything, he gestured Rhino over, and expertly searched him from head to foot. Rhino assumed that he was looking not only for weapons but, more likely, for recording devices that might suggest he was an undercover policeman. The man removed Rhino's wallet and checked the fake identification carefully, then handed it back. Beckoning to Gecko, he did the same, then stepped back and nodded.

Rhino went and opened the car door, and Natalie got out, every inch the regal rich princess. The Chinese man stepped towards her as if to search her too, but Rhino put a hand on his chest. The man stopped, stared at Rhino for a long moment, and then turned to look at the black rectangle of the open door.

A Chinese woman stepped out of the darkness and into the sunlight. It was difficult to tell her age, but Rhino thought she couldn't be much older than her late twenties. Her hair was black, and wound into a tight bun on the back of her head, and she wore a red silk dress embroidered with dragons.

'Mr Lang welcomes you,' she said in good English, 'and

hopes that you had a pleasant journey. Your visit is unexpected and unplanned, but welcome regardless. Mr Lang does insist, however, that all visitors be searched. It is a . . . requirement of this establishment.'

Natalie took her hat off and threw it in the back of the car, then followed it with her tiny handbag. She held her arms out from her sides and twirled round. The green silk dress that Rhino had bought for her didn't really leave anywhere that she could have hidden anything larger than a credit card.

'Do I look like I'm hiding anything?' she asked.

The Chinese woman paused, and then shook her head. 'Thank you,' she said, 'and I apologize for the necessity of asking. My name is Tsai Chen. Please to come inside.'

The inside of the warehouse was shadowed and mercifully cool. The smell reminded Rhino of the times he had gone to the zoo when he was a kid. It was the smell of the elephant house.

He hoped they didn't have any elephants there. He just knew that Natalie would want to take one home with her, for real.

From where the five of them stood, inside the doorway, rows of cages and crates stretched away into the darkness. Some of them stood on the floor, and others sat on metal shelving, three or four levels high. Rhino thought that he could make out, far away, some fenced-off areas of earth or water where animals would be free to roam and stretch their muscles. The warehouse wasn't silent either. From every direction Rhino could hear bleats, screeches, growls, barks and other noises that were more difficult to classify, but which obviously came from living things. He couldn't see how this many creatures could be kept in these conditions for very long. Just keeping them fed and watered would be a major undertaking in its own right. Presumably Xi Lang had some large open-air facility somewhere in the New Territories, and this was a staging post, somewhere close to the docks and the airport where the crates of 'merchandise' could be stored before they were sent to their final destination.

Rhino wondered how many of them actually turned up alive. Xi Lang must take precautions to minimize the fatality rate in transit. Maybe he drugged the creatures before they were dispatched. He wasn't going to ask – real customers wouldn't be that interested in the mechanics of the operation, whereas undercover police or other investigators would, and he wanted them to be counted in the former camp, not the latter.

'May I offer you some refreshments?' Tsai Chen said smoothly. 'Perhaps some jasmine tea?' Rhino noticed that the large man in the suit who had stepped out to meet them had come inside and closed the door, and he had been joined by two smaller men.

Rhino was about to say 'No,' but Natalie stepped in before he could open his mouth. 'Thank you – that would be lovely.'

As Tsai Chen gestured to one of the men, she said, 'We never established the name of the person who recommended our services to you.'

Rhino saw a fleeting look of panic on Natalie's face, mirrored by one on Gecko's . . . *Ah*, he thought, *this is where it all starts to go wrong* . . .

The door to Tara's room opened and one of the two short-haired Eastern European men entered. Tara wished she could tell what country he came from – Russia? Lithuania? Poland? – but her ear for accents wasn't good. She just knew he sounded like a baddie from a James Bond film.

He had a small gold earring in his left ear. She hadn't spotted that before.

He was also carrying a video camera on a tripod. Without looking at Tara, he plonked it down in the centre of the room, facing away from the window. Noticing Tara noticing that, he shrugged.

'No need to give away location,' he said.

'At the angle you'll be filming, there's just trees and sky out there,' Tara pointed out.

'Even so. Best not to take chances. I have seen these *CSI* programmes on TV – just one piece of a building, with a shadow showing which way the sun was shining, and they can tell where the video was made. Is very clever. That is why I use video camera instead of mobile phone to record you – harder to trace.' He nodded towards the tray on the floor, beside the mattress. 'You eat OK?'

'If you like fried chicken.'

'Who does not like fried chicken?' he countered.

'What kind of food do they have in your country?' Tara

asked, trying to get some kind of clue as to where he came from.

'Fried chicken,' he said. He looked up at her, from where he was fiddling with the camera, and smiled. 'We also eat goat, on special occasions. The tender parts of a goat, grilled.'

'Lovely.'

'If you like the tender parts of a goat.'

'Which are the tender parts?' she asked.

He frowned. 'If you do not know, it is best not to ask.' He gestured to her to come towards the centre of the room. 'Now, you stand there.'

Standing was difficult. Her muscles didn't want to obey her, and her legs were shaking with fear. She did as she was told though, and stood in the middle of the room, in front of the glass eye of the video camera. She cast a despairing glance at the door, but the man had closed it behind him, and she knew that his companion had to be out there somewhere. She could run for the front door, but she wouldn't make it, and things would just get worse for her. At least at the moment they were making her relatively comfortable. She'd lived in worse places, and eaten worse food.

The man handed her a piece of folded-up paper from his pocket. 'You read this out,' he said. He held up a hand, indicating that she wait until he had switched the video camera on, and then his hand swept down in an 'Action!' gesture.

She looked at the words on the paper, which were so predictable that she could have scripted them herself. She felt something shrivel inside her as she thought about the effect that the words would have on Gecko. It was loading a whole lot of guilt on to him that he really didn't need – and if he agreed to do what the gang wanted then it would be her fault!

Taking a deep breath, she looked up at the camera.

'Eduardo,' she said, and then improvised by adding, 'Gecko – I am being held by some men who say that they have talked to you before. They say that you have to come and work for them. If you don't, they say they will hurt me.' She could hear the tremor in her voice, and tried to suppress it. 'They say they will hurt me badly, and that it will be your fault. They say that you must come back to your flat, and that they will be waiting for you there.' She paused, reading the last sentence. 'They say you have three days.'

The man behind the camera paused, then clicked the *Off* button. 'That is fine. We will edit down and send to his mobile phone.' He glanced at Tara, and frowned slightly at her expression. 'You want to do it again? More feeling, maybe?'

'I think I've put all the feeling I can manage in there,' she said quietly. She looked at him. He didn't look like a bad man, particularly. He looked like someone you might find behind a bar, or running a stall in a market. 'Would you really hurt me?' she asked tremulously.

He grimaced, and shrugged. 'I have my orders,' he said. 'If I do not follow orders, then it is me that gets hurt. Given a choice . . .'

'I know,' she said. 'You're only following orders.'

'We have a saying in my country – "The fish eats the fly, the man eats the fish and the bear eats the man". You, I think, are the fly, and I am not the bear.'

'Which country is that?' Tara tried again. The man just smiled, picked up the camera and the tripod, and left.

Tara shivered, feeling a twisting sensation in the pit of her stomach. *Hurt badly*. That had been the phrase on the paper.

She didn't want to be hurt badly. She didn't want to be hurt at all.

But she didn't want Gecko to have to work for a criminal gang either.

She had been *so* stupid. This was all her fault!

'**D**o you remember my friend Savannah Drummond?' Natalie asked. Her heart was beating fast, but she kept a polite smile on her face. She kept telling herself, *This is a business discussion; there's no reason to panic*, but these were career criminals they were dealing with.

Tsai Chen inclined her head, but said nothing. It was obvious to Natalie that she didn't recognize the name – it would be unusual if she did, unless Natalie's friend Savannah actually *had* bought some exotic pet from Xi Lang – but she was too polite to say so, especially with a potential client standing just in front of her. And Savannah was careful enough of her own privacy that any enquiry from the Triads would hit a stone wall.

'She had the cutest little set of meercats, the last time I saw her,' Natalie continued. 'I asked her where she got them, and she mentioned Mr Xi Lang. As I was passing through Hong Kong on a shopping trip, I thought I would pop in to see what other things you might have.'

Tsai Chen didn't make any gesture or movement, but

the second suited man moved quietly away, presumably to check on their computer records. That left the larger man still standing there like a small but very threatening mountain.

'And what kind of . . . items . . . were you interested in?' Tsai Chen asked.

'Something that nobody else has,' Natalie replied. 'A speciality item.' She smiled her best, politest, whitest smile. 'Meercats are *so* last year. I want something that will make my friends green with envy.'

The first man came back with a tray containing a small teapot and two small cups. Tsai Chen carefully poured out two cups of honey-coloured tea, handed one to Natalie and then took the second one herself. Bodyguards don't get refreshments, Natalie mentally observed.

'Could I interest you in a dolphin?' Tsai Chen asked calmly.

'My local aquarium has seven dolphins,' Natalie countered, just as calmly. She took a sip of her tea. It had a delicate floral taste. 'Oh, how exquisite.'

'Do they have Yangtze River dolphins? They are very rare. Almost extinct, in fact. In another few years you might have the only living Yangtze River dolphins in the world.'

Natalie shrugged, doing her best to look bored. 'Dolphins are dolphins,' she said casually.

'Then perhaps a rhinoceros?'

Natalie tried not to look over at Rhino. 'Where would I put it?' she asked.

'One of our customers drained their swimming pool and put a rhinoceros in there.'

'Rather cramped, surely?' Natalie said. 'You would only have room for one, and it would get lonely.'

'That depends on the size of your swimming pool.' Tsai Chen's tone of voice didn't change, but Natalie could tell that she was becoming annoyed at Natalie's vagueness. 'Then let me ask a more general question: are you looking for something for the house, or for the garden?'

Natalie threw her head back and laughed. 'How quaint,' she said. 'A garden? No, we don't have a garden; we have grounds. *Extensive* grounds.'

'Then a pride of lions perhaps? Very good at keeping out intruders.'

'No, I don't think so.'

'Tigers, then? *White* tigers?'

Natalie raised an eyebrow, interested despite the undercurrent of panic that she was feeling. 'Hmm. I don't know *anyone* with *white* tigers, and they *would* go so well with my summer dresses.' She thought for a moment, and then shook her head. 'The problem is that I ride horses through the grounds, and I don't think the tigers would get on with them.'

'Have you ever ridden a zebra?'

Natalie winced. 'Stripes,' she said, 'are not in fashion this year.'

The second suited man returned with a slip of paper in his hand. He whispered something into Tsai Chen's ear. The

Chinese girl turned back to Natalie with a slight frown of concern. 'We do not appear to have dealt with a "Savannah Drummond". Can you provide . . . more details?'

'Well, she wouldn't have dealt with you herself.' Natalie didn't miss a beat, but she could feel her heart rate increase, and a slight giddiness made her vision go blurry. 'She has people for that kind of thing. I'm only here in person myself because I haven't quite decided what I want, and I thought I would check your stock out. But you have shipped some meercats to America, haven't you?'

Tsai Chen consulted her piece of paper. 'Yes . . .' she said dubiously. 'We have. Last year.'

'Then that would be for Savannah!' Natalie said, clapping her hands together and thinking, *That was a lucky guess.* 'Glad we could sort that out. Now, what do you have that nobody else has?'

The girl was obviously losing patience, but was too polite to show it. 'Mammal, reptile, amphibian, bird, fish or insect?'

'It sounds like a menu,' Natalie responded, trying to inject a sarcastic tone into her voice. 'Do I choose a sauce next?'

The girl smiled tightly. 'Actually, we do supply . . . exotic items . . . for very special restaurants around the world. But that is, I think, not what you want.'

'A mammal, then. Something that doesn't require a special diet, but will eat any leftovers. Something that will make people go "Ooh!"' Natalie paused for a moment, remembering the advice that Rhino had given her earlier, back at the hotel. 'Oh!' she exclaimed, faking a sudden idea, 'I remember when I was a kid, I used to have a pet rat. A white rat. It used to climb all over me, with its long whiskers tickling me. I remember when it died I cried for hours. Have you got anything like that – a rodent of some kind, only maybe, you know, *bigger*, like a dog, so it would live longer and I could take it for walks on a leash?'

Tsai Chen cocked her head on one side. 'A large rat?' she repeated. 'Are you *sure* that is what you want?'

Natalie shrugged in a deliberately vague way. 'I don't know – I haven't seen what you've got yet. Let's take a look.'

'It would be an *unusual* choice, even for us.' She paused, thinking. 'However, I believe we *do* have something like that in stock. Please to come this way.'

She led them along the main aisle between the crates and cages. Rhino and Gecko glanced left and right as they walked, ostensibly keeping watch for threats as a bodyguard should, but Natalie assumed they were surreptitiously trying to make out what was in the crates and cages. She could see patches of fur or scaled skin through the gaps, and the occasional pair of eyes watching her warily. Once or twice she caught sight of a mouth full of sharp teeth, or a claw clutched at the edges of a bar or a wooden strut, but it was difficult to put together a picture of anything definitive from the jigsaw of snatched images. The trouble was that she felt her heart going out to all of the animals. They hadn't asked to be there. This was not their natural habitat. She wanted to buy every one of them, just so she could set them free.

Sounds of snuffling, growling, barking and hissing grew louder as they approached each cage or crate, and faded as they moved away. At one point, just as they turned a corner into a narrower aisle, Natalie thought she heard a voice saying, softly, 'Help me! Please God, help me!' She twisted her head round, trying to determine where the voice came from, but the only thing she could see was a brightly coloured tropical bird, like an ornate parrot, sitting in a cage. She stared at it, and it stared back, but it didn't say anything, and she wasn't entirely sure that the voice had come from the direction of the bird. But, if it hadn't, then who or what had said those words? Natalie's skin began to prickle as she considered the only other possibility . . .

She kept walking: it was the only thing she could do. But she kept listening for something behind her asking for help. She wondered whether Gecko and Rhino had heard it too.

The door to Calum's room opened, and a man in a white coat walked in. It wasn't Dr Kircher. This man was excessively overweight, with a bald head and small, piggy eyes. He was carrying a tablet computer. He stopped in the doorway and assessed Calum for a few moments, then came further in. The door slowly swung shut behind him with a hiss, pushed by the hydraulic arm.

'Mr Challenger, my name is Laurence.'

'Is that a first name or a last name?' Calum asked politely

from the bed where he was sitting up.

The man shifted uncomfortably. 'Actually, it's both,' he said. 'Formally, my name is Laurence T. Laurence. I'm a psychiatrist. I've been sent to evaluate you.'

'Laurence T. Laurence? Whose bright idea was that? Your parents'?'

'We're not here to talk about me,' Dr Laurence snapped. He pulled a chair from the wall and placed it by the side of the bed, then sat down.

'What does the "T" stand for?' Calum asked.

'Do you mind if I call you Calum?'

Calum couldn't help but smile. 'Do I have a choice?'

Dr Laurence stared at Calum for a few moments, then made a note with a capacitive pen that he took from his pocket. It would work on the tablet's touch-sensitive screen. His lips moved as he wrote, and Calum thought he was saying: *Demonstrates aggressive responses.*

'Do you know why you are here?' Dr Laurence asked.

'I've been kidnapped,' Calum said firmly, but politely.

'Why do you believe that you have been kidnapped?'

'Because I didn't choose to come here, and I can't leave.'

Another note. This time, Calum thought that the doctor's lips formed the words *Firmly held persecution complex.* 'You know, don't you,' he said, 'that you have an injury to your knee, and that you are paraplegic?'

Calum nodded. 'The knee injury can be treated at any hospital,' he pointed out, 'not just one that's in a different country. And as for . . . as for the paraplegia – I have an apartment that has been modified to allow me to move around and live without any help.'

'And where is this apartment?'

'Back in England.'

'Where you claim you come from?'

Calum felt a sudden flash of anger. 'Where I *do* come from.' He paused. 'Can't you tell from my accent?'

'This is America,' Dr Laurence pointed out. 'Every second person I meet has an accent of some kind.' He made another note on the tablet PC. His lips moved slightly as he murmured *Issues with national identity* to himself. He consulted the clipboard again, turning a sheet back so that he could see something beneath. 'How exactly were you kidnapped?'

'I was sedated and put into an aircraft, then I was flown here.'

'That seems a lot of effort to go to, just for one boy.'

'Obviously I'm important,' Calum pointed out, 'otherwise Robledo Mountains Technology wouldn't have gone to all that trouble.'

Delusions of grandeur were the words mouthed by the doctor as he made more notes. He licked his lips. Calum wondered if he knew that he subvocalized when he was writing. 'And how are you feeling now?'

Calum shrugged. 'Still slightly fuzzy from the sedative, and angry about what has happened to me, but otherwise fine.'

'Good. Good.' He paused. 'Any hallucinations?'

'How would I know?' Calum asked reasonably.

Dr Laurence frowned. 'What do you mean?'

'Well, I think I'm sitting here talking to you. If you're really there, then I'm not hallucinating. If you're not there, then I *am* hallucinating.' He nodded towards the wall. 'I think there's a window there. The same thing applies to that. I have no idea if it's *really* there at all. That's also true about the blue giraffe standing over by the door.'

Dr Laurence twisted round to look behind him, confused. 'A blue *giraffe*, did you say?'

Calum sighed. 'I was joking about the giraffe. I just wanted to make a point that none of us actually know whether we're hallucinating or not.'

'So you can't see a blue giraffe?'

'No,' Calum said heavily, 'I can't see a blue giraffe.' He was beginning to realize Dr Laurence had no sense of humour.

The doctor wrote another note on the tablet PC. *Hallucinations, and denial of hallucinations* his lips said noiselessly. 'Thank you,' he said, standing up. 'I think I've got everything I need.' He smiled tightly. 'I'll send a nurse in later with some tablets that will make you feel better.'

'Great, thanks,' Calum said.

Dr Laurence stared at him for a long moment, obviously slightly perturbed at Calum's challenging sarcasm, then he turned to leave.

As soon as the door was slowly hissing shut behind him, Calum swung into action.

He had already detached the ladder-like rails that ran

along the sides of the bed, unscrewing them from their mountings. All the time that Dr Laurence had been in the room, the rails had been held up by the weight of the blankets. Now Calum pulled them out from underneath the blankets, used his arms to twist himself into a sitting position, then shuffled to the edge of the bed and manoeuvred the rails like crutches, allowing him to stand up.

The door was halfway shut now.

He rapidly swung himself towards the door, desperately hoping that Dr Laurence hadn't forgotten anything and decided to come back.

The door was nearly closed now.

Leaning on the makeshift crutches, Calum reached forward with his right hand and inserted a strip of plastic between the door and the frame, just where the lock was. The plastic had been taken from the sign above his bed – the one that said *Bed 1*. It had adhesive on the back, and Calum made sure that he pressed that side against the door, over the tongue of the lock. The plastic stuck to the wood of the door and the metal of the lock, stopping the lock from clicking home.

The door hissed shut, but the lock didn't engage. Despite the fact that there was no handle on his side, Calum could now pull the door open any time he wanted. Even better, anybody coming in would probably not notice his modifications.

All he had to do was to wait for nightfall, and then go exploring . . .

*

Another turn into a third aisle, and Tsai Chen stopped in front of a large cage.

'What about this?' she asked. 'Would this suit your . . . particular preferences?'

Natalie stepped closer to the cage. Rhino and Gecko both crouched down to get a better look.

The creature in the cage was buried underneath a large pile of straw. All Natalie could see was a whiskered nose poking out, but the nose itself was about the size of her fist. If this *was* a rat, then it was an amazing size.

She stepped back and to one side, trying to work out if this was the same cage that they had all seen in the photograph Tara had discovered. The angle seemed to be the same, and the boxes on either side were very similar to the ones in the photo. It was only when Natalie saw the reference number stencilled in black on the side of the crate – 119078B – that she knew they were in the right place.

'It's not very active,' she pointed out, trying to put as much disappointment in her voice as possible. After all, when you were buying a new dress, or a new pair of shoes, you could get a better bargain if you sounded uncertain than if you sounded ecstatic.

Tsai Chen picked a wooden stick up from the top of the cage and prodded the pile of straw through the bars. 'It just needs some encouragement,' she said. 'It is very friendly, and a very affectionate animal.'

The straw shivered, and then the creature inside lunged

out, grabbing for the wooden stick with its long teeth.

Natalie shivered, despite herself. It still looked like a rat. It was about the size of an Alsatian dog, with the rounded body, long tail and pointed head characteristic of rats. Its ears were large, corrugated and pink, like cauliflower leaves. It was covered in short brown hair, and its whiskers stuck out sideways from its snout, quivering. Its front teeth, now clamped on the stick, weren't as sharp as she would have expected. They were more like chisels than knives, in shape and in size.

Natalie saw Rhino glance at Gecko, checking his reaction. The boy seemed to be distracted by something on the floor behind him: he was bending over and looking at whatever it was. Fortunately Tsai Chen and her companions were all clustered around the cage, either looking at the giant creature or looking at Natalie to check her reaction. Rhino coughed quietly to attract Gecko's attention.

Natalie made an audible '*Hmmm!*' sound to make Tsai Chen and her men look at her, rather than at Rhino and Gecko.

Gecko looked up at Rhino, and then stood up, hiding something beneath his jacket. He looked into the cage and grimaced, then Natalie saw him glance at Rhino and shake his head. Whatever Gecko thought the creature was, it wasn't a giant rat.

'Is this more the kind of thing you were looking for?' Tsai Chen asked.

Natalie shook her head. 'I'm sorry, but –' she shrugged,

gesturing at the cage – 'this thing is a little too aggressive for my tastes. It wouldn't go down well at cocktail parties, and I can't see it taking well to a leash.' She gestured to Rhino and Gecko to follow her. 'Thank you for showing me your stock, but I think I'll pass. Perhaps another time.'

The woman bowed her head momentarily. Natalie thought she saw a flash of anger on her face. 'As you wish,' she said calmly. 'The customer is always correct.'

Natalie clapped her hands together. 'Wonderful!' she said brightly. 'I will still recommend you to all my friends, of course.'

'You are very kind.' The woman gestured to the large man by her side. 'Cho will escort you to the door. I presume I do not have to remind you that our service here is . . . very exclusive. We would not wish it to become public knowledge. Mr Lang would be . . . *most* upset.'

'Of course,' Natalie said as she turned to leave. 'The whole point about an exclusive service is that so few people have access to it.'

The three of them were silent as they were led back, but once they were outside in the oppressive heat and sunshine, and once Cho had shut the door behind them, Natalie felt strangely alone and sad. The warehouse had depressed her – all those animals that had been taken from the wild and were now destined for people's ornamental gardens or tanks in their massive living rooms. It was *wrong*.

She felt shivery, and she looked around. She had the

distinct impression that they were being watched. For a moment she couldn't see anything, and then she noticed a security camera on the side of the warehouse. It was pointed at them. Having spotted it, she quickly made out three other security cameras on the warehouse and other buildings around. They were *all* pointed at Natalie, Rhino and Gecko. They may have got out of the warehouse, but they were still the object of interest. Natalie caught Rhino's eye and glanced towards the nearest camera. He nodded slightly. He had seen them too.

Rhino turned towards Gecko. 'Well?' he asked. 'What's wrong? You don't look happy.'

'It was not a rat,' the boy replied quietly.

'It's pretty giant,' Rhino countered.

'Yes, but it's not a rat. It's a coypu.'

'Never heard of it.'

'They are also called "river rats". They are rodents, but they are semi-aquatic and they are vegetarians. They originated in South America, but they can be found all over the world now.'

'Can you be *sure* this is a . . . what did you call it . . . a *coypu*?' Rhino asked.

'I am. The tail is shorter than a rat's, and the front teeth are orange, and made for tearing at vegetation rather than ripping things. Those orange teeth are a distinctive feature of coypu.' Gecko hesitated, frowning. 'The large ear threw me for a minute, but I think maybe that was scarring due to a fight rather than a natural thing. The ear on the other side of the head was smaller, much more like I would expect on a coypu.'

'So,' Rhino said heavily, 'a wasted trip, then.'

'Not necessarily,' Gecko replied. He patted the bulge beneath his jacket. 'I have something to show you, but we need to get away from here.'

Rhino nodded, and turned to head towards the car, but he noticed that Natalie was still standing there, not moving. He walked across to her. 'That was great work back there. I believed you myself.'

She just stood there, not looking at him. Thoughts of the creatures in the warehouse were still weighing on her mind.

'Is anything wrong?' Rhino asked gently.

She nodded. 'That place . . .' she said quietly, and trailed off, then: 'All those animals . . . shoved together and waiting to be drugged and shipped out, just so someone can show them off to their friends. So they can boast about having something that nobody else has. It's . . . wrong. Those animals deserve to be in rivers and forests and plains, or wherever they live, not stuck in a warehouse.'

'What about your friend, Savannah?' Rhino asked gently. 'Did she really have meerkats?'

Natalie remembered how cute those meerkats had been, and how she hadn't even bothered to ask where they had come from or how healthy or happy they were. 'She did. But then, one day, she didn't. I asked her about them, but she just said she got bored with them. I never found out what happened to them. I never bothered to ask.'

'It's OK. We're out of there now.'

She looked up at him, and she could feel that her eyes were bleary with tears. 'But *they're* not.'

Gecko coughed. 'We have to go.'

Rhino pulled Natalie towards the car. 'There's nothing you can do about it,' he said. 'It's just one of those things in life that you have to accept.'

Natalie didn't say anything, but she could feel her jaw clench.

The three of them got back into the car – Rhino driving, Gecko beside him and Natalie in the back. Rhino drove quickly to the end of the warehouse and started to turn the corner.

Glancing out of the rear-view mirror, Natalie noticed a black car come round the corner of the warehouse and speed after them.

'I think we're being followed!' she announced to the rest of the car.

'How is it that you can spot a car following us so quickly?' Gecko asked.

'Hey, I live in Los Angeles,' she replied tartly. 'It's an occupational hazard.' She paused, thinking about what she had said. 'Not that I really *have* an occupation, but you know what I mean.'

'She's right,' Rhino said from the driver's seat. He accelerated the car, pressing the three of them back into their seats as they raced through the deserted warehouse district.

'It's Xi Lang's people – they must have got suspicious, and they want to see where we go.'

Natalie felt the panic in her chest expand to a point where it threatened to suffocate her. 'What are we going to *do*?'

'Do?' Rhino sounded grimly amused. 'We're going to get away from them, of course.' He glanced over his shoulder reassuringly – at least, it would have been reassuring if he hadn't taken his eyes off the road ahead. 'Trust me,' he said, 'I've done all the Special Forces driving courses. Twice.'

'Why twice?' Gecko asked.

Rhino smiled. 'Because I failed them the first time.'

Natalie looked over her shoulder again. The black car was keeping pace with them.

'It could be a coincidence,' she said, although she wasn't convinced.

Rhino wasn't convinced either. He suddenly swung the car right, into a side road, tyres squealing. The car behind them slewed round to follow. He did the same at the next junction, skidding the car to the left at the last moment. Again, the car behind them did the same, leaning precariously over as its driver only just managed to copy Rhino's manoeuvre.

'They know we're on to them,' Gecko pointed out.

'What does that mean?' Natalie asked.

'It means,' Rhino muttered, 'that they know that *we* know that they are following us, and, more importantly, that we *care* enough to do something about it. So rather than follow us back to the hotel, I think they're going to try to intercept us, and then ask us in some rather impolite manner involving guns who we are and what exactly we think we're doing.'

Even as Rhino spoke, the car behind them began to accelerate to overtake. Rhino sped up as well, keeping as much distance as he could between them.

Ahead, Natalie could see taller buildings in the gap between the warehouses. They were getting closer to the main areas of Kowloon. People began appearing on the pavements. Shops came into view, replacing the industrial buildings. Other cars beeped furiously as Rhino sped past them, weaving from side to side to avoid slowing down.

'If you're not careful, the police will stop us,' Gecko cautioned.

'Isn't that a *good* thing?' Natalie asked.

Rhino shook his head. 'Not if we don't want to spend the next few weeks in a prison cell while this thing gets sorted out. We have more important things to do.'

Without warning, he reached down and pulled the handbrake up, jerking the steering wheel right at the same time. The car slid for a few seconds, the back end coming round until they had rotated through ninety degrees and the car was pointed sideways. Natalie gasped, convinced that Rhino was going to drive straight into a shop front, but an alleyway appeared directly ahead of them and he accelerated into it.

'Market!' Gecko yelled, and indeed the alleyway ahead of them was filled with stalls, Chinese shoppers and tourists.

Rhino swerved. The left-hand wheels came up on to a narrow pavement, and Rhino kept driving, beeping his horn. Shoppers jumped out of the way as he pushed on through the market, steering close to the stalls in the road, but just missing them.

Natalie looked over her shoulder. Their pursuers had made the same turn, but people were gathering on the pavement behind Rhino's car, cursing and shaking their fists, and their pursuers were finding it difficult to get through. Natalie could hear shouts and curses in a variety of languages, and the sound of their pursuers frantically beeping their horn.

Miraculously, Rhino managed to get to the other end of the alley without hitting anyone or anything. As he pulled alongside the final stall, where dead snakes were hanging from pegs, he skidded to a halt, opened the window, held some cash out and yelled something. A Chinese youth ran forward to take the money. Rhino accelerated again, out of the alleyway. As he turned right again, into a wider road, Natalie saw the youth and some friends grab the final stall and push it towards the kerb, blocking the way for the pursuing car.

Rhino slowed to a more sedate pace and kept driving, looking at his rear-view mirror repeatedly for any sign of pursuit. Eventually he said: 'I think we're clear. Everyone OK?'

'If there was a motor-vehicle equivalent of free-running,' Gecko said, his voice too controlled for comfort, 'then you would get some kind of award.'

'Where to now?' Natalie asked. 'Back to the hotel?'

'No – I want to find somewhere quiet and stop for a while, just to check that we've shaken them off. And I want to look at whatever it is that Gecko picked up.'

Rhino kept going for a mile or so, until they were back in a more residential neighbourhood, then he pulled off into a side road and stopped. There was nobody around. Natalie turned to see if any cars passed by, following them, but the road was clear.

'OK,' Rhino said, turning to Gecko. 'What have you got?'

'Not in the car. You'll see why. Let's get out.'

Once they were out of the car, Gecko glanced around, then opened his jacket and pulled something out. It looked like a spiral mass of crumpled yellow cellophane. He straightened it with a rustling sound and laid it across the bonnet of the car while Natalie and Rhino tried to work out what it was.

'It was curled up on the floor,' Gecko explained. 'It had been kicked half beneath a crate. I wondered what it was, so I pulled it out to take a look. When I realized, I knew that I had to bring it with us to show Calum.'

The thing that Gecko had taken was about two metres long and a double-handspan wide. It drooped over the car's bonnet. It was hollow and cylindrical with a gap running from end to end. A kind of fringe ran along both sides, a little way from the split along its middle.

That fringe looked like legs.

They *were* legs. Hundreds of little legs, but hollow.

Natalie realized with a shock what it was – what it *had* to be – just as Gecko continued: 'This is a centipede's skin. It has been shed and left behind so that the centipede can grow larger.'

'*Larger* . . . ?' Rhino breathed.

'Yes,' Gecko agreed. 'Judging by this skin, it is already perhaps ten times as large as the largest centipede in the world. It is, I believe, an unknown species of giant centipede.'

There was a long pause as they all thought about the implications of what Gecko had said.

'And I thought giant rats were icky,' Natalie said, summing up everyone's thoughts perfectly.

ten

Standing there with the hot sun shining down on him, Gecko hefted the centipede skin in his hands. It was weightless, but it crinkled in his hands as it moved. He tried to imagine what the real creature – the one that had shed the skin – would be like, but it was almost impossible. Centipedes to him were things barely the width of his hand that scuttled out from beneath tables and out of cracks in walls, not things that were big enough to eat a cat whole.

'The question is,' he said, 'are we going to go back to Xi Lang's and change our order from a giant rat to a giant centipede?'

'I think,' Rhino answered carefully, 'that we've probably outstayed our welcome. A rich American girl buying a giant rat is unlikely enough, but just about plausible. A rich American girl buying a giant centipede on a whim is something else entirely. That Chinese girl will smell a rat – if you'll excuse the pun.' He thought for a moment. 'I need to talk to Calum, update him on what the situation is.'

Rhino reached into his pocket and took out his new mobile phone. While he dialled the number for Calum's phone, Gecko turned to Natalie. She was standing, hands crossed over her chest, holding on to her upper arms as if she needed comfort.

'Are you all right?' She looked up at him, and jerked nervously when she saw the centipede skin. He quickly held it behind his back. 'Sorry.'

She shook her head. 'That's OK. I think I've decided that keeping wild animals is wrong, which is not what I was expecting to happen here.'

'You are having an epiphany,' he said quietly.

'No,' she replied, frowning, 'Epiphany is one of my best friends, but she's in St Tropez at the moment. Why did you mention her?'

Gecko stared blankly at her for a moment. 'Never mind,' he said. 'What I meant was, you're having a life-changing moment.'

She nodded. 'I'm not used to thinking this way. I don't *do* "serious". I used to think that having a fur coat was the height of fashion, and if my boyfriends didn't have at least one pair of crocodile-skin boots in their wardrobe then they weren't my kind of person, but *now*? Now I can't stop thinking about the suffering that these animals endure, just so we can have something exotic to own – and if it's alive then all the better.' She paused. 'Something needs to be done,' she said as if the thought had only just occurred to her – which Gecko thought it probably had.

Behind Gecko, Rhino cursed. 'No answer,' he said. 'Gone straight to voicemail.' He thought for a moment, brow furrowed in concentration. 'I think we should go to the hotel and rethink our approach,' he said eventually.

They got back into the car – putting the centipede skin carefully into the boot – and drove out of Sham Shui Po and towards the hotel. None of them said anything.

Gecko felt the skin of his hands prickling as they sped through the Hong Kong streets. He glanced down at his palms. They were red and slightly blistered, as if he had a bad case of sunburn, but just in that area. It was probably the centipede skin. There could be some kind of toxin on it to deter predators – although he did wonder with some foreboding what kind of predators a giant centipede might have.

He took a tissue out of his pocket and wiped his hands carefully. The burning sensation eased slightly. He made a mental note to wash his hands and spread an antiseptic cream on them when he got to the hotel.

It started to rain just as they got back. Rhino let Gecko and Natalie out while he drove off to the underground garage. Natalie ran for the hotel lobby, but Gecko just stood there, entranced. The raindrops were *hot*, and it looked as if they actually began to evaporate before they hit the pavement. At least, there was a layer of steam rising up from the pavement to about waist height, and Gecko couldn't see any water on the pavement itself.

While Rhino parked, Gecko and Natalie headed to

their rooms to freshen up. There was something about the climate in Hong Kong that made Gecko feel sticky and grimy all the time. They met back together in the air-conditioned hotel lobby, away from any other groups. Rhino ordered cold drinks for everyone. While they were waiting for their drinks to arrive, he tried to call Calum again, but there was still no answer. Gecko tried to call Tara, just in case she was with Calum, but she wasn't answering either.

'OK,' Rhino said, 'let's take stock. The giant rat turns out to be an ordinary-sized coypu, and so we don't need a sample of its DNA. We think, however, that there may be a previously undiscovered species of giant centipede in the warehouse which Calum *would* want a DNA sample from. The question is: how do we get it?'

'Can't we get DNA from the skin that Gecko took?' Natalie asked.

Gecko shook his head. 'It is not likely. From what I know, insect and arthropod exoskeletons are made of chitin, and there is no DNA in chitin.'

'As I said earlier,' Rhino continued, 'I don't think that we can attempt to buy a giant centipede in the same way we would buy an ordinary animal. It's just not credible that Natalie would want one.'

'For a start,' Gecko pointed out, 'centipedes are carnivorous – they eat other creatures. I hate to think what animals a centipede that size would eat. Puppies, maybe? And most of them are venomous too – they have poisonous bites, and often they can excrete poison from their skin.' He held his hands up, showing the blistering and the burn. It was better than it had been – the pain and the redness were receding – but Natalie winced anyway. 'They do not make good house pets. Nobody in their right mind would want a giant centipede as a pet except for a villain in a James Bond film, perhaps.'

'Why would this Xi Lang be selling giant centipedes in the first place?' Natalie asked. 'What is in it for him? Who would buy them?'

'Maybe the people who supply him just happened to pick them up, and he's trying to work out what to do with them,' Rhino suggested.

Natalie frowned. 'Maybe they can be used in Chinese herbal remedies. I remember reading somewhere that a lot of animal parts go into those remedies – rhino horns, bear gall bladders, all kinds of icky stuff.'

'It's possible.' Rhino nodded. 'The trouble is that we've shot our bolt. We can't go back and ask to see any giant centipedes he happens to have lying around.' He thought for a moment. 'I think there's only one answer – I'm going to have to break into the warehouse and find those centipedes myself.'

It took Gecko a few seconds to process the words that Rhino had spoken.

'You are going to do *what*?' he asked, astounded.

'I'm going to break into the warehouse, find the giant centipedes and take a sample of their DNA.'

'You are going to break into a warehouse that is quite

probably run by the Chinese Triads, and secretly take a DNA sample from a giant poisonous creature?'

'Yes.'

'Not without me,' Gecko said.

Rhino shook his head. 'Not going to happen,' he said firmly.

Gecko pushed on. 'Think about this logically,' he said. 'I am smaller and lighter than you, and probably faster. I am also used to high places. I can get up on to the roof of the warehouse and find a skylight that I can get through. There is bound to be one. No building that big is completely sealed, and it is old enough that there will be gaps between sheets of cladding, or broken windows, that I can use. Once I get in I can find a way for *you* to get in, and then I can keep watch for guards while you look for the centipedes. Alone you have a much smaller chance of success.'

Rhino looked grim. 'I still don't think it's a good idea,' he muttered. 'I'm meant to be responsible for the two of you. What if something happens to you while we're out there?'

'What happens to us back here if something happens to you alone out there?' Gecko countered with remorseless logic. 'By maximizing your chances, I am maximising all our chances.' As Rhino continued to look grim, he added, 'You know it makes sense.'

Eventually Rhino nodded: once, briefly. 'OK, then – you can come. But not you, Natalie.'

The American girl held her hands up defensively. 'Hey, I wasn't even *thinking* of coming with you. Testosterone-fuelled gymnastics are your thing, not mine. But I really don't think this is a good idea. These people are *dangerous*.' She paused, looking from one to the other. 'Look, what if,' she said quietly, 'we call in the police now? They could raid the warehouse, and in the confusion you could sneak in and get the DNA sample. Doesn't that make sense?'

Rhino shook his head. 'Firstly, it's likely that Xi Lang is paying protection money to the police, and they would either ignore anything we said or they would give him advance warning of a raid, and secondly, there's a good chance that the animals we're interested in would be impounded and might die while we were trying to get to them.'

Natalie obviously wasn't willing to give up. Gecko could tell that from the firm set of her jaw. 'Let's say the police are out of the picture,' she said. 'Isn't there some *other* organization that we could contact to tell them about Xi Lang and what he's doing? Anything that prevents you two having to go back in and that gets those animals out of there! I know you've got this boys' machismo thing going, but these people are *dangerous*. I don't want to be the one to explain to Calum that you've both been killed by Chinese criminals while searching for an *insect*.'

'Arthropod,' Gecko corrected.

'I guess there's the United Nations,' Rhino said, shrugging, 'but the chances of us just sneaking in on the back of any raid they make are slim, to say the least.' He sighed heavily. 'Look, Natalie, we're not a law-enforcement agency. We're an independent group of travellers who just happen to want some DNA. This isn't our fight. I don't particularly relish the thought of Gecko and me going in, but I can't see any realistic alternative. We need to do what we need to do and get out. Someone else can deal with Xi Lang. It's not our job.'

Natalie was about to say something else, but changed her mind. Gecko saw her clench her jaw and stay quiet. It was obvious, however, that she was deeply unhappy. She glanced from Rhino to Gecko and back. 'Actually, I'm not feeling too good. I think it might have been the smell of that warehouse. I'm going to go and lie down for a while.'

Rhino nodded his agreement. 'You go and get some rest.' He looked at his watch. 'It's late afternoon now. Gecko – we'll get some rest as well, and meet back here at about eight o'clock. We'll grab a quick bite to eat and then head out when the sun goes down. Best that we do this kind of thing in darkness, I think.' As Natalie got up to leave, Rhino continued: 'I'll have a look on Google Maps to see what the warehouse looks like from above – maybe there's a lower-level cabin at the back that would give you easier access to the roof. And I need to look for somewhere we can park where the car won't be discovered, but where we can get to it quickly.'

'Reassure me about one thing,' Gecko said.

'What's that?'

'Please tell me that we are just going to get a sample of the centipede's DNA – not to retrieve an actual centipede.'

Rhino laughed. 'If I was going to pick up a pet,' he said,

'then it wouldn't be a giant centipede, and I wouldn't do it in Hong Kong. It's just DNA – don't worry.'

Gecko smiled. 'Later, then,' he said.

As he headed towards the lifts, he saw Natalie waiting.

'You ready for your little expedition?' she asked

Gecko nodded. 'There is only one thing that worries me,' he said.

'Only one? What's that?'

'I'm not sure that Rhino has thought through the difficulty of getting a DNA sample from a creature with a hard, thick exoskeleton . . .'

Back in her room, Natalie stood by the window.

Hong Kong was shrouded in mist. The office blocks and high-rise buildings materialized from it like geometric islands emerging from the cloudy waters of a lake. The hotel room was cooled by air-conditioning to a point where Natalie was shivering, but she only had to put a hand on the window to feel the heat pressing through from outside.

She couldn't pull her mind away from the warehouse, from the animals that she'd seen there pent up in cages too small or too dirty, and from that voice she thought she had heard calling out for help.

A parrot. It had to have been a parrot.

This was all *wrong*. Things like Xi Lang's business, and the warehouse, shouldn't be allowed in a civilized world. If people wanted to buy pets, then they ought to go to a well-lit, well-ventilated place where happy animals were cared for by trained assistants and there was a qualified vet on call, not something that looked and smelt as if it was one step up from a slaughterhouse. What was the mortality rate like among Xi Lang's animals? she wondered. And if those animals had been ripped away from their natural habitats and their family – if they had families – only to end up as a trophy roaming around someone's carefully manicured lawns, then maybe death was a preferable option for them.

Her thoughts kept circling around in her head like lazy black flies, and somewhere in the background she could hear, like the tolling of some huge, cracked bell, the unspoken words 'This is wrong! This is wrong!' as a backdrop to her confusion.

She held her iPhone in her hand, and her hand was by her side. As soon as she had got away from Gecko and back to her room, she had done an internet search on the words 'United Nations', 'exotic animals', 'Hong Kong' and 'smuggling'. Within a few seconds she had the phone number for the local UN office dealing with animal smuggling. All she had to do was tap the screen and the phone would dial the number for her. It was that simple. She glanced at the slip of paper. This was a big step, but she had to do it. She *had* to. She wouldn't be able to live with herself otherwise.

Rhino would be furious, she knew, but she was doing it for him as well. He was dead set on going back to the warehouse and breaking in, despite the risks. He was so focused on completing the *mission* that he was blind to the dangers.

Natalie had to stop him. She had to get the UN, or the police, or someone to raid that warehouse before Rhino and Gecko went back into danger.

She walked across to the table where the hotel phone was located. She didn't want to do this from her own mobile, just so she didn't leave an obvious trail back to herself. The way hotel phones operated, the call could only be traced back to the hotel switchboard.

She dialled the number.

'*Wei?*' a woman's voice said.

'Hello,' Natalie said, 'do you speak English?'

'Yes, I do. Can I help you?'

'Could you put me through to whoever deals with the illegal import and export of exotic animals, please?'

The request didn't seem to faze the operator at all. 'Please wait for a moment, and I will transfer you,' she said.

Natalie waited, still shivering but feeling a bit better about herself.

Calum sat in bed, restlessly waiting, until the sun set behind the desert horizon outside his window and the sounds outside his room faded.

His mind raced all the time, trying to work out his options. He was a prisoner, that much was certain, but the prison was comfortable and the bars were almost invisible beneath their padding. Nobody was threatening him – not directly, anyway – and he was being fed. The food was good as well – mainly TexMex specialities, where everything came with red or green chilli peppers. The problem was . . . well, *one* of the problems was . . . that he didn't know what was wanted from him. He didn't know why he was there, or what he had to do to get home again – if he ever could. At some stage, he presumed, someone would offer him a Faustian bargain, but he hated having to wait until *they* came to *him*. He wanted to be able to anticipate their offer so that he could think about his answer in advance.

The useful thing was that he wasn't in a hospital. If he had been, then there would have been nurses on duty all night. The fact that the sign behind his bed said *Bed 1* indicated more than just the fact that he was their most important patient. It implied that he was their *only* patient, otherwise what were the odds that he would randomly have been given bed number one?

So, if there weren't any other patients, and there weren't any nurses on duty all night, then the place probably went down to skeleton staffing overnight. He was, as far as Robledo was concerned, locked in his room, and he couldn't leave. There wasn't even an emergency button – they were banking on the fact that, having been examined, he wasn't going to have any medical crisis before everyone came to work the next morning. At best there would be a security guard on patrol every couple of hours.

Calum decided to test out his reasoning. At midnight he settled down in bed and pulled the covers up to his chin, and waited.

At half past one in the morning, according to his watch,

the door opened, spilling in light from the corridor. He glanced up, trying to look as if he had just been woken.

'Wha–?' he muttered.

A uniformed security guard stood in the doorway. 'Sorry to disturb you, sir,' he said, and moved back out into the corridor. The door hissed shut behind him. The last thing Calum saw of him, he was turning right.

So, one guard, on patrol, and probably only checking the rooms every couple of hours.

Calum waited for ten minutes, then pulled the ladder-like sides out from his bed, swung himself round and moved across the floor to the door, using the sides as crutches.

He got the tips of his fingers into the crack between the door and the frame, and pulled. The door moved towards him, the tongue of the lock having been prevented from engaging with the hole in the door frame by the sticky plastic strip he had placed there earlier.

He stuck his head out and glanced along the corridor in both directions. Most of the lights were dark, leaving only the emergency lighting.

Nobody in sight. More importantly – no security cameras that he could see.

Dr Kircher, Dr Laurence and the nurses had all exited his room and turned left. He did the same, using the crutches to move down to a corner where the corridor turned left again. He poked his head round the corner.

About halfway along the next section of corridor was what looked like a lift lobby and stairwell. Just before it was a desk in a wider section of the corridor, opposite what looked like a little kitchen area. The desk looked like a nurses' station, but there didn't seem to be anyone on duty.

Checking behind him, just in case the guard was coming back, Calum scuttled down the corridor, swinging the makeshift crutches back and forth and wincing every time they went *clunk* on the carpet-tiled floor.

He felt exposed in the middle of the corridor, like a cockroach running from the safety of one set of shadows to another.

He got to the desk without being observed.

There was no paperwork scattered around – he suspected that the Robledo Mountains Technology management mandated a clean-desk policy – but there was a tower PC stashed beneath the desk with its LCD screen blank, and more importantly there was a plastic rack filled with tablet PCs just like the one that Dr Laurence had been using to make notes on earlier.

Calum glanced yearningly at the lift lobby, just the other side of the desk. The lifts would lead down to the ground floor, and there would be a door leading out into the open. There would be cars out there, and . . .

. . . And that's where the dream of escape would end, of course. He couldn't drive, for two very good reasons. Firstly, he had never learned and, secondly, his legs were paralysed. He couldn't operate the accelerator or the brakes.

He sighed, still feeling the pull of freedom emanating like a magnetic field from the lifts and the stairs. He could phone for help, he supposed – what was the emergency code in America? 911? – but even if the operator believed him and sent a police car to investigate, the security guards would have a cover story.

No, he had to be cleverer than that.

He took one of the tablet PCs from the plastic rack. He turned away, then turned back again and took another one. He might as well be hung for a sheep as for a lamb.

Tucking the tablets beneath his arms, he scuttled back along the corridor, round the corner and back to his room. He knew that turning the handle would make no difference, given his slight modifications to the lock, so he just pushed the door open and slipped inside, then let it *hiss* closed as he moved towards the bed, dumped the tablets on the sheets, climbed in and put the sides back.

He glanced around, slightly panicky, to make sure that everything was exactly the same as it had been when the guard had looked in earlier.

He was safe. He let his head sink back into the pillow in relief. His plan had worked – or, at least, the first phase of his plan. Now he just had to figure out a way to use the tablet PCs to get some kind of message out.

He stashed one beneath his mattress, and held the other one in front of him. It seemed like a fairly standard design. He was pretty sure that, with the things that he had picked up from Tara over the past couple of months, he could get past whatever security protocols it had and perhaps even connect up to the internet.

His fingers felt something on the other side – a sticky plastic label. Robledo did like their sticky plastic labels. It was probably just a security tag, or a serial number. He turned the tablet over to take a look.

And felt his breath catch in his throat.

It was a white rectangular tag, stuck to the back of the tablet, and it read:

PROPERTY OF ROBLEDO MOUNTAINS TECHNOLOGY
LAS CRUCES, NEW MEXICO
A SUBSIDIARY OF NEMOR INCORPORATED

eleven

Rhino crouched in the shadow of the corner of a warehouse, just across the road from the back of Xi Lang's emporium, and looked around. It was night, and as dark as it ever got in Hong Kong, with the neon lights of the island reflecting from the low cloud in a chromatic glow.

Rhino was trying to match the things he could see from the ground with the view from above that he had memorized from Google Maps. Yes, that low cabin that had been fixed to the back of Xi Lang's place was exactly where the computer image had said it would be, and the gap between it and the building across the road wasn't any wider than it had appeared while they were planning this. Apparently, according to Gecko, the gap was narrow enough to jump, except that Rhino wouldn't have done it on a bet. That, he reflected, was probably because he wasn't as young, as fit or as foolhardy as Gecko.

Xi Lang's warehouse didn't have any drainpipes leading down from the roof, which immediately cut off Gecko's preferred route of access. The few doors in its walls were heavy and locked – the only exception being the one at the front. Discreet visual and infra-red CCTV cameras were attached to the corners of the warehouse, scanning all the approaches. Rhino assumed that they would be continually monitored.

'Ready?' he asked.

'Ready,' came a voice from behind him.

Rhino turned his head. Gecko was dressed all in black, in clothing that was loose enough not to restrict his movements but not so loose that it would get caught on anything. His gaze met Rhino's, he nodded once, and then he was gone, climbing up a drainpipe that was attached to the side of the warehouse in whose shadow they were sheltering. He climbed like a cockroach – fast and scuttling, pressed close to the corrugated metal wall. As soon as he reached the top, he squirmed over and was gone. Rhino knew that if *he* had tried it, the drainpipe would have peeled away from the wall under his weight, but Gecko was a lot lighter.

Rhino waited patiently, picturing Gecko running back across the warehouse roof, turning round, judging distance and wind direction, then running full-tilt back the way he had come. Just as Rhino imagined that Gecko's sprint had reached the edge, a black shape sailed silently across the gap between the warehouses. It was like watching an owl swooping between trees. A faint thud reached Rhino's ears as Gecko landed on top of Xi Lang's warehouse. He imagined Gecko rolling forward on the roof and coming up running to absorb his momentum, then slowing, turning and coming back to the edge.

A black shape appeared, hunched against the neon-coloured clouds. Rhino saw a hand wave briefly, and then a rope appeared, snaking down from the roof. Gecko had wound it round his waist before climbing the drainpipe. Now he had apparently attached it to some fixed point on the roof.

The rope would be invisible to the infra-red cameras, but Rhino wouldn't. He waited while Gecko moved to one corner, reached down to put black cardboard covers over the infra-red CCTV lenses, then moved to the other corner and did the same thing. If they left the covers there for too long, then whoever was watching the screens would notice something, but a few minutes would probably be OK.

Rhino reached down and picked up the bag that was by his side. It contained two items they were going to need inside the warehouse. He sprinted for where the rope hung down, then stopped and quickly attached the bag to his belt. He grabbed the rope and scrambled up it to the roof: feet gaining purchase on the metal wall while he pulled himself up with his arms. He had already wrapped torn strips of the bed sheet from his hotel room around his boots to make them quieter when hitting the metal of the walls. It was just like being back in training.

He pulled himself over the edge, hands burning at the roughness of the rope, and lay flat as Gecko removed the cardboard covers from first one and then the other IR camera. Rhino indicated the expanse of flat roof, punctuated with occasional skylights and labouring air-conditioning systems, with a quick wave of his hand. Gecko shook his head. There were no other cameras up there.

Rhino half stood and pulled the rope back up. No point leaving it for someone else to find and, besides, they were going to need it again in a moment. He coiled it up, and then followed Gecko across to a skylight. The glass was grimy, and had metal wire wound into it in a grid, but a corner of it was broken. Rhino could smell a faint hint of the zoo-odour of the warehouse drifting up through the hole. Gecko reached in through it and fished around, shoulder pressed hard against the glass. Rhino heard a *click* as Gecko disengaged a catch. The skylight moved inwards under the pressure of Gecko's shoulder. He quickly withdrew before he fell into the dark space beneath.

The two of them paused for a full minute, waiting to make sure that they hadn't been heard. While they were waiting, Rhino detached the bag from his belt and took out the contents – two sets of night-vision goggles that he had brought with him from England.

He handed Gecko one set of goggles and slipped the other set over his head and turned them on. Rather than seeing heat as the infra-red cameras around the warehouse did, they amplified low levels of light into something much brighter. Suddenly the world was filled with a ghostly green glow – almost too bright, given the reflections of the neon advertising signs on Hong Kong Island from the low clouds.

Gecko switched his goggles on, flinched slightly at the

sudden brightness, then gave Rhino a 'thumbs up' sign.

Confident that they hadn't been seen, Rhino tied one end of the rope round a ventilation duct and fed the other end through the open skylight. He was sweating now in the oppressive heat.

They had already worked out the rough area of the warehouse that they wanted to enter, based on where they had been earlier in the day, and chosen a skylight close to that location. There was no point getting in all the way across the warehouse, away from the coypu and hopefully the giant centipedes, if it meant increasing their chances of being spotted, even if the entry turned out to be easier that way.

Rhino turned round and dangled his legs through the open skylight, holding on to the roof with his hands and making sure that he was on top of the rope. He squirmed backwards and clasped his legs, vice-like, on the rope, then slid further inside the warehouse. When his shoulders reached the edge he reached down with one hand to find the rope, and then lowered himself fully down, finally bringing his other hand inside the skylight. Now he had two hands and his legs clamped on the rope. He lowered himself slowly down.

The night-vision goggles allowed him to see all the way to the far side of the warehouse. Everything was flooded with green light. He couldn't see any of Xi Lang's guards – as far as he could tell, the warehouse was empty, although he had to work on the assumption that there were people around somewhere.

The skylight they had used as their entry point was near to one of the columns holding the roof up – and he used the column as cover while he slid down the rope. The problem was that directly underneath the skylight was a row of crates and cages, rather than one of the aisles, and Rhino's feet touched down on a crate. The slack of the rope – the bit that would have hung down to the ground had the skylight been above an aisle, was curled loosely on top of the cage. The zoo-smell was almost overpowering, overlaid with an acrid scent that stung Rhino's nose, like bleach.

Rhino glanced down, trying to make out through the narrow gaps between the bars what was inside the cage, but he could see only a shadowy mass curled up in a corner. Maybe it was just a pile of hay, or something. Maybe the crate was currently empty.

Gecko landed beside Rhino. His foot caught the rope and pushed it sideways. The end fell between the bars, into the cage.

And it touched the dark mass that was curled up below.

The shadowy shape lunged explosively upward. A massive paw tipped with scalpel-sharp claws hit the bars. It was too large to go through, but the cage shook and two of the creature's claws managed to get through the gap and rake at Rhino and Gecko. Somewhere below them Rhino heard a growl so deep that it was only part sound. The rest of it was a deep vibration that he could feel through his boots.

Rhino jumped backwards one way, Gecko another. Gecko was agile enough to make sure that his jump took him to the nearby column. He grabbed it, lifted his feet up, swung round the column and jumped lightly to the ground.

Rhino wasn't as agile, or as lucky. He jumped badly. One of the claws caught the heel of his boot, and he toppled sideways, hip banging against the top edge of the crate. His momentum carried him over, into one of the aisles between the crates and cages, and he started to fall towards the ground, head first.

Everything seemed to be happening in slow motion. He could see grit on the floor and footprints in the dust, as well as the seams on the cage where the bars had been welded together. He hoped desperately, in that long eternity of falling, that whoever had soldered those bars had done a good job.

Without thinking, he reached out and grabbed hold of the bars as he fell. His fingers bent backwards and he thought for a terrible moment that they were going to break, but he twisted his body, clenched them against the metal and pulled himself closer, allowing himself to pivot so that his legs came past his head and he was falling the right way up.

Something massive and dark hurtled towards him from inside the cage. He released the bars just as a mouth big enough to crush his head, lined with dagger-like teeth and wet with saliva, crashed into them. A wet fetid wave of hot air crashed against his face. Inches away from his face a huge yellow eye glared at him, full of hatred.

His legs connected with the ground, absorbing the impact of the fall. He sprang backwards just before a paw the size of his head raked its claws downward, slicing the air inches away from him.

He ended up sitting on the ground and staring at the cage. He still didn't know what was inside; he just knew it was incredibly dangerous. Even with the night-vision goggles – which, thank heavens, still worked despite the fall – all he could see was a black shape that was curling itself up again, somehow knowing that its prey was out of reach.

Gecko appeared round a corner. He looked like some kind of strange insect–human hybrid with the goggles over his eyes. He reached out a hand and pulled Rhino to his feet.

'What was *that*?' he asked.

'I don't know and I don't *want* to know,' Rhino replied. 'But I can't imagine who would want it as a pet!'

'It might be a tiger,' Gecko said, gazing at the cage in awe. 'In Chinese medicine, powdered tiger bones are highly prized for their supposed medicinal properties. Chinese healers make something called "tiger wine" out of them.'

'Great,' Rhino said breathlessly. 'I'd hate to have to be the guy who does the powdering.'

Gecko's mouth was set into an unpleasant line. 'I'm sure there are plenty of ways to kill a tiger in a cage,' he said bleakly. 'Anything from a rifle to a long stick with a knife on the end. They are magnificent creatures. They deserve better than that.'

Rhino clapped him on the shoulder. 'It's an unfortunate situation,' he said, 'but we can't let it distract us. We have a job to do.'

'It's a good thing Natalie isn't here,' Gecko murmured. 'She's taking this whole thing surprisingly hard.' He led the way back to the corner where the aisles crossed. Rhino glanced around, trying to orientate himself, based on what he remembered from earlier on. If the main door was over *there*, and the skylight they had entered through was up *there*, then the place where Gecko had discovered the moulted centipede skin was over . . .

'There,' said Gecko, pointing. 'That's where the coypu was.'

'Are you sure?'

'I am sure. Now all we have to do is find the crate with the centipede in, get a sample of its DNA and get out unobserved. How hard can it be?'

A sudden loud crash echoed through the warehouse. It was followed by two more crashes from different directions.

'You had to ask, didn't you?'

'What was *that*?'

'That was the sound of doors being smashed in,' Rhino answered grimly. He'd heard that noise before. He'd caused it more than a few times.

Lights flared as the overhead illumination suddenly came on. Rhino and Gecko pulled the night-vision goggles from their eyes before they were blinded. A heavily amplified voice announced something harsh in Mandarin. Rhino translated it roughly as 'This is the police! Stay where you are! Do not move or run!'

The noise level in the warehouse suddenly rose as the

various creatures protested in whatever way they could at the sudden intrusion. Growls, barks, snarls and screeches filled the air. There was also panicked shouting in Mandarin from Xi Lang's various employees who had been taken by surprise.

'It's a raid!' Rhino told Gecko grimly. 'What are the chances that the police would choose to raid this place just as we get here?'

'That depends on how they knew about it,' Gecko answered, thinking of Natalie. There was a strange tone in his voice.

Rhino sprinted down the aisle to the place that Gecko had indicated earlier. He saw the coypu straight away: it was pressed against the far side of its cage, shivering. Looking at it now, head on, Rhino could see that it was very different from a rat – its legs were longer, and its head was squarer.

'You check that way,' he said to Gecko, pointing right, 'and I'll look this way.'

Separately the two of them went from crate to crate, cage to cage, trying to work out what shadowy creature was in each one. The animals were on edge and wary now, bothered by the sudden activity, and most of them were easy to see. Within the space of thirty seconds Rhino spotted hyenas, crocodiles, a brown bear and a tangle of pythons as thick as his arm.

He passed a crate where the wooden slats were closer together, and moved in for a better look. A big, black eye was looking back at him, at the same level as his own eyes. The creature inside screeched at him; the eye blurring as the creature whipped its head forward, and something hard hit the wood by Rhino's face. A beak, maybe? Was it an ostrich? He wasn't sure, but he knew that it wasn't a centipede, so he moved on.

The air was suddenly filled with noise as another harshly amplified announcement came over the tannoy – in English this time, and spoken by a different voice – American. 'This raid is being carried out by the Hong Kong Police on behalf of the United Nations Office on Exotic Animal Trafficking,' the voice said. 'My name is Evan Chan. Please stay exactly where you are. If your paperwork is in order and you are *not* dealing in the illegal sale of protected species, then you have nothing to fear.' The announcement was repeated in Mandarin by the same voice that had spoken earlier.

There was a pause, filled only by the sounds of the various animals in the warehouse protesting, and then Rhino heard gunfire. Semi-automatic weapons, he thought. Probably Israeli Uzis or Ingram MAC-10s, judging by the sound. He'd been on both ends of those weapons before in Special Forces. Nasty little things.

Single shots responded to the gunfire – probably Heckler & Koch pistols. That would be the police.

Xi Lang's people were fighting back. Presumably the announcement had not reassured them.

'Over here!' Gecko called, not bothering to be quiet now that the warehouse was filled with noise. His voice sounded strange. If Rhino hadn't known better, he would have said that Gecko was frightened, but he'd never known anything to scare the plucky Brazilian boy before.

Rhino moved to join him, passing the coypu again. Gecko was crouching beside a crate and shining a small flashlight inside. He turned his head towards Rhino, and his eyes were wide. 'I think,' he said, 'I may have found them.'

'*Them?*' Rhino echoed. Over to one side, another speckle of gunfire punctuated the warehouse air, along with more shouting in Chinese.

'Oh yes,' Gecko said softly. 'I mean, who would want just *one* of these things?'

Rhino knelt beside the boy and glanced through the wooden slats of the crate.

And saw something straight out of hell.

At first sight it was a tangle of vivid red cable, wet and glistening. It was about as thick as a loaf of bread and as long as a car. It was writhing, apparently unknotting itself from the tangle that it had got into. As the smell hit him – something unpleasantly vinegary – he realized three things: firstly, that the thing he'd thought was a cable was actually flattened rather than rounded, and made of numerous segments that were wider in the middle than at the places where they were joined; secondly, that a row of bright red legs ran along each 'edge', one leg to each segment and each leg terminating in a claw that looked as if it could cut through metal; and thirdly, that there were two of the things, wound around each other. They separated as he watched. One of them reared up towards the top of the crate, exploring it with long twitching feelers that emerged from its head. Now that he had a better look at it, Rhino saw that there were blue rings marring the vivid crimson of the creature's hard exoskeleton. The other one, also ringed with blue, wove its way across the crate's floor, moving like a snake, from side to side, right towards where Rhino and Gecko were crouched. Its head was blunt, with two feelers emerging from the top that twitched as if with a life of their own, and a pair of pincer-like jaws on the bottom. In between was a symmetrical scattering of hard black spots that Rhino assumed were primitive eyes. They glittered in the light, and there was something about that glitter that almost suggested a malign intelligence.

Rhino shook himself. This thing was a monster, but there was no need to get carried away. It was just a centipede – big, yes, but not housing some bizarre intelligence.

'I tell you what,' Gecko muttered. 'You hold it and I'll take the DNA sample.'

'Can we toss a coin?' Rhino whispered back.

The creature's feelers waved at them – first at Rhino and then at Gecko. It could see them, and it knew that they were interesting. Perhaps even edible. A sudden explosion from the direction of the front of the warehouse didn't faze it at all. Maybe centipedes were deaf.

Which reminded him . . .

'You did say that centipedes are carnivorous, didn't you?' Rhino asked.

'And poisonous,' Gecko reminded him.

'Great.' He reached into a pocket of his lightweight

anorak and pulled out the DNA sampler – a metal probe with a handle at one end and a rounded section at the other. Pulling a trigger on the handle opened up the rounded part to reveal a small, sharp-edged circle. The idea was to push that into the skin of whatever creature you wanted to sample, cut out a very small plug of flesh, and then close the end to protect the sample.

That was fine if you were dealing with an animal that had soft skin – like a giant rat. It wasn't so useful if the creature had a hard exoskeleton, like a centipede.

'It's possible that we didn't think this through properly,' Gecko pointed out.

'You think?' Rhino rejoined.

A sudden burst of semi-automatic fire sounded close by. Several single shots from an automatic pistol followed it.

'That's too close,' Gecko hissed.

Rhino glanced from the centipede to where the gunfire had come from, and back again. They didn't have enough time to work out what to do.

'I'm going to try to pull off one of those legs,' he announced. 'It's not like it'll miss one. Let me know if you hear anyone coming.'

The centipede's head was still weaving hypnotically back and forth in front of him, its feelers caressing the wooden slats. He glanced down to where a couple of the legs were waving through the gaps in the wood. The claws on the ends of the legs snapped open and shut with little *snick, snick, snick* noises. He should, he thought, just be able to grab one and twist it off. It probably couldn't even feel pain. Did any insect feel pain?

Somewhere off in the distance Rhino could hear a crackling, like flames. He glanced in that direction. A red glow was reflecting from the roof. Something was on fire.

Not much time. He turned back to the centipede and braced himself, feeling vaguely sick.

Before he could close his fingers on one of the legs, Gecko grabbed his shoulder.

'People coming!' he hissed.

Rhino retreated to the other side of the aisle, pulling Gecko with him. Most of the cages and crates were separated by narrow alleys, and the two of them sheltered in one that was just wide enough to take them. The cage on one side held a trio of red pandas – small, furry creatures with black circles round their eyes who cowered in a corner, hugging each other. On the other side, the cage was lined with glass and was half filled with an object that looked like a small mountain and which Rhino thought might be an anthill, although he couldn't see any ants.

Moments after they got out of the aisle, two men raced down from the direction of the front of the warehouse. Behind them was Tsai Chen. The men were holding guns, while the Chinese woman grasped a removable computer hard drive to her chest. It took Rhino less than a second to work out what was going on – the explosion he had heard a few moments before was probably Tsai Chen trashing Xi Lang's computer files and written records – probably with a thermite grenade chucked into the office – and now she was running off with the only back-up copies. Without records, all the police and the UN would have was a warehouse full of animals. No names, nobody to track down. Xi Lang, Tsai Chen and everyone else who didn't get caught would just relocate somewhere else and start again.

A voice shouted 'Stop!' in Mandarin, then again in English. Tsai Chen didn't even blink. She just kept running, but the two men with her stopped and turned round. They raised their guns.

A shot rang out from the direction the voice had come from. One of the men fell back, blood blossoming from his shoulder like an exotic flower. His fingers tightened on the trigger of his own gun, which fired a stream of bullets uselessly into the air. Some of them hit the crates near Tsai Chen. She dropped the hard drive, glanced at it for a moment, glanced back to where the police were running down the aisle, then ran off, leaving it behind. Stray bullets caught the top corner of the centipedes' crate, smashing it to wooden splinters.

The second man looked at his injured friend, then at the police at the end of the aisle. He threw his gun to the ground and raised his hands.

A movement and a flash of colour caught Rhino's eye. He glanced over at the centipede crate.

The corner was now missing, replaced by a large hole in the wood.

A hole through which one of the centipedes was crawling.

The man who had thrown down his gun glanced at the centipede, glanced back at the police, then turned and ran.

The centipede flowed sinuously down the side of the crate, more and more of its body emerging from the hole that had been blasted by the gunfire. Rhino, almost hypnotized by the sight, heard shouts of disbelief and shock from the policemen.

The end of the centipede emerged from the crate just as its head got to the injured man on the floor. The touch alerted him that something was going on: he opened his eyes and stared directly into the centipede's open jaws.

And screamed.

Gecko sprang forward, grabbed the man's arm, and pulled him away just as the arthropod's jaws snapped closed. Foiled, the centipede snaked its way across the floor and out of sight into the shadows of another gap between crates.

Rhino's gaze went back to the hole in the crate. The second centipede was emerging. It was larger than the first. Its body was almost as wide as the hole, and its legs made a rasping noise as they caught against the wood. Instead of following its companion it twisted its body round and went directly upward, on to the top of the crate. From there it headed for a nearby pillar and crawled higher, towards the roof.

The injured Chinese man was curled up on the floor, talking rapidly to himself in a hysterical voice. Gecko left him and stood up.

'I think we need to go,' Rhino said to him, bending to

pick up the discarded hard drive. 'We can't get any genetic samples now. The things have gone.' He looked around. 'Come on – we can still get to the rope and get out, sheltered by the column. If we get arrested now, who knows how long it will take to get things straightened out!'

Rather than emerge into the aisle, with the police at the far end, the two of them backed along its length to the parallel aisle. This one was empty. They ran down it, away from the police and towards the place where they had come in.

The creature they thought was a tiger was prowling angrily around its cage, disturbed by the activity. It saw Rhino and Gecko approaching and snarled, baring its teeth in an unmistakable 'Keep away!' signal.

They ignored it. Rhino turned and made a stirrup with his hands, boosting Gecko to the top of the cage. The tiger sprang for him, but Gecko danced out of the way and extended a hand, pulling Rhino up after him with incredible strength for his young frame. Rhino pushed Gecko towards the rope. It was still hanging down from the open skylight, but the bottom part, the bit that had hung into the cage, had been shredded.

Gecko scrambled up the rope. Rhino kept moving across the cage, not letting the tiger get its claws through the bars and into his boots. When Gecko was clear of the cage, he grabbed hold of the rope and began to pull himself up.

Looking downward, he saw a furious yellow eye glaring up at him from between the bars.

'Stop! Hey, you! Stop!'

It was the English voice that Rhino had heard making the announcement about the UN and the raid earlier on. He looked off to where the sound was coming from. A man was standing near the centipedes' crate. He was Chinese, young, with his long black hair pulled back into a ponytail. He wasn't with the police, unless he was plainclothes: he was wearing jeans, hiking boots and a green hunting jacket. His gaze locked with Rhino's.

Rhino smiled at him, made a sketchy little salute with one hand, and then scrambled up the rope towards the relative safety of the roof. The police would be surrounding the warehouse, but Rhino was pretty sure that he and Gecko could get past them and get away.

But what then?

twelve

Calum waited for a while under the covers in his comfortable cell, just in case some silent alarm had been triggered, but nobody came into his room to investigate. All the time he was there, his brain was trying to wrap itself around the fact that he had been kidnapped by *Nemor Incorporated*. The thought made him shivery. They had been interested in him for months, and it looked as if that interest had now translated into something larger. That was how he and Tara had met – she had been blackmailed by them into trying to spy on his website, and he had caught her. Or, rather, he had spotted the intrusion, worked out where it was coming from and then sent Gecko to find out who it was. Nemor had also tried to break into his apartment to get information on the trip his friends had made to Georgia in search of the legendary Almasti. They had even set up their own rival expedition and taken Natalie captive so they could get to the Almasti first. Calum didn't know what Nemor Incorporated wanted with him, but it was obviously something to do with the Almasti and Calum's search for missing or rare DNA. Now he was being held captive by them.

This wasn't good. This really wasn't good.

He needed to get out of there, and fast, and that meant he needed help.

He was interrupted in his dark thoughts by the door opening again. A security guard was standing there, looking into the room. When Calum didn't move, the guard retreated into the corridor, letting the door shut behind him.

Calum glanced at his watch; it was exactly an hour and a half since the guard had last checked on him.

He sat up in bed and turned the tablet on. Within a few moments he had established that it was a basic Android device, which meant that he knew a number of ways around the security systems, thanks to Tara.

Not that there were a lot of security systems set up on the tablet. Robledo Mountains Technology didn't seem to be particularly security minded. Maybe they didn't kidnap people that often. Whatever the reason, he pretty quickly had a map of the building's various floors on the screen, and had established a connection to the internet through some kind of company Wi-Fi. Presumably there would be a record of his access somewhere, but he was hoping to be long gone by the time anyone realized.

He checked the top of the tablet. Yes, it did have a camera, and that meant he could send a video message to his friends to tell them where he was and to ask for help. He could even Skype them in real time, if they were on their computers at the same time he was. He thought for a few seconds, and then decided it was too risky. If some passing guard or late-working member of staff passing his door heard voices inside, then they might just get suspicious and check in on him – and then the game would be up for sure. No, he was better off sending an email.

He thought for a moment, then rather than start up the email app on the tablet he went straight to the web browser and accessed his own email account that way. It was clumsier than using an app, but less likely to be traced.

Hi, he typed.

This will probably come as as much of a shock to you as it has to me, but I think I've been kidnapped, and I think it's by Nemor Incorporated. I had an accident with the robotic legs that Robledo had loaned to me, and some people from the labs came to rescue me. They sedated me and flew me to their labs in Las Cruces, which is where I am now. They keep pretending that I'm not a prisoner at all, but I'm trapped in bed here and they aren't letting me communicate with anyone. I'm sending this email on a tablet that I've 'borrowed'.

I really don't know what to do, which is why I'm emailing you. I need you to get me out of here! I don't care if I never see those robotic legs again – I just want to be back in my own apartment.

I really hope I hear from you soon. I'll keep hold

of this tablet for as long as I can, and I'll check in on my emails whenever I get the chance. Please, please reply soon.

Oh, by the way, the name of the doctor who has been treating me is Kircher – he came with me from England. The name of the psychiatrist who has provisionally labelled me as being 'paranoid' – presumably as a way of justifying keeping me here – is Dr Laurence. Laurence T. Laurence.

Please get me out of here.

Calum

He read the message back a couple of times. It sounded desperate, but then he *was* desperate.

He thought for a moment about whom exactly he should send it to. Ideally it would be Rhino, but he was in Hong Kong with Gecko and Natalie, and he had a job to do. Calum didn't really want him to be distracted from that – and he didn't want him bursting in all guns blazing. Tara was a possibility, but she was in London and he didn't see what she could do.

In the end he typed the only realistic name into the *To:* section of the email, and pressed *Send*.

He leaned back in the bed. Hopefully, his guardian, Gillian Livingstone – Natalie's mother – would get the email soon and know exactly what to do . . .

*

There were five trays stacked up in the corner of her room now, and Tara was beginning to think that everything smelt of fried chicken. The view outside the window didn't change much either: sometimes it was night, sometimes day; sometimes a red car went down the street and sometimes it was a blue car; sometimes a kid in a hoodie was standing by the bus stop and sometimes it was an old woman with a shopping trolley, but that was about the extent of the variation. Life was pretty tedious. Tedious and scary.

Without a laptop or a tablet to keep her amused, Tara was at her wits' end. She spent a lot of time either looking out of the window at the ever-changing yet ever-similar scene or lying on the mattress staring at the cracks in the plaster ceiling, imagining what might happen to her if Gecko didn't respond, and then trying *not* to imagine what might happen to her. She felt nauseous with terror all the time.

And Gecko *hadn't* responded. That was the thing that terrified her most. Or he had responded but her captors hadn't told her, which she thought was unlikely. She'd got to know them slightly over the past day or so, and they seemed to be straight talkers who were vaguely embarrassed about what they were being asked to do, but who would do it diligently because that was how they worked. They, in their turn, had become almost protective of Tara – making sure she was well fed and well rested and that she had frequent toilet breaks, and chatting to her about inconsequentialities. One of them had even popped out to get her some fresh clothes and toiletries from a pound shop down the road. Under other circumstances she would have enjoyed their company.

If they hadn't been planning to cut her fingers off if Gecko didn't respond.

And they still wouldn't tell her what country they were from. Or what their names were.

She was lying on her back on the blanket, watching the sunlight slowly crawl across the carpet and trying not to be sick, when the door opened.

'Just put the tray down by the door,' she said wearily. 'I'm not sure I can face fried chicken again. Not right now, anyway. If nothing else, you could always vary the sauce. Maybe some barbecue, or some garlic and herb. Anything apart from tomato ketchup.'

'Actually,' a voice she recognized said, 'I brought pizza. I hope that's OK.'

She jerked upright. Tom Karavla – the boy who had lured her to the coffee shop and then abandoned her – was standing in the doorway. He was looking very uncomfortable, and he was holding two large, flat cardboard boxes that were giving out steam from their seams.

'Deep pan?' she asked, despite the sudden flush of anger she felt.

'Yes.'

'Meat feast?'

'Yes.'

'Stuffed crust.'

'Oh yes. And extra cheese.' He paused, staring at her. 'Can I come in?'

'Do I have a choice?'

Karavla walked in, letting the door close behind him, and sat cross-legged on the floor beside the mattress. He slid a pizza box across to Tara and kept the other one for himself.

'I got one meat feast and one barbecued pork. I hope that's OK? We have a saying in my country,' Tom continued, opening his box, '"Hunger is the best sauce".'

'I'm not exactly hungry,' Tara snapped. 'I'm just bored of the same thing all the time.'

'Yeah, my uncles have no imagination.'

Tara caught the admission straight away. 'Your uncles?'

He shrugged, not looking at her. 'Yes. That's how they got me to do what I did. Family pressure.'

'So they're brothers?'

'Both older brothers of my mum. They managed to get her to England. Things were bad back in Croatia.'

She filed that one away as well. 'Croatia? That's where you came from?'

He nodded, eating a slice of pizza himself.

'But you don't have much of an accent,' Tara pointed out.

'We came over when I was eight years old. I speak English almost perfectly, but I'm told I speak Croatian with an accent.'

'And your name – is it really Tom?'

He nodded. '"Tom" as in "Tomas" – Tomas Karavla.'

She glanced at him. 'And you lured me to a coffee shop by making me think you were interested in . . .

in cryptids and in thelostworlds.co.uk.'

He shifted uneasily. 'I didn't know why they wanted me to do what I did. I was just told to get close to you on email, and get you to meet up somewhere.' He paused. 'It wasn't hard.'

She scowled. 'I know. I fell for it hook, line and sinker.'

He sighed and closed his eyes. 'My English phrasing does sometimes let me down. What I mean is, it wasn't difficult for *me* because I *wanted* to do it. I actually do like the idea of cryptids, and your website is incredible. And talking to you on email was really fun. I'm just sorry that . . .'

'Yeah,' she said. 'So am I.'

They ate in silence for a while.

'So, your uncles – they know you're here?' Tara said eventually.

'Yes. I asked them if you were OK, and they said you were, apart from the fact that you were complaining about the food. I asked them if I could bring you a pizza, and they said yes. I think they want to make sure that you're not going to go mad and try to beat them up with a tray the next time they come in.'

'Don't think I haven't thought about it,' she said darkly. 'The trouble is that they both look like they've taken a fair share of hits to the face before. I'm not sure there's anything else I can bring to the party.'

Tomas laughed and, in spite of her anger and fear, Tara felt herself relax slightly. The sick feeling in her stomach receded. 'Yes, they both do cage-fighting in their spare time,' he said.

That kind of stopped the conversation for a while.

'Did they also ask you to get me to record another message for Gecko?' she asked.

He frowned. 'Gecko?'

'My friend. They want him to come back so he can be a thief for them.'

He nodded. 'Ah yes – I heard about that. I didn't know the boy's name, but I knew that my uncles – and the man they work for – are really impressed with the way he can run and jump and climb.' He frowned, and looked away. 'So – is he your boyfriend, then, this "Gecko"?'

Tara felt her eyes widen at the thought, and her face flush. 'No!' she said quickly. 'He's not my boyfriend.'

'Oh,' Tomas said quietly. 'Good.'

That kind of stopped the conversation for a while longer.

'Tomas, can you help me escape?' Tara said eventually, in a very soft voice, not looking at his face.

'I wish I could,' he replied, as if he had been waiting for her to ask. 'I really do. I've been thinking about whether there's anything I can do to get you out. The problem is that my uncles will know it was me who helped you, and they'll beat me.'

'Your uncles would beat you?' she repeated, disbelievingly.

'Oh yes. They would do it because I had failed to show them respect, and because I had disobeyed them, and because the man they work for would have them beaten for losing you, and they would pass that beating down to me.'

'Oh,' she said quietly.

'It would be worth it,' Tomas added, almost diffidently, 'if I thought I could actually get you out without them seeing, but I couldn't. They are on guard all the time.'

'Well,' Tara said eventually, 'thanks for even thinking about it.' She glanced at him. 'If this was a prison-break film then you would have smuggled a small saw or a knife in here inside the pizza.' She paused. 'You didn't, did you?'

'If I had, then you'd have eaten it by now. I've never seen anyone eat that fast.' He looked at the empty pizza boxes and sighed. 'I suppose I ought to be going,' he said.

'More girls to abduct?' Tara said bitterly, and then wished she hadn't when she saw the pain on his face.

'Look, I really *am* sorry about this. I wish it wasn't happening – I really do. I just wish we had met under different circumstances.' He got up, brushing pizza crumbs from his hands on his trousers.

'Are you going to come back some time?' Tara asked.

He nodded. 'I will,' he said. 'I promise.'

'Chinese next time?'

He smiled. 'Sounds good.'

Tara got up too, and stepped forward towards Tom. He tensed slightly, but she slid her arms round his waist and pressed her head against his chest. 'Thanks for visiting,' she said, her voice muffled by his shirt. 'And thanks for the food.'

He didn't seem to know what to do, so he just stood there while she hugged him. Eventually she let go and stepped away, hands behind her back. He smiled uncertainly at her, and walked towards the door.

'It will be OK,' he said, opening it and turning to look at her. 'I know it will.'

'I wish I could be sure of that,' she replied.

He left, closing the door behind him. She heard the bolt slide into place.

She stood there for a few moments, feeling the rectangular shape of Tom's mobile phone in her hand. He hadn't noticed her slip it out of his pocket. If she was lucky, she might have it for an hour or two, and that would be more than enough time to call for help.

She smiled for the first time in days. He was an idiot. All boys were idiots.

'Calum?'

Calum turned over and stared at the open door. He had already known that there was someone there, by the sound of the door opening, but he hadn't wanted to acknowledge them. Instantly reacting any time the door opened, like a puppy hearing the rattle of a packet of biscuits, wasn't cool. He wanted *them* to wait on *him*, not the other way round.

It was a minor psychological victory, but it *was* a victory.

Dr Kircher was standing in the rectangle of freedom revealed by the open door. 'Calum? I have someone here who wants to talk to you.'

'And if I don't want to talk?'

Dr Kircher smiled a thin smile. The glow from the overhead fluorescent tubes reflected from his glasses, turning them into flat sheets of light. 'Oh, I wouldn't be uncooperative if I were you. We all want the same thing here.'

'And what is that?'

'You up and about on your own two feet, of course.'

'And, speaking of that, is there any progress on finding out what happened back in my apartment?' Calum asked. 'Only, I can't help but notice that, apart from a rather crude psychological evaluation, I've not been involved with any tests or anything.'

'We're still going through the data from the processor on the bionic legs and from the ARLENE robot,' Kircher said. 'Once we have done that, we can move towards looking at what's best for *you*. He frowned slightly. 'I have to say that the data from the robot is very inconclusive. It almost looks as if it's been edited – there's no information in there about where it has been used. But, anyway, our initial hypothesis – that the robot reacted to stray electromagnetic signals from the processor on the legs – appears to be false. The robot seems to have been operating under the influence of a separate signal from outside. It's all very puzzling.'

Someone coughed in the corridor. Kircher straightened up slightly – not quite coming to attention, but not far short.

'Yes, of course,' he said. 'Calum, this is Mr Pournell. He's here from . . . our head office.'

Kircher moved backwards, and another man stepped forward to take his place. He was wearing a dark suit, a white shirt and a blue tie with red stripes. His hair was black, and swept straight back off his forehead. He was probably in his mid-forties, Calum estimated. A slight waft of expensive aftershave came with him.

'Hi,' Calum said, beating him to the punch.

'Hi,' the man said brightly, entering the room. Kircher moved to follow him, but Pournell shut the door in Kircher's face. 'Calum. Can I call you Calum? You can call me Dave.'

'So, Dave,' Calum said, 'when can I leave?'

Pournell's expression didn't change from the bright smile that almost seemed to have been painted on, but his next words sent a chill down Calum's back. 'Why, you can walk out of here any time you want, kid.'

'Very funny.'

'Sorry – you're right, that was in poor taste. But my intent was serious – do you *want* to walk out of here?'

'Once those bionic legs are fixed, I fully intend to. And I'm going to walk into the British embassy and put in a strongly worded complaint about having been brought here against my will and locked up in this room for reasons that are still a mystery to me.'

Pournell frowned in an exaggeratedly theatrical manner. He turned to the door, slid his fingertips in between the door and the frame and pulled the door partially open. Dr Kircher's face was momentarily visible in the gap. Pournell let the door hiss shut again. 'No locks there,' he said. 'Looks as if you could get out whenever you want.' He looked around. 'Actually, that *is* a point. We should provide a wheelchair for you. Nothing fancy, I'm afraid. Not motorized. Very basic. But if you want to leave, you can. We'll even call a cab for you to the airport.'

Calum knew that the door had opened so smoothly because he'd taped the tongue of the lock down last night, and he suspected that Pournell did too. 'And will you fly me back home?' he asked.

'Ah, I'm sorry: the corporate jet is being used elsewhere, but I'm sure you can afford a ticket. I recommend the seats by the emergency doors – there's more leg room.'

'You're from Nemor Incorporated,' Calum said quietly.

'That I am. Good work, Calum – you're as intelligent as your reputation suggests, and that means you'll listen to the proposal I have to make and react to it in an intelligent manner.'

Here it is, Calum thought, *the reason for this visit, and probably the reason I'm here in America in the first place.* 'What's your proposal, Dave?'

Pournell walked forward and stopped just in front of the foot of Calum's bed. 'How would you like to *properly* walk again? Not just with the bionic legs – we both know that's a poor substitute for the real thing – but how would you like to actually be able to *control* your legs, and *feel* things touching them again?'

'You know I would,' Calum said darkly.

'Of course. Who wouldn't?' He paused. 'We can make that happen.'

Calum let the silence run on for a few moments. He wasn't sure what to say, how to react – even what to think.

'How?' he said eventually.

'You've heard about stem cells, haven't you?'

'Stem cells are cells that haven't decided what they want to grow up to be yet.'

Pournell nodded. 'Slightly simplistic, but basically accurate. Good enough for me, anyway – I'm a businessman, not a scientist. Well, we've made some significant strides in stem-cell research in the past year or two. We now have the ability to inject stem cells into the site of an injury – a spinal injury, to take a random example – and then persuade the stem cells to repair the nerve damage by using appropriate triggering drugs. It's an experimental treatment at the moment, but we're working up to small-scale trials and we're looking for volunteers. Volunteers with crippling spinal injuries and a strong desire to walk again.' He paused. 'Do you know anyone like that, Calum?'

'And what do I have to do to qualify for the experimental trials?' Calum asked. His heart was racing, and he could hardly breathe. To suddenly be given the chance to walk again . . . it was incredible. And scary – especially considering where the offer was coming from. 'What do you want in return?'

'Something very simple. Something so simple that you wouldn't even miss it.'

'Name it.'

'The genetic samples from the Almasti that your friends brought back from Georgia.'

'The expedition was a bust,' Calum said calmly. 'They never found the Almasti. It's just a legend, like the Yeti, or the Sasquatch.'

'Please,' Pournell said, 'don't insult my intelligence. My people did enough background interviews to know that something was being covered up by the villagers you met. We know you found the Almasti, even though you managed to send our team in the wrong direction. Anyway, rather than keep looking out there ourselves, searching all the valleys in the Caucasus Mountains until we hit the right one, it's more cost-effective to get the samples from you.'

'If there are any samples.'

'Let's assume, for the purposes of conversation, that there are.'

'And what will you do with them?'

'The same as you would have done – sequence the genes, work out what each of them does, see if there are any genes that we don't already see in nature, splice them into living tissue and see if we can replicate their effects.' His face took on an earnest expression. 'Just think about it, Calum – you could help us cure cancer, or malaria, or any of a hundred different diseases.'

'And you would charge for the cures,' Calum pointed out, feeling anger raging beneath his calm surface. This was a replay of the argument he'd had with Gillian Livingstone a few days ago. 'You would make a profit from curing suffering – and if people couldn't pay then you wouldn't cure them.'

'It takes billions of pounds to fully investigate a new genome and test the genes,' Pournell pointed out, 'and that money has to come from somewhere. Universities and charities just don't have the resources. You know that already – you just don't want to admit it. We're the only ones who have the resources to do the job – and, yes, why shouldn't we be rewarded for putting all that money into it?'

'You tried to hack into my website, using Tara Fitzgerald,' Calum pointed out, shifting the argument sideways. 'You kidnapped Natalie Livingstone and tried to get to the Almasti before we did. Why should I trust you?'

Pournell smiled. 'Industrial espionage is everywhere, Calum. What – you haven't tried to investigate *our* website, find out more about *us*? I can't say I blame you. I would have done the same thing in your position – but don't try to pretend that you are somehow better than us.'

'I haven't kidnapped anyone,' Calum pointed out.

'Give it time,' Pournell replied. 'If you find a good enough reason, you'll do it.' He sighed, and shook his head. 'Look, kid, I don't want to get into a philosophical argument with you, I really don't. The offer is on the table. Think about it. Give us the Almasti genetic material and we'll give you functioning legs again. It's a bargain, whichever way you look at it. I'll come back tomorrow, and hopefully by then you'll see your way clear to giving us what we want.' He turned to go, and then casually turned back again. 'Oh, by the way – Dr Kircher said that one of their diagnostic computer tablets has gone missing. I don't suppose anyone left it in here, did they?'

Pournell stared at Calum, and Calum could see despite his perfectly bland expression that the Nemor Inc.

representative knew perfectly well that Calum had the tablet. He frowned for a moment, pretending to think, then reached down and took it from the side of his bed, where he had stowed it beside the mattress. 'Oh, yes, Dr Laurence left it here yesterday. I meant to tell someone, but I forgot.'

Calum held out the tablet, and Pournell reached out and took it. He stared at it for a moment, and then looked back at Calum.

'Thanks, kid. I'll have a word with Dr Laurence. He really shouldn't leave these things lying around.'

He pulled open the door, then turned to glance back at Calum. 'Did you know you talk in your sleep?' he asked casually. 'Well, if you're sedated, anyway. You had a lot to say about Hong Kong, and a cryptid that your little friends are looking for. It was so interesting that I decided to put together a little team of my own to find it. Much better equipped than your friends, and much more . . . professional. I'll let you know how it all pans out.' He walked into the corridor, pausing only to reach down and tear off the strip of adhesive plastic that Calum had stuck across the lock. 'Messy,' he said quietly. 'I do so hate it when things get stuck over walls and doors. I much prefer a clean working environment.' He left, and the door shut behind him. Calum very distinctly heard the *click* as the tongue of the lock engaged with the hole in the door frame. He was locked in again.

He waited for a few moments, until he was sure that Pournell wasn't going to come back, then he reached down and reassuringly felt the edge of the second tablet computer that he had taken. He had slid that under the mattress so that it would be harder to find.

He didn't mind losing one tablet – in fact, he had almost expected it. He still had the second left, and he intended to keep on using it.

Calum had a dilemma now, and he wasn't sure what to do. His dream ever since the accident had been to get back the ability to walk, but he had assumed that it would take a lot of time and a lot of work. Now he was being handed the solution on a plate, and all he had to do was give up on his moral position with regard to the Almasti genetic material.

Which was, he thought, what it must be like being offered eternal life by the Devil, at the small cost of your soul.

thirteen

It was next morning, some indeterminate time between breakfast and lunch, that Dave Pournell came back to visit Calum.

The tablet computer was hidden beneath Calum's mattress. He had already realized that daytime was the riskiest time for using it. Instead he just sat there quietly in bed, apparently staring at the wall but in reality working through in his head all the possible permutations of what might be happening to his friends, in England and in Hong Kong.

Pournell stood in the doorway. He was still neatly dressed in suit and tie. He checked the edge of the door to see whether Calum had 'fixed' it again, and then grinned at Calum as he entered the room.

'Hey, kid, how's things?'

'What can I say?' Calum responded with a shrug.

'The standard phrase is "Same old, same old",' Dave said. 'But, just to save you the trouble, let me say that I know what you're going to say – you've been kidnapped, you can't communicate with anybody, you want to get out of here and go back home, blah, blah, blah. Am I right?'

'Pretty much,' Calum admitted. 'I *was* going to complain about the lack of entertainment as well. Would it kill you guys to put cable TV in these rooms?'

Pournell laughed. 'I like your spirit, Calum, I really do.' He walked to the end of Calum's bed and put his hands on the rails. 'It's crunch time, kid. I offered you a bargain, last time I was here. Now I need your answer. It's a very simple choice: you can walk again, or you can keep the Almasti DNA to yourself.'

Calum was silent for a few moments, staring at Pournell's smiling face. He had been mulling the choice over for hours, and it all came down to a very basic question – was he searching for cryptids so he could use their DNA to help cure a whole load of people of a whole load of diseases, as he had told Gillian Livingstone, or was he in it just to cure himself and damn the rest. If it was the former, then he had to keep the Almasti DNA to himself until he could get it into the hands of a laboratory that would sequence it for free and distribute it widely. If it was the latter, then he might as well give the DNA to Nemor Inc. in return for them treating him with their stem-cell technology – if it existed and if it worked as well as they said it did. Was he as altruistic as he liked to think in his better moments, or as selfish as he believed himself to be in his darker moments? What kind of person was he?

'Can't do it, Dave,' he said, surprising himself. He hadn't meant to say anything, not that quickly anyway, but it seemed as if his subconscious mind had already decided for him. He was a better person than he had feared.

Pournell looked disappointed. 'You sure? You're throwing away a lot.'

'I'm sure.'

'I wish I could say I respected your principles, but I don't. I just think you're being stupid.'

Calum shrugged. 'What can I say? Look, there's no point in you keeping me here any more. You've tried your best, but I haven't played ball. Take me back home, and we'll call it quits. I won't make any trouble over the kidnapping. If you can't take me home, at least take me to an airport, and I'll find my own way back.'

Pournell stared at him for a few long seconds, and Calum realized as he watched the man that his smile was just a muscular reaction. It didn't mean anything. He wasn't happy, cheerful, friendly, or anything else that a smile might indicate. He was a deeply dangerous man, behind that mask.

'You know, let's not do that,' he said. 'Let's go to plan B instead.'

'Plan B?' Calum asked, feeling his spirits drop.

'Yeah.' Without turning his head, Pournell called, 'Hey, Kircher, get in here!'

Dr Kircher hurried through the door. 'Yes, sir, what is it?'

'You were telling me earlier about some conclusions you'd come to about that mental link to the bionic legs.'

'Yes, that's right.' Kircher sounded as if he was reading

from a script. 'I think that the problem with the stray signals affecting the ARLENE robot can be solved by reducing the wireless signal strength.'

'Great!' Pournell said. 'And how do you go about doing that?'

'Well,' Kircher went on, 'having the sensors on Calum's scalp gives us a level of signal blockage that has to be overcome by high sensitivity. If we can actually implant the sensors in Calum's brain, then we can reduce the sensitivity by a factor of a hundred or so.'

'Wonderful! So brain surgery is the answer. Let's start preparing the operating theatre!'

Kircher looked uncomfortable, but all he said was, 'Yes, sir!' He turned to leave, and didn't even look at Calum as he went.

'For the record,' Calum said in a shaky voice, 'I don't want brain surgery.'

'Nonsense. You want this problem fixed, don't you?'

'Not this way!'

'Unfortunately, that release document you signed – you really should have read the small print – it gives Dr Kircher carte blanche to do anything he needs in order to get those bionic legs working, up to and including radical surgery. Of course, there *is* a risk of possible side effects, including brain damage, coma and death, but then any serious surgery carries risks. I'm sure you understand.'

'I looked at the small print. I'm a fast reader. It didn't say anything about you being able to conduct surgery on me.'

Pournell smiled. 'It does now. You wouldn't believe how easy it is to add an extra page or two to a document that's already been signed.'

'I want to rescind my permission,' Calum said. His stomach was churning, and he could hear a loud buzzing in his ears.

'No can do, kid.' Pournell turned to go, and then turned back. 'You can stop this any time you want,' he said, still smiling. 'Just tell us where that Almasti DNA is.' He stared at Calum for a moment. His smile faded, and Calum got a clear sight of the single-minded insanity underneath. 'After all,' he added, 'is it *really* worth losing your mind over?'

He turned and left.

Calum sat there, trembling, unable to believe what had just happened. This wasn't going to end until either he gave in or Nemor performed whatever torture they could on him. And it seemed there wasn't any limit to the torture they were prepared to perform. Eventually he would crack, but would that be too late to save himself?

He didn't know.

By the time Gecko and Rhino got back to the hotel it was well after midnight and Rhino was furious.

'Natalie tipped the police off,' he said as they entered the lobby. 'I know it was her.'

'I doubt that she alerted the police,' Gecko said, trying to calm Rhino down. 'Your reasons for not involving them were good. However, I think she may have followed through with her second option of alerting the United Nations. If they have an office covering illegal animal shipments here in Hong Kong, then they may have been able to mobilize the police through their own contacts and move quickly.'

'The UN!' Rhino snarled, making it sound like a curse. 'When you actually want them to do something, it takes nine months and a unanimous resolution to get them moving, but when you *don't* want them to move they're like greased lightning!'

'To be fair,' Gecko interrupted, 'I think Natalie *did* want them to move. She has taken this animal stuff to heart. I think it has hit her somewhere personal.'

'Why does she choose *now* to suddenly get a conscience?'

Gecko shrugged. 'I think it has been building for a while.'

'I ought to go up to her room now and have a strong chat with her, culminating in her flying straight home, alone! I can't have her undermining our missions like this!'

Gecko held up a warning hand. 'That would not help. I'm sure she didn't mean to undermine our mission. I think she was just trying to do something for those animals.'

'Maybe that's the case, but because of her those two giant centipedes have escaped. Who knows what they're capable of?' Rhino looked at Gecko with sudden interest. 'You live in Brazil, don't you? What do *you* think they're capable of?'

'What?' Gecko said, feeling a flush of anger. 'Just because there's a rainforest within fifty miles of my family home, you think I'm some kind of expert on strange animals?'

'Yes,' Rhino said, looking confused, 'of course I do. You knew about capybaras and coypus, didn't you? That's more than I did.' He sighed. 'Look, I was born on Canvey Island. I can do seagulls and that's about it. At least you *have* exotic animals in your country.'

'What's your point?'

'My point is that I can predict people. I can't predict animals.'

Gecko nodded, calming down. He knew that Rhino was frustrated and angry, and didn't really mean what he was saying. 'I guess I understand. OK, then, the centipedes are carnivores, yes? And they have a poisonous bite. They have presumably not had very much food during their captivity. They will be hunting.'

'Hunting for what?'

Gecko closed his eyes briefly. Images of what the centipedes might be hunting for were flashing through his mind, and he didn't like what he was seeing. 'Live food,' he said quietly. 'Smaller centipedes hunt other insects. For ones this size, insects won't be enough. I would imagine that their usual food, wherever they come from, is likely to be small mammals – monkeys, maybe, or rodents. In a city like this –' he shrugged – 'cats, maybe. Dogs. Even small children.' In his mind he was imagining the carnage that could result from the release of the two centipedes, and the thought made him feel sick. 'Rhino, it's worse than you think.'

'What do you mean?' Rhino asked warily.

'What if they are male and female centipedes – a breeding pair? What if they mate, and lay eggs? In a few months' time Hong Kong could be swarming with these things!'

Rhino didn't reply for a moment, but he lost colour from his face as the thought hit home.

'We have to do something,' Gecko urged. 'We have to kill them, or recover them somehow.'

Rhino nodded. 'You're right. We caused this situation. We need to fix it.'

'But how are we going to find them?'

Rhino thought for a moment. 'We obviously need to know more about them.' He lifted his hand, which was still holding the hard drive that he had retrieved from where the fleeing Tsai Chen had dropped it on the warehouse floor. 'There might be something on this about the centipedes, if we're lucky – their likely habitats, their diet, something we might be able to use. I've got a laptop in my room – I'll connect it up and see what I can find. Do you want to join me?'

Gecko shook his head. 'I need a shower and a change of clothes. Can I join you in half an hour?'

'OK.'

The two of them split up, each heading to his own room. When Gecko entered, he saw that his mobile phone was sitting beside the bed where he had left it. Instinctively he checked it for messages. There hadn't been any calls – which was strange, because he would have expected to have heard from Calum or Tara by now – but he had received a text message. It was from an unknown number. Gecko half thought about deleting it, on the basis that it was probably some kind of advertising scam, but he clicked on it anyway, just in case.

The message was very plain and simple:

> We have the girl – Tara Fitzgerald.
> Watch the video file.

It was not signed, but Gecko was pretty sure he knew who had sent it.

He felt as if he was standing on the deck of a boat in a storm. The ground seemed to be moving beneath his feet, rocking up and down, and his stomach was churning. He didn't want to watch the video file, but he knew he had to. So he pressed on the *Play* button.

He watched with increasing feelings of nausea and guilt as Tara read out her brief message. He listened to the words, but more importantly he watched her expression as she spoke them. She was frightened. She was trying to hide it, trying to put a brave face on things, but she was frightened.

She had good reason to be. He knew what these men were capable of.

The video finished. Gecko stood there, in the centre of his room, his thoughts whirling as if there was a hurricane inside his head. Tara was in danger. *Tara*.

He had to go back. He had no choice.

Without showering or changing, he headed straight for Rhino's room.

Rhino was sitting at the desk. He had connected the removable hard drive to his own laptop using a USB cable. As Gecko knocked and entered, he glanced up. 'No good,' he said grimly. 'It's encrypted. We need Tara to take a look at it. She can do that from England, can't she?'

'I do not think she can,' Gecko said. He played the video for Rhino. The ex-soldier stood there for a good thirty seconds after it had finished, staring into space and thinking.

'I need to go back,' Gecko said.

'Don't overreact,' Rhino cautioned.

Gecko moved to where he could stare Rhino in the face. 'I have to go back,' he repeated.

'Look, Gecko, I'm trained in hostage rescue. That means I'm also trained in negotiation. The first rule of negotiation is: work out what the kidnappers actually want. The second rule is: don't give them anything until you have proof of life. The third rule is: don't give them anything until you can be sure that you'll get their captive back alive and well.'

Gecko knew that Rhino was talking sense, and he tried to calm himself down. 'Are there more rules?' he asked.

Rhino nodded. 'As far as I'm concerned, there's a fourth rule as well: don't give them anything at all, if you can help it. Take swift and harsh action to get the captive back, if you can do it without the hostage getting hurt.'

'And what about the kidnappers?'

'Oh, nobody cares about them.'

Gecko sighed, feeling dark thoughts swirling around him again. 'This is my fault. I caused this. I need to fix it.'

'Not by giving yourself to them. Let's think this through.' He was quiet for a moment. 'I'm surprised that Calum hasn't told us anything about this. Maybe he doesn't know. We need to talk to him, and quickly. The trouble is he's not answering his phone. I've tried him on his computer – he's usually glued to that like football fans glued to a sports-bar TV set – but he's not answering that either.' He raised a hand to his head and pushed his hair back. 'I'm not sure what the next move is,' he said with an uncertain tone in his voice.

Tara listened nervously at the door to her cell/bedroom until all the noise from the flat died away apart from the murmur of a television set. Her pulse was racing. It was dark outside, and she guessed that one of the Karavla brothers had gone to bed while the other one sat up on watch. After all, it wouldn't be good for them if they were both asleep and Tara managed – somehow – to get out. If she could work out what that 'somehow' was, then she might even try it, but short of pulling the pins out of the door hinges – and her nails were bitten too short for that – she was out of ideas.

But she did have a mobile phone – Tom's mobile phone.

It was security locked, but it was a simple four-digit code and she knew all kinds of ways past that. Within seconds she was in.

Who to call? Rhino would have been the best bet at getting her out, but he was in Hong Kong. Gecko she was worried about – he apparently hadn't got in touch with the Karavla brothers yet, and Tara was beginning to wonder, with a feeling of dread in the pit of her stomach, whether something had happened to him, despite the fact that Rhino was meant to be looking after him. Natalie was . . . well, just Natalie. Which left Calum.

Actually, Calum had resources and courage, and nothing fazed him. He was also the de facto leader of their little group, despite (or maybe because of) his physical issues. He would know what to do.

Tara worried about whether she should send him a text message or call him and risk being overheard, but she needed to know that her words were actually getting through to someone, rather than just being dumped in a recorded message bucket on a server somewhere in the world. She could call Calum, but then when he asked her to describe what was outside so he could locate her she would have to resort to words, or take a photograph and email it to him. No, the best bet was a video chat. That way she just had to turn the camera round and actually show him what was outside.

Fortunately Tom's camera phone had a front lens as well as a rear one. That made things a lot easier.

She quickly downloaded a few specialist apps that Tom hadn't got, and then used one of them to set up a video chat. Calum usually spent every waking hour in front of his computer screens, and he didn't sleep much, so she was bound to get hold of him.

Unless he had gone out walking with his new bionic legs. That thought momentarily brought her up cold, before she convinced herself that he would be following Dr Kircher's instructions and not going out without company.

When Calum's face appeared on the screen of Tom's phone, Tara was ecstatic. That faded away after a moment and was replaced with surprise. He wasn't in his apartment. The background was white and sterile, like a hospital, and she could see a sign behind his head that said: *Bed 1*. The bottom of the sign was rough-edged, as if part of it had been snapped off.

Calum was wearing pyjamas. That was odd. Tara had *never* seen him in pyjamas.

'Tara!' he exclaimed. 'Thank God!'

'Calum, be quiet. I have to talk quickly. I've been kidnapped, and I'm being held prisoner. You need to help me get out. Do you understand?'

'I've been kidnapped and I'm being held prisoner,' he repeated. 'You have to get me out of here!'

'That's right,' she said.

'No, that's what's happened to *me*!'

She frowned. This wasn't the conversation she had imagined in her head. How long had he been awake for? 'No, Calum,' she said slowly, '*I'm* the one who has been kidnapped. I'm somewhere in east London. I don't know exactly where.'

'Stop talking for a minute and listen! *I've* been kidnapped, and flown to America. I'm in a Robledo Mountains Technology facility in Las Cruces, but Robledo is actually owned by Nemor Incorporated. I stole one of their tablet computers and I've tried sending a message to Gillian Livingstone, but I've had no answer.'

'If you're in Las Cruces, how come I was able to get hold of you on your computer system?' Tara asked, puzzled.

'I used the stolen tablet to log into my own system remotely. As far as the internet is concerned, I'm in London, in my apartment. I wanted to try to link up with Rhino and tell him what's happened, but he hasn't been at his computer.' He paused for a moment, and frowned as he caught up with *her* news. 'Hang on – you've been kidnapped too? Who by?'

'Two brothers with the surname Karavla. They're Croatian. They belong to the same gang who wanted Gecko to work for them as a thief. They want to use me to influence him. They got me to record a video message to send to him, but they've not heard back yet. I hope he's all right.' She stopped to catch her breath. This was all going too fast for her. 'What does Nemor Incorporated want with you?'

'They want the Almasti genetic material you retrieved from Georgia.'

'Well, give it to them.'

He shook his head. 'It's not that simple. I don't think I have the right to do that.'

'How did they get through your security to kidnap you?'

'Long story,' he said, wincing. 'Back to you. How did these Croatians get past your well-known paranoia to kidnap *you*?'

'Ah.' She could feel herself blushing. 'There was this

boy, named Tomas. It turns out that he is their nephew, but I don't think he actually wants to work for them. I think they frightened him into it.'

'And he was the one who managed to get you out of your shell?' Calum raised an eyebrow. 'There must be something special about him.'

'He's very convincing,' she said through clenched teeth. 'But I got my revenge. I stole his phone.'

'Oh, he visits, does he?'

'Leave it, Calum. Seriously – leave it.'

There was a long silence as they both looked at each other. Eventually Calum summed it up: 'We've *both* been kidnapped, and we *both* need rescuing.'

'That appears to be the situation.'

He closed his eyes, frowning in concentration while he thought. 'OK, here's what we'll do. In case anything happens to one of us, we'll *both* do this so at least one of us will be successful. First thing you do is to phone Mr Macfarlane – you remember him?'

'Small man, tight suit, strange taste in music.'

'That's him. I'll give you his number in a second. We need to tell him roughly where you are, and he can come and get you out.'

'I don't *know* exactly where I am!'

'OK – leave that to Macfarlane. If you can describe the buildings outside your window, he might be able to locate you. He knows east London like the back of his hand. How many of them are there in the flat?'

'There's at least two of them, and they have guns and knives and stuff. Isn't that, like, overwhelming odds?'

'It is,' Calum agreed, 'but they've got it coming to them.' Before Tara could correct his understanding of her question, he continued: 'The second thing is to get in touch with Rhino, whenever he switches his laptop on again. I need him to try to contact Gillian Livingstone for me. I've tried to get hold of her myself but nothing's happened. Maybe she didn't get the message. If he can't get her, then he has to find some way of getting me out of here. The British embassy might be a good start – I'm sure he knows people who know people. So, I'll talk to Rhino and you talk Mr Macfarlane, then *you* talk to Rhino and *I'll* talk to Macfarlane.'

'What's his number?'

Calum recited it from memory.

The two of them stared at each other in silence for a long moment, neither one wanting to break the call in order to make another one. This was human contact. This was a rare moment of warmth and a reminder of better things.

'We need to go,' Calum said eventually.

'I know,' Tara said. She paused, then, 'You first.'

'No, *you* first.'

'Calum!'

'OK, then – both at once. On a count of three. One . . . two . . .'

'Calum!'

'What?'

She felt her breath catch in her throat. 'Good luck.'

'You too, Tara. Right – one . . . two . . . three!'

Her finger came down on the *Disconnect* button at the same time his did. Her screen went blank.

She felt desolate. Lost.

Shoving the desolation and the fear to one side, she quickly got into the operating system of Tom's mobile and deleted any logs of her video call. If anything went wrong, the Karavla brothers wouldn't know she had used the phone. She would do the same after she had made the call to Mr Macfarlane.

She was just about to dial the number that Calum had given her when the door suddenly opened. She tried to hide the mobile behind her back, but in her panic she dropped it.

'So – you have mobile.' She felt her heart go cold. One of the Karavla brothers was standing in the doorway. 'I think we need to have a talk with young Tomas.'

'It's not his fault,' Tara said, trying to keep the tremor out of her voice. 'I stole it from him.

'Then it *is* his fault,' Tomas's uncle said grimly, 'and he will be punished. If you have actually made call, then he will be punished in a way he will never forget!'

Despite the sinking feeling in the pit of his stomach, Calum tried to contact Rhino again via video link. This time the electronic request was answered. A window opened on the tablet's screen and Rhino's worried face appeared.

'Calum – we have a problem,' he said quickly.

'Actually, we have several problems,' Calum corrected. 'Do you know about Tara?'

'We've just found out, and we also have two giant poisonous centipedes on the loose in Hong Kong.'

'And I've been kidnapped by Nemor Incorporated.' Calum explained where he was, and took a deep breath. 'It looks like we're all in trouble, then.' He hesitated for a moment, replaying the conversation. '*Centipedes?*'

'It's a long story. We think we might have some intelligence on a removable hard disk, but it's encrypted and I can't read it. That's why we need Tara.'

'And Tara's kidnapped as well.' Calum thought for a moment. 'OK – priorities. We need to get Tara out first. She can hopefully decrypt your hard drive, so you can locate the centipedes. Once that's done, you can all come for me.' He remembered Dave Pournell's parting comments, and felt another shiver run through him. 'If I'm still here.'

'What does that mean?'

'I'm facing non-elective brain surgery if I don't give Nemor Inc. the Almasti DNA.'

Rhino frowned. 'Well, give it to them, then.'

'I may have to, but I'm holding out.' He paused again, thoughts racing. 'I can get Tara out, but I need to know her location first. I'll work on that – you get in touch with Gillian Livingstone and tell her where I am. She might be able to exert some leverage. I'm working on a stolen tablet at the moment, so I don't know how much longer I've got, but I'll try and get back to you in an hour or two. OK?'

'OK.' Rhino looked as if he was going to say something else, but Gecko's head appeared in the video window, pushing the ex-SAS soldier out of the way.

'Calum, I could fly back to England and give myself up to them!'

'Not a chance,' Calum said. He could hear Rhino saying something similar in the background. 'Tara has seen their faces. They won't let her live, even if they get you.' He tried to look earnest and believable. 'Gecko, trust me – I'll get her back. I promise.'

Gecko nodded, reluctantly. 'You have to, Calum.'

'I know. Talk soon.' He suddenly remembered the other thing he'd meant to say. 'Oh, by the way – there's a Nemor team headed your way. Be careful.' Calum cut the connection. He felt a wave of depression and loss wash through him, but he pushed it away. There was no time for that now.

Tom Karavla. He was the key to this.

Calum knew that he wasn't as good at computing and hacking as Tara was, but he knew a lot and he'd learned more from her. Using the Robledo Mountains Technology tablet, and knowing that someone might come through the door any moment, he remotely accessed his system back in London to search for the name *Tomas Karavla*. Within a few seconds he had an email address and IP address. Tomas Karavla was logged on at a coffee shop in central London. Calum hacked into the boy's laptop and activated the camera above the screen. Within seconds he was looking at Tomas's face. The boy had obviously been in a fight. He had a black eye, a bruised cheek, a split lip and a gash on his forehead.

Calum activated a two-way interchange. He knew, from

Tomas's amazed expression, exactly when a window had opened up on the boy's computer with Calum's face in it.

'My name is Calum Challenger,' he said. 'You are Tomas Karavla, and you helped kidnap Tara Fitzgerald.'

'Not through choice,' the boy said. He frowned. 'You are not the way I imagined you.'

'Never mind that. I need your help. Where is Tara being held?'

Tomas tried to lick his lips, but when his tongue touched the bloody split in his lower lip he winced. 'Why should I help? My uncles – they beat me up just because Tara took my mobile without me knowing. If they do that for an accident, what would they do if I deliberately betrayed them?'

'They are going to kill her,' Calum said quietly but urgently. 'You know that, don't you?'

'No! They said they would release her unharmed when this Gecko boy comes to work for them.'

'And do you believe them?'

Tomas was silent.

'You know that she knows what they look like. Do you really think they'll let her go?'

'If they frighten her enough,' Tomas said, as if the words hurt him, 'then she will keep quiet about them.'

'Even if that was true, and we both know it isn't, do you really want them to hurt her badly enough to scare her forever? That doesn't seem to be something you'd be comfortable with.' Calum didn't know that for sure, but Tara seemed to think that Tomas was OK, and Calum didn't have much choice but to go with that.

Tomas's face was tortured. 'No,' he whispered, 'but they will hurt me. Badly. They will *cripple* me.'

'Not if they don't know what you've done. And not if *they* get hurt first.' He paused. 'Do they still have your phone?'

'Yes. They smashed it in front of me.'

'Then they probably think you can't talk to anyone. Tell me where they are holding Tara. I promise that nobody will know you're involved.'

'I don't want her to be hurt.' Tomas looked as if he was trying to convince Calum of what he was saying. 'I don't even want her *frightened*.'

'Then tell me.'

A long pause, then: 'St Alkmund's Court, in Stratford. It is a block of flats. She is in number forty-five.'

'Thank you,' Calum said.

'Get her out. Get her out alive.'

'I will,' Calum said, cutting the connection.

He looked around. He was immobilized in a medical facility in a different country, and someone might come through the door any moment and take the tablet away. How come this was all on *his* shoulders?

He sighed. Now he just had to get hold of Mr Macfarlane . . .

fourteen

Tara was alternating between states of euphoria and depression. On the one hand she knew that Calum, at least, was aware that she was in trouble, and that the Karavla brothers didn't know she had managed to get a message to him. On the other hand she knew that Calum himself was in trouble and might not be able to help. So sometimes she would stay pressed to the window, mind racing, looking for signs of rescue, and other times she would just curl up into a terrified ball on the mattress, trying not to think about anything.

Angry as she still was with him, Tara kept wondering what Tom's punishment had been. Part of her wanted him to be hurt, but she also knew that he hadn't wanted to betray her, and he didn't deserve punishment for trying to help. And it wasn't as if he had *given* her his mobile – she had taken it from his pocket. She hoped he was OK.

When the lock clicked and the door swung open, Tara was at a low point, lying on the mattress curled into a ball. She glanced up. One of the Karavla brothers was standing in the doorway. She didn't know which one. He was holding something in his hand: a metal object that glittered in the light shining through the window.

'It is time,' he said without any trace of emotion.

'Time for what?'

'Time to prove that we mean what we say. Your friend Eduardo has not been in contact with us, so we need to remind him that we are serious men.' He lifted his hand, and Tara could see that he was holding a pair of gardening shears.

She had a terrible feeling that gardening was not on the menu today.

'Come,' the thug said. 'We do this in the main room. Very quick, very hygienic. We have put down sheets. There is no reason to get blood on carpet.' He shook his head. 'It is very hard to clean up afterwards if you do not use sheets.' When she didn't move, he said, in a harsher voice, 'Come on, girl. Do not make me angry. Let us do this quickly and with small amount of fuss.'

If she didn't get up, Tara knew that he would come over and pull her roughly to her feet. Part of her was thinking, *Why make this easy for him?* while another part was thinking, *Let's at least do this with a little dignity, and without screaming if possible*.

She climbed slowly to her feet and walked across to the door. She was trembling all over, but she tried not to show it. She would get through this. She *would* get through this.

But why hadn't Gecko been in contact? She didn't expect him to rush back and make everything all right, but at least he could have called the thugs and *pretended* that he was coming back. That might have delayed the torture she was about to endure. Didn't he care that she was in trouble? Maybe something had happened in Hong Kong. Maybe he hadn't sent a message because he *couldn't*.

This was all so messed up.

The thug stood back and let her through into the living room, which she had only glimpsed when she was brought into the flat. There was a sofa, an easy chair, a wide-screen LCD TV and, as promised, a white sheet laid down in the centre of the room. A glass door on the far side gave out on to a balcony. The second of the brothers was sitting in the easy chair, with a beer bottle in his hand. He was watching a sports channel on the TV. The fact that he wasn't even bothering to watch while Tara's finger was cut off was somehow the worst thing. How often had he done this kind of thing before to make him so blasé?

'Stand on sheet,' the first brother said. He had taken up a position between her and the little hallway that led to the front door, just in case she tried to make a run for it. Not that she could: her legs were like jelly. 'We take little finger on left hand first. You will not even miss it.'

Before she could move, the front door exploded inwards with a stunning burst of noise and smoke, propelling the man with the gardening shears forward. He stumbled, feet catching in the sheet, and fell. The sitting thug sprang to his feet. A gun suddenly appeared in his hand. He peered through the smoke, trying to make out what was happening.

A black object like a cricket ball bounced into the room, coming to rest on the sheet. The two brothers looked at it, puzzled. Instinct made Tara turn away, towards the glass door to the balcony. There was something odd about it . . .

A bright flash of light from the bouncing object turned the room into a white void. Tara, looking away, was only momentarily blinded, but the two brothers cried out and put their hands to their faces, covering their eyes in shock. The one with the gun started shooting blindly at the door, where he expected the attackers to enter.

Tara saw the glass in the balcony door shatter into jigsaw pieces that still somehow held together. It looked as if a transparent film had been stuck across the glass, so that the broken bits stayed in place.

The shattered door fell slowly inwards and hit the carpet.

A dark shape sprang in from the balcony outside.

Whoever it was, he was about Tara's height but a lot bulkier. He wore a black balaclava over his head, and black overalls. He raised a hand that was holding, bizarrely, a water pistol: all bright red and yellow plastic, with a water reservoir bulb on top.

The brother with the gun turned round, still blinded by the blast but aware that someone had entered from the balcony. The intruder fired the water pistol at the thug's face. He screamed, dropped his gun and clawed at his eyes frantically. Tara smelt something simultaneously sharp and rancid. Her nose suddenly itched and her eyes started watering.

Tara glanced at the thug's brother, who was still on the floor. He had rolled sideways and was desperately pulling a gun from his jeans. The intruder hadn't noticed. He was checking the rest of the room for threats.

Tara stepped sideways, grabbed the edge of the LCD TV and pulled it, hard. It topped off its stand and fell on to the second thug, crushing him. Tara kicked the gun out of reach.

The intruder pulled off his balaclava. The face revealed was one that Tara had seen before – Mr Macfarlane, the chauffer who worked for Calum's great-aunt and who had driven them both to Farnborough.

'Afternoon, miss,' he said. 'I was told you was lookin' to be rescued.'

'And just in time too,' Tara said shakily.

Macfarlane looked around. 'Anyfing you want from 'ere, or shall we go?'

'Let's go, please.'

'Right – just 'ang on a minute.' He handed her the water pistol, then reached into his pocket and took out some plastic ties. Quickly he secured the wrists and ankles of the Karavla brothers – one of whom was still rubbing his eyes and moaning while the other was unconscious beneath the TV. Having secured them, he carried them out through the shattered glass door and fastened their ankles to the balcony.

'How did you find me?' Tara asked as they left through the front door. No neighbours had come to see what had happened. Perhaps this kind of thing occurred all the time in this neighbourhood.

'Young Mr Calum got in touch with me. 'E told me what 'ad 'appened, an' where you were. Asked me to come an' get you, 'e did.'

'But how did he know where I was? *I* didn't know where I was!'

''Pparently some bloke named Tomas told 'im.'

Tara felt conflicted about Tom. He had come through for her, in the end, but he'd got her into this situation in the first place.

She handed back the water pistol. 'What have you *got* in this? It smells *terrible*!'

'It's a mixture of lemon juice an' onion juice,' he replied. 'I didn't want to bring a gun, cos that makes the police really narked if they get involved, an' I couldn't get 'old of any tear gas in a hurry, so I 'ad to improvise. The water pistol belongs to me nephew. I'll 'ave to wash it out before I give it back to 'im.' He sniffed. 'The next best thing would've been a shotgun loaded with salt instead of pellets, of course, but me mum had used all the salt for a tongue she's curin'.'

'A *what*?' Tara felt as if the conversation had taken a sudden left turn.

'Ox's tongue. Sweetest meat ever, but it needs to be cured in salt for a few days before you can eat it. Shame, that, cos a shotgun commands a lot o' respect. A water pistol, not so much.'

They hurried down a set of concrete steps and out into the open. Mr Macfarlane had parked a couple of streets away – not the big black limousine that he had been driving the last time that Tara had seen him, but an old and more anonymous BMW.

'I meant to ask,' she said as he held the back door open for her, 'I know the front door blowing open and the flash grenade were both distractions so they weren't looking at the balcony, but how did you do it? Remote control?'

'I 'ad, 'elp, didn't I?' Macfarlane said as he slid into the driver's seat. 'That Tomas kid.'

Tara looked around wildly. 'He's *here*? He's all right?'

''E said 'e thought you wouldn't want to see 'im right now, so 'e's makin' 'is own way 'ome.' He paused before starting the car, and shook his head. ''E's been roughed up. Don't look too hot.'

Tara felt a spike of guilt run through her. She hoped she would get the chance to see Tom again. They had things to resolve.

As the car pulled away, she noticed that a laptop with an internet dongle sticking out of one of the USB ports was sitting on the seat beside her.

'What's this for?'

'Mr Calum asked me to tell you that there's a problem in 'Ong Kong,' Mr Macfarlane said. 'There ain't much time, apparently. There's an 'ard disk that needs decryptin' in an 'urry. 'Pparently that laptop there can take remote control of the one that this 'ard disk is connected to. He said he knows you're tired an' stressed, but could you take a quick gander at it for 'im?'

Tara grinned. 'Can *I* use a computer? I've been going cold turkey for days now. Just let me at it!'

'Good girl!' He paused momentarily as he pulled round a corner. 'I'll take you back to Mr Calum's apartment, an' I'll stay there to make sure nothin' 'appens to you. In the meantime, do you mind if I put some music on?'

'Dubstep?' Tara asked, ready to give it a go, given how much she owed Mr Macfarlane.

'Nah, Beethoven!' he said, shocked. 'The Choral Symphony. Can't beat a bit of Beethoven after a good workout!'

'No problem,' she said, then hesitated for a moment. 'Look, is there any chance we could stop for a takeaway coffee somewhere? I've been looking forward to one!'

It was morning in Hong Kong, and the sun was shining sideways through a haze of pollution. In Rhino's hotel room he and Gecko were sitting together on the sofa staring at Natalie, who was sitting in an easy chair. Rhino had called and asked her to join them for a room-service breakfast. The atmosphere was tense.

Gecko watched Natalie as Rhino told her briefly what had happened the previous night. She was sullen and disinterested, looking away to stare out of the window.

'I suppose you think I called the United Nations and

told them about the warehouse?' she said when Rhino had finished.

'I do,' he said.

'You're right – I did.'

'Why?'

Her face suddenly creased into an expression that was part anger and part distress. 'I kept thinking about those animals, and the conditions they were being kept in. I couldn't stand it. I had to do something!'

'I understand,' Rhino said, surprising both Gecko and Natalie. 'But you put both of us at risk. Next time, tell me first if there's something you feel you *have* to do. If it really is something that can't wait, then we'll work around it. OK?'

She glanced up at him, and her eyes glittered with tears. 'OK,' she said in a small voice, 'I promise. And I'm sorry. But I'm not sorry.' She shook her head in confusion. 'You know what I mean!'

Rhino was spared the necessity of answering by the voice that came from his laptop, on the desk. 'Hello? Anyone there?'

Gecko sprang off the sofa and got to the desk. Tara's face was gazing from a window on the screen.

'Tara!' he cried, a wave of happiness crashing over him. 'You're OK!'

'No thanks to you!' she said, sending a pang of guilt through his heart.

'Look, I left my mobile behind in my room, and I had it turned off anyway, after the flight, and I didn't get the message for a long time, and—'

'It's OK,' she said. 'I forgive you. Things turned out OK, and I wouldn't have wanted you to get sucked into a life of crime just because of me. Is Rhino there?'

'I'm here,' Rhino said from behind Gecko. 'Where are you?'

'In a car heading for Calum's apartment. We've got to get him back!'

'We have,' Rhino said, 'but right now we've got an encrypted hard disk to examine. Can you access it from where you are?'

Tara leaned forward and typed something into the laptop, and the removable hard disk connected to Rhino's computer whirred into life. 'Do bears wear funny hats?' she murmured. 'Is the Pope—'

'Can you do it or can't you?'

'Of course I can. Running some decryption algorithms now.' She paused. 'Fortunately it's not encrypted using the PGP algorithm. That's more or less unbreakable. This is some commercial off-the-shelf stuff they bought in a computer shop. Should have it decrypted in a few minutes.' Another pause. 'You'll be pleased to hear that it's in English, rather than Chinese. Thank heavens for Microsoft and Apple's domination of the computer market. You want me to copy the unencrypted files to your own hard drive?'

'Please,' Rhino replied, 'but could you also do a quick search for the word "centipede" and give me a separate file with all that text in it?'

'Will do.' Silence for a few moments, apart from the growl of a car engine, the click of keys being pressed and, bizarrely, the sound of a choir singing. 'Right – here it comes.'

'Thanks, Tara – you go and rest now.'

'It feels like I've been resting for days,' she said. 'I want to go out and have fun. And I want to see what I can do to help Calum.'

'Talk later.'

'OK.'

Tara's window on the laptop screen closed. Rhino brought up a file listing and clicked on a particular file. The screen filled with text.

'Jeez,' he murmured, 'there's a lot of this!'

'Let me have a look,' Natalie interrupted, pushing past Gecko. 'I can speed-read faster than anyone I know. It's probably a genetic thing. God knows I never asked for it.' She sat down and quickly scanned down the text. 'Right, there isn't a lot of stuff about the centipedes, although much of it is repeated in different places. They don't appear to have a buyer – the centipedes were discovered in a rainforest in some place called Hainan Island, and Xi Lang was emailing various people to see if they were interested. OK . . . this is interesting. Apparently the centipedes had GPS RFID microcircuits attached to their backs so they could be tracked. All of the animals had these microcircuits stuck on or implanted somewhere inside them so that Xi Lang always knew where they were.'

'So we can track their locations!' Gecko said. 'That

suddenly makes the problem a lot easier.'

'Have you got the identification codes for the centipedes?' Rhino asked.

'Yes – they're here.'

'Right. Get Tara back on the line. We need her help in locating those critters.'

Natalie pushed her chair back and stood up. 'I can speed-read,' she said, 'but I'm not a telephone operator. Gecko can do that.'

Gecko rolled his eyes, slid into the chair and called Tara back. When her face appeared, she was obviously still in the car. 'Hi!'

'Tara, we've got codes for GPS chips on the two escaped giant centipedes. Can you locate them for us?'

'Should be able to. It's no different to locating a lost or stolen mobile phone. There are apps that can do it easily. I'll let you know what they are and you can download them to your mobiles. What are the codes?'

Gecko read them out from the screen of the laptop. Tara typed away, scowling in concentration. 'Right – I've got them. I'm also installing an app on your laptop that will put markers on a map so you can find the little critters.' She caught herself. 'Sorry – *big* critters.'

'Thanks, Tara.' Gecko hesitated. 'Look –'

'Don't worry,' she said softly. 'We're OK, OK?'

'OK.'

'Now I've got to go. Things to do.'

Tara's window vanished, and a few seconds later a map

sprang to life on Rhino's laptop screen. Two red dots were flashing in locations in Kowloon. They weren't that far from the warehouse where the centipedes had been kept.

'Right,' Rhino said grimly. 'This is now a search-and-destroy mission. Everyone good to go?'

'Yes,' said Gecko.

'Yes,' Natalie added.

'No qualms about hunting down giant centipedes?' Rhino asked pointedly, looking at Natalie. 'You don't want to save them and return them to this Hainan place?'

'Eeuw!' she said. 'There are limits.' She paused, staring at Rhino. 'But when we've finished, can we give that hard drive to the UN animal exploitation team. There's a man named Evan Chan I spoke to. They might find it useful as evidence.'

'OK,' he nodded. 'It's a deal. Get ready to leave.'

'What happens if one of the centipedes escapes while we're chasing the other one?' Gecko asked, concerned.

Rhino grimaced. 'Good point. We may have to take that risk.'

'No, we don't,' Natalie said quietly. They both turned to look at her. 'You go after one; Gecko and I will go after the other.'

Rhino's face reflected his indecision. 'Are you sure you can cope?' he asked.

Natalie shook her head. 'Of course not, but it's the only practical solution, isn't it?'

He nodded reluctantly. 'Be careful,' he said. 'These

creatures are poisonous and vicious.'

Gecko looked at his hands, which still hadn't fully recovered from picking up the centipede's shed skin back in the warehouse. He knew all too well how dangerous those things were.

Calum managed to slide the tablet computer beneath his mattress before the door to his room fully opened and Dave Pournell and Dr Kircher entered, along with two bulky orderlies in white uniforms. They looked like bouncers heading for a fancy-dress party.

'Ready to have those electrodes implanted in your brain?' Pournell said cheerily. 'I've talked it over with Dr Kircher here, and we've decided that rather than shove them all in at once we're going to do one a day for the next ten days. That's the good news. We're also not going to use any anaesthetic, because Dr Kircher assures me that the brain doesn't have any nerves. That's the other good news. You may, however, experience an unpleasant *drilling* sensation. That, I guess, is the bad news. Isn't that right, Dr Kircher?'

Kircher was looking pale. He nodded, once, and Calum noticed that he was looking anywhere but at Calum.

'So – about that Almasti DNA . . .' Pournell continued, as if the two subjects were linked. Which, of course, they were. 'Any update on when Nemor Inc. can take those samples over and evaluate them?'

'Not any time soon,' Calum said in a whisper. He could feel fear building within him like a growing core of ice, but he wasn't going to give in. He *couldn't* give in. It was just plain wrong. And maybe, just maybe, Gillian Livingstone or Rhino or Tara would find some way of rescuing him, although right now he was wondering how late they were going to leave it.

Pournell gestured to the two orderlies. 'Take him away,' he said. 'Nearest operating theatre.'

The two orderlies moved to the head of the bed and started pushing it towards the door.

'Last chance, kid . . .' Pournell murmured as the bed passed him by.

Calum told him to go and do something biologically improbable.

'Hey,' Pournell said, 'let's maintain a little politeness, shall we?'

The bed was out in the corridor by now. As the orderlies tried to turn it round, the tablet computer slipped out from beneath the mattress and crashed to the floor. Pournell bent down to retrieve it. He shook his head disapprovingly. 'Naughty boy, Calum. Just for that I'm going to tell Dr Kircher to drill *extra* slowly. Purely for safety's sake, you understand.'

Calum's last link to the outside world was gone.

The bed trundled down the corridor towards the nurses' station, and then past it and round the bend in the corridor. Calum cast one final despairing glance at the lifts in the lobby as they disappeared behind him.

Halfway down the corridor was an open double door. The orderlies stopped there, and turned the bed to steer it through.

Calum could feel the pressure building within him to agree to give Pournell the Almasti DNA, but he had a terrible feeling that the man would proceed with the brain surgery anyway, just because he enjoyed having that power over Calum.

The operating theatre was dominated by a large white MRI scanner, like a doughnut on its side. A bed with a sliding top allowed the patient to be moved into the scanner. It was similar to the one that Calum had been in at the Robledo place in Farnborough, except that this one looked as if it allowed surgery to be carried out at the same time.

Dr Kircher confirmed this as he followed the bed into the room. 'We'll put you into the scanner and ask you a series of questions,' he murmured. He didn't sound as if he was enjoying himself. 'Depending on how your brain lights up, we'll decide where to insert the electrodes.'

'I might be being stupid here,' Calum said, his voice scratchy, 'but isn't there a bloody great magnet inside that thing? Won't that make it hard to do any drilling and inserting?'

'Nice try,' Pournell said from behind him, 'but all the medical implements are made of ceramics rather than metal. They won't be affected by the magnetic field. The electrodes are metal, sure, but what we're going to do first is insert some long ceramic tubes, like straws, through holes in your skull. We can slide the electrodes down the straws when you're out of the scanner.' He paused. 'Any last words, kid? Anything you want to tell me?'

'Lots of things,' Calum replied shakily, 'but they all break that politeness rule of yours.'

'Remember – you can stop this any time. Just raise a hand.'

Calum raised a hand.

Pournell laughed. 'Somehow I think you're just joking with us now.'

At a signal Calum couldn't see, the two orderlies pushed the bed up parallel to the scanner and lifted Calum across. They strapped him down so he couldn't move, and then they put a white plastic frame down over his face so that he couldn't turn his head. All he could do was stare straight up.

'It's . . . normal procedure,' Dr Kircher said as he checked the lights on the scanner. 'We need you to remain perfectly still while we're . . . working.' He licked his lips.

'Keep telling yourself that,' Calum said. The frame held his jaw closed, and he had to speak through clenched teeth.

He was then slid inside the scanner until his head was tight up against something rounded, something that his skull fitted into snugly like it was a cap. There were sharp bits around the inside of the cap that touched against his scalp.

'Really, really, really last chance,' Pournell called from outside. He was so sure that Calum was going to crack that the boy felt a hot spike of anger piercing the icy cold of his fear. He was *not* going to give that DNA to Nemor Inc. He *wasn't*.

Except that part of him knew that this was sheer

bravado. He was going to give in sometime in the next few seconds . . .

Suddenly an alarm went off.

'What the hell is that?' Pournell shouted.

Then a *bang!* and the sound of breaking glass.

'What *is* this?' Pournell screamed. He sounded as if he was somewhere between furious and terrified. Calum got the impression he didn't like to be in situations where he didn't control everything.

'Don't know,' one of the orderlies said. Calum could hear the other one talking frantically on a mobile phone.

A series of heavy thuds shook the room now. They were getting louder, as if something very big was getting closer and closer . . .

'OK, get him out of there!' Kircher shouted. 'Get him *out* of there!'

Someone grabbed hold of Calum's feet and yanked him out of the scanner. The metal frame was pulled away from his head. He sat up, staring at the closed doors in wonder as the thuds shook them.

And then the doors exploded inwards, scattering wood and metal everywhere.

Something enormous stood there.

fifteen

The signal from the giant centipede that they were chasing was coming through strongly on their mobiles, so Gecko and Natalie set out after it. They took a taxi as far as they could, out through the streets of Kowloon, before the press of people and other traffic got too much. After they'd abandoned the taxi they ran through the crowds of people and market stalls towards the point where their mobile phones told them that the giant centipede was located. It wasn't moving, which worried Gecko more than if it *had* been moving. Was it already dead, he wondered as he ran, or was it feeding?

The heat was oppressive, and Gecko found himself covered in sweat almost instantly. The humidity was so high, however, that the sweat had no way of evaporating to cool him down, so it just soaked into his clothes and pooled in his trainers, making them squish each time he took a step. Every few minutes he had to wipe a sleeve across his eyes to get rid of the stinging sweat. His sleeve was already dark and dripping. His lungs were also labouring to pull the thick, wet, hot air into his lungs. It had been a long time since he had experienced conditions like this.

He knew he was going to get dehydrated very quickly. He and Natalie would have to stop and get a bottle of water from somewhere, if they could.

He glanced sideways as his feet pounded against tarmac and pavement, wondering how Natalie was holding up. She seemed fine, and he remembered that she had been a runner, back in school in America. She obviously had a lot of stamina, and he found he had to exert himself to keep up. He was better at short sprints and long jumps.

There seemed to be no rhyme or reason, no grid system to the alleys and streets that they ran through. The city's layout appeared more organic than planned, like the veins and arteries in some massive biological system.

Through the half-open doors of the buildings they passed, Gecko could see fragmentary flashes of life in the city: dried fish hanging on strings from the ceilings; women with bundles of steaming noodles wrapped round sticks in their hands, which they pulled apart to thin and stretch the food; men crouched over paper rolls on which they painstakingly painted Chinese characters in thick strokes of black ink; entire families crowded into single rooms, all talking or eating or sleeping at the same time. It was mesmerizing and confusing, a kaleidoscope of foreign life.

Natalie shouted across to Gecko. 'Up ahead! We're nearly there!'

'Up ahead' turned out to be a pair of ornately carved

pillars that marked the entrance to a park. The two of them ran unhesitatingly inside. Paths led, twisting and rising, towards a central low hill. Bushes and flowers of all colours lined the paths, providing plenty of cover.

Gecko indicated that Natalie should go left while he went right. Hopefully, if one of them didn't find the giant centipede then both of them would converge on it somewhere near the top of the hill.

As he ran across a narrow stone bridge that crossed a stream, Gecko checked his mobile. The centipede was only a little way ahead – and it was still motionless.

He diverted left, leaping over a bush covered in small red flowers, and found himself running across a clearing where elderly Chinese men and women were performing t'ai chi – a form of exercise that looked to the idle observer like martial arts being performed underwater.

Gecko threaded his way between them and over another bush – to find the creature they were looking for curled round a pigeon that it had partially consumed. Its bright red exoskeleton, mottled with blue rings, was stark against the lush green grass.

His heart, which was already hammering in his chest, suddenly speeded up. He could feel the *thud, thud, thud* of blood in his neck and his temples.

He reached into a pocket and removed a green string sack that Rhino had bought from a fruit-and-vegetable stall. Without pausing, he threw it.

The sack fell across the creature, which twisted round

and reared up, trying to locate whatever was attacking it. Gecko could tell that it was the smaller of the two centipedes they had seen back in the warehouse.

Its flat, blunt head weaved around like a snake's. The scattering of black dots that acted as eyes glinted with anger and hunger. Its legs – many more than a hundred, surely, Gecko found himself thinking – scrabbled at the taut strands of string that made up the sack, making strange plucking noises.

Gecko moved to grab the sack's handles and scoop it up, intending to hold it well away from his body so that the thing couldn't bite him. His plan was to dunk the giant centipede into the water, assuming that it wasn't aquatic, and wait for it to drown. He would then crush it with a large rock, just in case it *was* aquatic.

The centipede had other plans. Its scissor-like pincers closed on the string covering its head, and cut them with an audible *snick!* The strands parted. The centipede's scrabbling legs managed to pull the sack downward, along its segmented body, while its head bobbed around free. For a moment it seemed torn between wanting to attack Gecko and wanting to escape. Gecko could hear a hissing noise coming from its head. Its black eyes fixed on him, transfixing him. Its feelers waved hypnotically.

It attacked. The giant centipede lunged through the hole in the sack, heading straight for Gecko's face, pincers snapping in fury.

Something spun in from one side, hitting the centipede

in the side of the head. It whirled around in mid-air, trying to locate the source of the sudden attack.

The thing that had hit the centipede fell away to the ground. It was a green string sack, just like the one Gecko had used.

Natalie's sack.

Gecko looked sideways to see Natalie standing in a gap between flowering bushes. She was breathing heavily, and her skin was glistening with sweat, but her face was full of concern for Gecko.

'Run!' she cried.

The giant centipede fixed on Natalie. It bunched itself up, and then it launched itself like a missile at the girl.

Gecko did the only thing he could. He grabbed its rear end and pulled it backwards.

The giant centipede's pincers snapped shut just inches from Natalie's face. She recoiled, horrified. The creature turned round, twisting muscularly in Gecko's grip, and tried to fasten itself on to him instead. He whirled it round like an Olympic hammer thrower, letting the centipede's weight propel its body away from him. It felt heavy, like a duffel bag full of wet clothes. He let go of it when its body reached the top of its low arc and watched it fly across the bushes . . .

And fall among the people doing t'ai chi that Gecko had seen earlier.

There were screams and curses, and volleys of rapid Chinese from the other side of the bushes.

Gecko grabbed Natalie's hand and pulled her along,

following the path of the giant centipede. The elderly Chinese were running in all directions. For a moment Gecko couldn't see the creature, but then he caught sight of a flash of scarlet heading through the bushes. He gave chase, with Natalie running behind him.

His palms were burning from touching the creature, and he could see Natalie brushing her hands against her trousers as she ran.

This wasn't going the way that it had been supposed to . . .

Something large stood in the doorway of the operating theatre where Calum was strapped down. Something large and metallic, covered in wires and cables. It had a head, made up of cameras and lights and other sensors. It also had six legs, four of which were on the ground while the front two were held up like those of a praying mantis. It had obviously used those limbs to push the doors in.

It was ARLENE.

Calum had never in his life been so glad to see something that had once tried to kill him.

The robot advanced into the room. One of the orderlies rushed towards it. ARLENE lashed out with a single leg and he went flying across the room, crashing into the wall. The other orderly backed away, hands up to protect himself.

The sensor head turned to look at Calum, and the raised front leg seemed to wave. Or maybe it was just a random electrical misfiring, like the one that had caused

Calum's leg to be broken in the first place.

Or maybe . . .

'Tara?' he said.

ARLENE's head nodded.

'You're OK?'

Another nod.

'And you're at my apartment, controlling ARLENE?'

If the robot had been fitted with speakers, Calum suspected he would have heard a very feminine 'Duh!', but all ARLENE did was nod again.

'I bet you regret having ARLENE shipped over here with me,' Calum said to Dr Kircher. He seemed to be transfixed by the robot's menacing presence.

Dave Pournell stepped forward, hands raised. 'Now look,' he said, 'we can talk this through like reasonable people, surely? There's no need for violence.'

'I'm getting out of here,' Calum said forcefully, 'and you are going to let me.'

'Really?' Pournell made a big play of considering Calum's words. 'I can't really see *how*. I mean, yes, you've got a big scary robot which you managed to take control of and get out of the warehouse we were storing it in – and, believe me, I'll be asking some pointed questions about who exactly let that happen. But what are you going to do now? Correct me if I'm wrong, but the robot can't pick you up and carry you – it's got six legs, but no arms. You might be able to pull yourself up on to its back, but then what? You're going to ride it out of here like a cowboy? Again, I think not. Where would you go? No, all things considered, I think you're bluffing. Good card, I'll grant you, but it's still a bluff.'

Calum's mind raced. Pournell was right – he wasn't in a position to ride away from Nemor Inc. on ARLENE the way that Natalie had done in Georgia. He was still stuck, except . . .

'Tara,' he said to ARLENE, 'come over here and get ready to smash the scanner.'

'No!' Kircher screamed, jumping forward with outstretched arms. 'It's one of a kind. It took five years to develop and build. Do you know how much it *cost*?'

'I don't,' Calum admitted, 'but I know how much it *will* be worth in a few minutes if you don't release me and arrange for me to be flown home *right now*!' The last two words were shouted rather than said, but Calum forgave himself. It had been a stressful morning.

ARLENE stepped further into the room, its weight cracking the tiles on the floor as it walked. It came right up to the scanner and rested both front legs against it, very gently but very firmly. Dr Kircher whimpered.

'Remember,' Calum said, looking at Dave Pournell, 'you can stop this any time you want. Just raise a hand.'

Pournell at least had the good grace to smile at the words being thrown back at him. He glanced at ARLENE thoughtfully. 'You know, I suspect that the fuel cell on that thing will need recharging at some stage. We could all just wait here until it runs down, and see what happens then.'

'Before ARLENE runs out of fuel, this scanner will be

trashed,' Calum responded, 'along with any other expensive equipment we can find in this building. Just how much is the Almasti DNA worth to you, Dave? What kind of loss can your superiors afford before they fire you?'

'It's a Mexican stand-off, kid,' Pournell said, but he was looking concerned now. 'And given how close we are to the Mexico border, that's very apt. Even if we agree to fly you home, you can't get this robot on to the jet. The minute you're away from the robot, you've lost your bargaining chips.'

'Not if he gets on to *my* jet,' a voice said from the smashed doorway. 'He retains all his chips, and we get to take ARLENE home as well – disassembled and in nicely wrapped boxes.'

Calum looked over to the doorway. Gillian Livingstone was standing there, as immaculately dressed as ever. She smiled tightly at him, and nodded. 'Calum, we need to have a long talk, I think, but not just yet. Let's get you out of here first.'

'Professor Livingstone, isn't it? I've been told about you. I thought we were working to the same ends,' Dave Pournell said, gazing in puzzlement at Calum's legal guardian.

'There are times when the ends do *not* justify the means,' she replied. 'If I had known just how far you were going to go, I never would have agreed to this.'

Agreed to what? Calum wondered. Yes, he and Gillian were going to have to have a long talk, but then they had a long flight ahead of them. He felt himself relax. He wasn't exactly out of the woods yet, but he could see a clearing up ahead.

'And while we're waiting,' he said, 'could I get a Coke? I'm parched.'

Having lost track of the centipede underground, Rhino left the gleaming glass, metal and black-tile air-conditioned heaven of the Tsim Sha Tsui metro station, took the escalator up to the surface and emerged into the oppressive heat and humidity of Kowloon's Nathan Road.

He was surrounded by square concrete buildings of various sizes, but it was the one directly ahead of him that was his target. Tungking Mansions. Seventeen storeys tall, consisting of five separate blocks all connected together, it was possibly the most famous – or infamous – location in Hong Kong since the bulldozing of the lawless Walled City collection of accommodation towers. Somehow, over the course of the fifty-odd years since it had been built, it had developed, changed and mutated to the point where it was almost a city inside a city, a separate environment that had its own rules and laws, its own population and its own way of doing things.

The problem being that it was where Rhino's giant centipede was located, according to the map display on his phone.

Rhino looked up at the complex in dismay. It was smaller and squatter than most of the buildings around it, studded with the blocks of ancient air-conditioning units. Mostly a dull, rain-swept grey in colour, it stuck out in a way the other buildings didn't. Not only did it have character –

so much character that you could sense it spilling from the thousands of balconies, running down the stained walls and dripping on the ground – but Rhino knew, from his research on the way over, and from his previous time in Hong Kong, that the place was home to some four thousand people. Many of those were locals, large Chinese families crowded into one-room apartments. Some were workers in the small shops, restaurants and guesthouses that were located in and among the apartments. The rest were international travellers taking advantage of the legendary cheapest accommodation in Hong Kong. Walking along a corridor deep inside in Tungking Mansions, far away from natural sunlight, one was liable to pass restaurants, guest houses, apartments, electronics shops, clothes shops and food shops, all mixed together and all within a hundred metres. And this was where his giant centipede was located.

He found himself hoping that Natalie and Gecko were having better luck with their creature.

The map was a two-dimensional display, he realized. It showed where on the ground the signal was coming from. The problem was that the building was not a two-dimensional object. Yes, the map would tell him where, looking downward from space, the signal was coming from, but it might actually be on any of the seventeen floors, or the roof. And while he was trying to discover which level it was on, people might be dying in there.

Shaking his head, he walked off Nathan Road, through an entranceway beneath a large cracked marble sign saying

Tungking Mansions and into the building. The first two levels were large open spaces, like car parks, shadowy and dripping with condensation, lit only by streetlights. People moved slowly – old women pushing shopping trolleys, young kids in gangs shoving each other around, girls in slinky silk dresses who watched him from lowered eyes as he passed, old men with leathery, emaciated faces and wispy white beards walking with sticks. He moved past them, trying not to be noticed, but he was European and reasonably well dressed, and so he stood out like a badger at a vicarage tea party.

The place stank of a thick mixture of curry houses, urine, rotting pak choi leaves and animal waste. Rhino tried to breathe through his mouth as he moved, but quickly found that even if he couldn't smell the place any more he could taste it. He found a stairwell, dripping with moisture, the origins of which he didn't like to think about, and he climbed up, past the first floor, to the terrace from which the five main blocks actually started.

As he left the stairwell and tried to walk out on to the terrace – a flat expanse of concrete open to the sun, peppered with sunken areas of soil in which scrubby plants grew, and from which the five towers erupted like great concrete cliffs – a group of young men pushed past him and surrounded him. He felt hands expertly running across his pockets and trying to get inside his jacket. He had to stop this, and quickly. Grabbing one particularly invasive hand, he twisted it hard, ducking underneath and taking the arm behind its owner's back so that the kid had to suddenly bend forward, cursing and grunting with the pain. There was silence and an abrupt cessation of the movement that had surrounded him. Seven sets of eyes were directly on him. He could sense hands moving to belts and pockets, ready to pull out knives.

'No harm, no foul,' he said quietly but with force. 'I'm here on business, and I'm going to leave as quickly as possible, with everything I came in with.'

No sound, no movement – just the watchful eyes.

'There are eight of you,' he went on calmly, 'and that's probably enough to take me down, if you want to, but I promise you that I can kill two of you and cripple another two before you manage it. The question you have to ask yourselves is: is the chance that you get killed or crippled worth it, compared to the chance that you get to search me for the money I may or may not have?'

He looked around, meeting all the eyes of the youths who were watching him. He didn't see any acceptance of his points, but he didn't see any argument either. Blank, watchful faces all round. He just had to hope that he'd been promoted in their minds from *victim* to *potential threat*.

He released the man he was holding. The man staggered forward. He turned as if to lunge at Rhino, but one of his friends caught him and pulled him back. And then the group of eight was moving on into the stairwell, chatting and shoving as if nothing had happened.

That had been close. Too close. Despite the heat, Rhino felt a sudden chill run through him.

Checking his mobile again, he noticed that that the

flashing symbol was moving. He zoomed in, trying to track it. The symbol was moving through Block D – on some unknown level – and it was travelling quickly between apartments – probably through ceiling or floor spaces or ventilation gaps.

Then it seemed to pass through the block wall and out into empty space, and Rhino suddenly knew, with a rush of euphoria, where it was. The only places that there was a continuous stretch of ground over which the centipede could travel were the first two levels – the common spaces beneath the blocks. It was somewhere near him, and downward!

He looked around reflexively. He had to check each of the two lowest levels and locate the thing before it moved up into one of the blocks. If it did that, his chances of catching it would plummet to almost zero.

He was at Block A, and he needed to get to Block D. The quickest route was to go through blocks B and C. He ran for the nearest entrance and raced down a corridor that was redolent with curry fumes and filled with backpackers. He ran past shops selling dresses, handbags and high-end electronics, most of them probably counterfeit. He came out the other side of the block, bursting from shade into light, and raced across the terrace to the next block. The corridor that ran across it was much the same as the previous one, and for a second he thought he was trapped in a recurring dream. Out the other side and into another wide corridor, identical to the previous two. He found a stairwell and rapidly clattered down the steps to Level 2.

A market had been set up in the open common level – rows and rows of stalls beneath tarpaulins selling, strangely, only one thing – jade. Every stall was covered with either jade jewellery in gold or silver settings, jade carved into small figures of people or dragons, or polished but unset and uncarved lumps of the green stone. The stalls were lit by fluorescent lights, and the thousands of pieces of semi-precious stone glittered like a galaxy of stars. Tourists who had been lured into the market by the promise of cheap jewellery bartered with the stall owners.

Rhino pushed his way through the crowd. He was about to check his map again, but a commotion at the far side of the market caught his attention. Someone was screaming. It might be just an attempted pickpocketing, like the one he'd narrowly avoided, but it might be something else. It might be the giant centipede. He quickly shoved people out of the way, heading like an arrow towards the source of the disturbance.

A fist caught him beneath the ribcage, and he folded up on the damp, dirty ground, agony blazing through his body.

On the other side of the bushes was a stretch of grass, which gave on to a set of wide white stone steps. Gecko noticed that every second step had a long wooden pole stuck in a hole in the stone. At the stop of each pole was a triangular yellow silk banner. Some of the banners had sinuous blue dragons embroidered on them, while others had red

Chinese calligraphy in vertical columns.

The stone steps led up to the top of the hill, and to a typically Chinese gate: four square red pillars with inset Chinese calligraphy, topped with a complicated double-beamed roof. Through the gate was a Chinese temple: many single-storey wooden rooms in a variety of sizes, apparently all open to the air and connected to each other, all under tiled roofs that curved upward at the end.

The scarlet pillars on the gate confused Gecko for a second, but then he saw the scarlet of the giant centipede's exoskeleton rippling its way up the steps towards the temple, seeming to spend as much time weaving left and right as it did going straight ahead. Tourists on the steps screamed and jumped out of the way. Maybe the noise and the movement were confusing the centipede, because it didn't attack anyone but just headed for the relative safety of the dark temple.

Gecko and Natalie ran up the steps, following the creature. Gecko's breath burned in his chest; despite his years of free-running, the heat and humidity were getting to him. His legs felt like those noodles he'd glimpsed being stretched earlier.

The two of them burst into the temple. It was a spacious building: made of red and gold-painted wood and hung with long silk banners. Light came in from all sides, giving it an airy feel, but its ceiling was wreathed in smoke and covered in soot. Stone and metal statues of various Chinese figures, all life-sized or larger, were set into niches in its walls. Bowls containing smouldering bunches of incense, chrysanthemum flowers and fruit were set all over the floor space. Worshippers who had been sitting or kneeling in front of the statues, some throwing wooden sticks on the flagstones and some apparently burning money as an offering, looked around in confusion at the sudden noise. Priests in long yellow robes and flat black hats who had been chanting from scrolls or banging small drums dropped whatever they were holding and ran in from all sides to see what was desecrating their temple.

The giant centipede headed for one of the pillars that held up the ornate ceiling. Reaching it, the creature scrambled up the column, vanishing into the smoke that hung there.

Without thinking, Gecko rushed forward towards the pillar. Almost immediately he realized that it was too wide to climb, so he diverted sideways towards one of the statues.

Behind him he heard Natalie shout, 'No, Gecko, this is a *temple*! People are *worshipping*!' but it was too late. He was committed.

A priest grabbed at his shirt as he ran past, but he tore himself free and speeded up.

The statue was a tarnished bronze colour, about twice his size. It seemed to be a representation of a muscular warrior, clad in a sheet wrapped round his waist. His face was grimacing and his ears were stretched out to unusual proportions, the lobes dangling down to his shoulders. Some kind of strange ribbon wound round his neck and shoulders, and floated free around his body. The great thing about it as far as Gecko was concerned was that there were various projections that he could use to climb up – bent knees, outstretched hands, the ribbon . . . He leaped for the statue, and scrambled upward with as much grace as he could muster under the circumstances. From behind him he could hear shouts of dismay from the priests and worshippers, and gabbled apologies from Natalie.

Standing on the statue's head, his own head was in the layer of smoke that hung from the ceiling like gauzy curtains, shifting back and forth with the breeze. He could see the underneath of the roof, dimly, two metres or so above his head. It was supported by horizontal wooden rafters and braced by smaller diagonal ones. He jumped for one of the rafters. His hands caught the rough wood and he pulled himself up until he was crouching on top of it. He glanced around rapidly, feeling the sweat running down his sides and back. His hands burned, partly with the effort of pulling himself up and partly because of the giant centipede's poison.

Somewhere up here the creature was either running, hiding or preparing to attack.

The coiling smoke made it difficult to judge distances. As it moved it revealed momentary glimpses of distant rafters, beams, parts of the roof, the tops of other statues and the stone floor below. For a second he saw Natalie, surrounded by gesticulating priests, and then the smoke covered the scene up again and revealed a crowd of worshippers all heading for the temple steps.

He tried to quell his beating heart and rasping breath, listening out for the *scritch* of claw on wood, or the *hiss* of a scared and angry arthropod.

Something crimson flashed towards him from his left side. Something with pincers held wide.

sixteen

Rhino came round within seconds, cheek pressed against the gritty concrete. He didn't move – just listening in case he could pick up anything from whoever had hit him. It didn't do any good.

'He's still conscious,' a familiar voice said. 'You'd have to hit old Rhino a lot harder than that to knock him out. Get him to his feet – I want to have a word with him.'

Hands clamped on his shoulders and pulled him up into a standing position. He opened his eyes.

Craig Roxton was standing in front of him.

The man's long blond hair was brushed backwards, and his face was as pale as Rhino remembered. His blue eyes were as cold as chips of agate. He was wearing chinos and a polo shirt beneath a light cotton jacket. The heat didn't seem to be bothering him at all.

The two men standing on either side of Rhino were dressed similarly, but they were bigger than him. Despite the size difference it was clear, however, that Roxton was the leader.

'Mark Gillis – my word, it's been an age since we last saw each other.'

'Not long enough,' Rhino said quietly. His thoughts were racing. Apart from Roxton's meeting with Gillian Livingstone, the one Rhino had glimpsed at Waterloo station, his former colleague's last known whereabouts were in Georgia, working for Nemor Incorporated. He was a mercenary, a trained Special Forces man who was prepared to hire himself out to anyone if the money was right. Calum had told Rhino that Nemor was sending a small team to Hong Kong – Roxton must be the man in charge.

'Still working in hostage rescue?' Roxton asked. 'Not much money in that. More to be made in the actual taking of hostages, I think.'

'Still working for some big, anonymous corporation, taking orders from men in suits?' Rhino riposted. 'I wouldn't have thought that was your idea of a perfect career path.'

Roxton smiled. 'Ah, I see that the young girl – Natalie, was it? – has been talking. Yes, I work for Nemor Incorporated, but believe me, Rhino, they are so much more than just another big American corporation.' He paused. 'I could arrange a job interview, if you like?'

'Or I could give you the names of some charities you could donate some time to,' Rhino countered. 'Greenpeace, maybe, or the World Wildlife Fund . . .'

'Funny.'

Rhino was about to say something else when a fourth man, dressed the same anonymous way as Roxton and the other two, appeared from behind Rhino.

'There's a tracking app on his mobile phone,' he said in a grating voice that sounded as if he'd been hit in the throat once too often. 'I think he's got a location for the creature. Looks as if it's not too far away.'

Roxton nodded decisively. 'Good. Bring the phone – we'll use it.'

'What about this bloke?' one of the men holding Rhino asked.

'Kill him,' Roxton said. 'Do it quietly, and out of the way. Don't be seen, and leave the body underneath a pile of rubbish.' He grimaced. 'There's certainly enough of it around.' He glanced at Rhino, then looked away, dismissing Rhino from his thoughts completely.

Rhino opened his mouth to shout for help – not that there was any around, but it would get people looking in his direction. Before he could make a noise, one of the men holding him punched him in the stomach again. He folded up, pain exploding through him like a supernova. He nearly retched.

The two men dragged him off. Through a red haze, he saw Roxton and the man who had his mobile phone walking away, not looking back.

The two men pulled him towards one of the large pillars that studded this level. It was thick enough to shield them from the marketplace. They released Rhino, and he fell to his knees, still feeling as weak as a kitten.

'You want to do it, or shall I?' one of the men said.

'Whose turn is it?' the other one asked.

The first man shrugged. 'I've lost track. Tell you what – I'll take this one; you take the next.' He unclipped something from his belt and flicked his hand. A spring-loaded knife flashed into view, blade gleaming in the meagre light. 'Don't worry,' he said reassuringly. 'I've done this loads of times. There won't be any pain – apart from the obvious.'

'There's something you forgot to do,' Rhino said quietly, reaching to a small leather holster attached to his belt behind his back.

'What was that?' the man asked, stepping closer. Rhino felt the comforting rubber grip in his hand.

'Search me.' Rhino sprang to his feet and lashed out with the weapon he had retrieved. The impetus of his swing extended the weapon from a short tube to a long club made of hollow telescopic sections of steel and terminating in a solid steel ball. It was called an ASP, and it could break bones.

Which is what it did.

Rhino caught the first man in his chest. The man crumpled, gasping in agony as several ribs cracked under the impact of the metal. He still had his knife in his hand, and he scythed it round, desperately trying to catch Rhino, but Rhino brought his ASP up and then down again on the man's forearm. It snapped, bending in a highly unlikely fashion. The man screamed once; then passed out.

Rhino stepped forward towards the second man, snarling. The man was reaching behind his back. Rhino thought for a moment that he might have a gun, so he stepped closer, ASP raised up ready, but the man brought his hand sweeping back low and fast. Rhino heard another mechanical clicking noise, but before he could react the man's own telescopic baton caught him just below his waist. Only the thick fabric of his chinos protected him from serious damage, but the impact of the weighted steel on the point of his hip sent spikes of sickening pain arcing through his body like lightning. He tried to take a step back, but his leg was numb and he fell, rolling away on the gritty concrete as best he could.

The second man stepped closer, raising his baton over his head so that he could bring it crashing down on Rhino's skull.

Rhino kicked out with both feet, catching the man on his shins. His legs shot backwards and he fell forward, arms outstretched to brace himself. Rhino rolled out of the way and sprang to his feet. By the time he had turned round, his assailant was also upright, and facing Rhino, baton extended like a sword.

'Let's dance,' he said, and lunged forward, the heavy steel ball at the end of the baton heading straight for Rhino's throat.

Rhino blocked the lunge with a parry of his own. The impact of the two metal batons clashing sent shockwaves up his arm, numbing it.

The man stepped backwards. He considered for a moment, and then came at Rhino with a flurry of blows from left, right and above. It was all Rhino could do to keep blocking them as he took small steps backwards, but each strike got closer and closer to his head. It was only a matter of moments before his skull was fractured and the fight was over.

He had to do something, and he had to do it fast.

Still blocking with his right hand, holding the extended ASP, Rhino jerked his left hand forward, thumb extended. He pulled his head back, away from the other man's ASP, and used his right leg to push himself forward, inside the man's guard. His thumb, aimed precisely, hit the man's right eye. The man jerked backwards, bringing his hands up to cover his face. Rhino brought his baton down, catching the man's own baton close to the rubber grip. The man dropped the baton, nerves temporarily paralysed by the impact. The baton clattered on the floor.

The man cursed, and reached towards his belt with his left hand. He had a knife there, like his companion, and Rhino realized with sudden shock that the man was ambidextrous. He could fight equally with both hands!

Rhino had to finish this.

He aimed a backhand stroke at the man's head, hoping to knock him unconscious, but the man's right hand moved quicker than Rhino could see, catching the steel ball on the end of the baton and holding it still with amazing strength. His muscles bulged with the effort of overcoming the swing of the weapon, and he snarled.

'Weren't expecting that, were you?' he said tightly. He jerked his knife towards Rhino's stomach.

Rhino pressed a small button in the base of the baton's grip. The battery inside sent a huge pulse of electricity through the steel ball on the end. Rhino heard a sudden crackle. The man's eyes went wide, and his hand clenched even tighter on the ball. A small curl of smoke escaped from his fingers. He toppled forward slowly, like a tree, and Rhino had to step out of the way and pull the baton from the man's grip so that he could hit the ground face first.

'How about that?' he muttered. He took his finger off the button and pushed the ASP against his leg, folding it back up. Thank the lord for unauthorized modifications . . .

High up in the Chinese temple, the centipede's pincers snicked together a few inches from Gecko's eyes. Liquid dripped from them and towards the floor. Knowing what he did about centipedes, Gecko was sure it was poisonous.

The centipede turned its head towards him. Its black eyes stared at him. He saw nothing but pain and death in them. He could smell something sharp and acidic that made his eyes water and his nose sting.

Time seemed to slow down. Gecko became fascinated, and repelled, by the complexity of the centipede's mouthparts. The pincers curved into sharp, black points, but behind them and around them were other, smaller pincers, and thick hairs, and things that he couldn't even name, all of them waving and moving in a strange choreography around the central wet hole of the thing's gullet.

He knew this was it. He was crouched in the space

between the rafter and the roof. The centipede was in front of him, and there was nothing behind him but bracing beams and empty space. His only option was to jump, but it was a long way down to the stone floor, and he didn't think he would survive the fall.

Still, it was better than ending up with that obscene, incredible, complicated mouth fastening itself on his face.

He was just about to push himself off the rafter and jump down when something from below caught the centipede beneath its head segment. The creature's mouthparts spasmed as the thing – whatever it was – went straight through the exoskeleton and into the soft innards. Gecko heard a *crack* and then a *squish*. The centipede jerked, pincers gaping wide while all the way down its body its legs spread wide, claws groping at empty air. The ammonia-like smell intensified to the point where Gecko felt sick.

The giant centipede seemed to float away from Gecko. He watched it go with amazed eyes, but then the smoke momentarily cleared and he realized that the thing he'd seen coming up from beneath was a wooden pole. Its sharp end had been the thing that went through the creature's head segment.

He followed the line of the pole downward, to where Natalie was holding it like a long spear. A yellow silk banner lay by her feet. It was one of the banners from the steps outside.

She let the pole drop. The end she was holding hit the ground, and the rest of it pivoted, carrying the twitching centipede to the ground where the pole clattered and the creature splattered like a fly on a car windscreen.

'That was . . . good work,' Gecko called down in a voice that contained too much sheer panic for his liking. 'How did you do that?'

'Lots of cheerleader practice,' she shouted up. 'Banners, flags, pom-poms – you name it!' Despite her bantering tone, her face was white. 'Are you coming down, or are you going to stay up there all day?'

'I don't know,' he said. He felt as if his muscles were locked in place. 'Is it dead?'

Natalie glanced over to where the giant centipede had landed and burst sickeningly. Some of the priests and the worshippers were in the process of covering it up with the yellow silk banner.

'I really hope so,' she said, with feeling. 'If it's not, then I don't see what else we can do, apart from get hold of a rocket-launcher.'

'I'm sure Rhino could do that, if he felt it was necessary,' Gecko said, beginning the climb down.

Rhino raced through the market stalls, desperately trying to work out where Roxton and his friend had gone. He couldn't let them get to the giant centipede first. They might actually capture it, which in a sense would solve Rhino's immediate problem, but Nemor would then get the DNA, and Rhino had no idea whether or not Natalie and Gecko had retrieved any DNA from their own target creature. The people of

Hong Kong would be safe, but Calum Challenger's aim would have been thwarted. More likely was the possibility that Roxton and his friend would scare away the creature, and it would go to ground somewhere. That way it would be free to wreak havoc whenever it came out for food. And what if it was pregnant? Rhino had no idea about centipede biology – how *did* they reproduce? – but he knew he couldn't take the risk. He had to be the one who got to the giant centipede first.

He ran in the direction in which he'd seen Roxton heading, past the edges of the jade market and out into a less crowded surrounding market of stalls selling food, silk, mobile phones and fireworks. He was feeling lightheaded after the fight, and he was limping after that blow to the hip, but he had to keep moving. He had to.

Up ahead he saw blond hair. There weren't many blond Chinese, so it was highly likely to be either Roxton or his friend. He increased his speed.

Outside the final ring of stalls, in the shadows of the area beneath the blocks, he came upon a macabre sight. The scarlet and blue creature was halfway up one of the pillars, claws digging in hard to the concrete, head turned round to face Roxton and his companion, who were approaching it carefully. Roxton had a long rod with a grip on the end. Presumably he intended to catch the creature in the grip. His companion had a sack, which looked pitifully small compared with the size of the centipede.

The creature obviously had no intention of being

captured. Its head spun round to face Roxton's sidekick, and it seemed to spit a stream of venom across the distance between them. The man jerked backwards, hands clamped to his eyes, screaming.

Roxton looked down at him dismissively, then took a silenced pistol from inside his jacket and shot him. He scooped up the sack and approached the creature again, long-handled grip extended.

Rhino's first impulse was to let Roxton find out just how dangerous this thing was, but he feared that once the creature had incapacitated or killed Roxton it would vanish. There was a hole at the top of the pillar, and if the creature got up there it would be impossible to find.

Rhino looked around desperately.

Market stalls. Jade. Food. Silk. Nothing he could use.

Except . . .

He turned and rushed back past a stall where the holder was cooking soup in a tureen over an open flame and to the stall he'd seen selling fireworks. The Chinese had invented fireworks, and loved to use them on all occasions. Rhino grabbed a handful of rockets in cardboard tubes. The stall-holder tried to catch hold of his arm, but Rhino pushed him away. He bent down and scooped the cold end of a piece of burning wood from beneath the tureen as he ran past the food stall.

Up ahead of him, Roxton was facing the creature, and looking scared.

Rhino dumped all the rockets on the ground apart from

one. He held the wooden stick by the end and aimed it at the creature. He quickly inspected the firework. There was a hole in the tube, about halfway down, through which he could see the fuse. He lit the fuse with the burning wood, pointing the tube towards the giant centipede as it reared up and prepared to attack Roxton.

Holding lit fireworks is dangerous. Holding lit fireworks is *stupid*. He knew people had blown fingers and even whole hands off doing this, but he couldn't think of anything else to do. He had to kill that creature. Because he – or, rather, one of the kids he was meant to be looking after – had been responsible for releasing it.

The rocket *whished* out of the cardboard tube and away from him with a horizontal spray of golden sparks. He felt his hand burning as the sparks peppered it.

The rocket flashed a few inches away from Roxton's face. He screamed and clutched at his eyes, just like his friend had done, but for a different reason.

The centipede seemed to sense something. It scuttled upward, and the rocket hit the column just below where it hung, exploding in an expanding cloud of red, green, blue and yellow stars. Rhino's eyes were dazzled, but he could just see the centipede turn and head upward, towards the hole between the top of the column and the ceiling.

Rhino lit another rocket, and aimed high.

Another *whish!* as the rocket launched from the tube towards the giant centipede. More golden sparks. Rhino's hand was an agony of burning, blistered flesh. For a second he thought he had misjudged it, and the creature would be inside the hole before the rocket could get to it, but the rocket went in and exploded outward, blasting the centipede apart in glowing colours. Even at that distance, Rhino could smell something cooking. Bits of centipede fell to the ground, still burning.

Rhino looked around, cradling his injured hand. One or two people from the market were looking over in their direction, but mostly they were being ignored.

He walked across to where Roxton was writhing on the ground, holding his burnt eyes. He would collect the bits of giant centipede later, see if he could retrieve a chunk of unburned flesh, and then put the rest of it in the sack and burn it all, but first he had something to do.

'You never go anywhere unprepared,' he said to Roxton. 'Where's the first-aid kit?'

'My eyes!' Roxton moaned. 'I need help!'

'First-aid kit?' Rhino prompted.

'The man who got spat at by that damned creature,' Roxton said, seemingly forcing the words out, 'he has the first-aid kit. It's a pack on his belt.'

'Thanks,' Rhino said. He crossed to the other man, who was lying on the ground and twitching. He did, indeed, have a first-aid kit attached to his belt. Rhino unclipped it and walked away, opening it up as he went. There had to be a burn ointment in there somewhere.

'What are you doing?' Roxton screamed, hearing the footsteps moving away. 'I'm injured!'

'Yes,' Rhino said quietly, 'but I've hurt my hand, and that's *much* more important. I'll see you around, Craig.' He smiled as he walked. 'Although I'm not entirely sure you'll be seeing me.'

Despite the long time he'd spent in bed at the Robledo Mountains Technology establishment in Las Cruces, Calum slept for a good few hours aboard Gillian Livingstone's jet. The stress of the past few days had pushed him right to the edge, and he needed to recharge his physical and mental batteries. The last thought he had before he slid into welcome unconsciousness was to wonder whether the aircraft actually *belonged* to Gillian, or whether she'd hired it or borrowed it from some corporation that owed her a favour. However she'd got it, it was nice: small, with a main cabin that had eight comfortable chairs in it, and a full bathroom in the back.

Getting out of Nemor Incorporated's clutches was A Good Thing, but An Even Better Thing happened as they were leaving. Dr Kircher came up to Gillian's limousine, outside the Robledo Mountains Technology building, with a plastic crate just like the one that Gillian had brought to Calum's apartment days ago.

'Oh, more bionic legs,' Calum said without any noticeable enthusiasm. 'Just what I want.'

'These ones aren't controlled by your brain impulses,' Kircher said, obviously embarrassed and guilty, 'but they are the next best thing. There's a small hand-held controller that straps round your wrist and sits in the palm of your hand. You can use it to operate the legs – forward and back, up stairs and down, fast or slow.' He shrugged. 'There's obviously a design flaw in the brain-impulse software we tried to use. It's too vulnerable to interference from other equipment in the vicinity.' He frowned. 'Although we never tied down exactly what happened with the ARLENE robot to make it react like that. Anyway – take these as a form of apology. Things went too far – much further than I should have let them.'

'Thanks,' said Calum, genuinely touched. He knew that Kircher had just been a tool, and that Dave Pournell had been the man wielding the tool, but Pournell had already left after taking a long phone call from, presumably, his bosses during which he had said very little and listened a lot, mostly with a dark expression on his face. Based on the expression on *Gillian*'s face, the phone call had had something to do with her. Calum was surprised, and disturbed, at how far her influence extended.

But at least he managed to walk on to Gillian's aircraft, rather than being carried, using the new legs. That was a small victory of his own.

When he woke up from his deep, dreamless sleep, Gillian was sitting opposite him, staring at him. She looked . . . tired. Unhappy.

'How are you feeling?' she asked.

'Physically – a bit shaky,' he said. 'Mentally – what do you think?'

She nodded softly. 'You're wondering how deeply I'm

involved with Nemor, or how deeply they're involved with me.'

He said nothing, just staring at her until she looked away.

'I've done some work for them before,' she said. 'I've done work for a lot of companies. Nemor have fingers in a great many pies, and they've got a lot of influence in high places. It doesn't do to cross them.'

'But you did,' he pointed out.

'I had to. I honestly didn't know that they would go so far as to kidnap you and threaten you. I'd been asked by them to talk to you, see if you could be persuaded to release the Almasti DNA, but I didn't know they were going to take their own action.' She sighed. 'I'm sorry, Calum. I should have told you. I should have been honest.'

'Yes,' he said, but he was remembering how Gillian's daughter, Natalie, had been put into physical danger in Georgia, and how neither he nor Natalie had told Gillian the full story. Maybe there was fault on both sides.

'How did you find out I'd been kidnapped?' he asked. 'I sent you emails, but I didn't get any answer from you. Did you *get* my emails?'

Gillian looked away, out of one of the aircraft windows. 'I did,' she said slowly, 'and I was trying to get hold of someone high up in Nemor Inc., to find out what was going on. I only decided to take more direct action when Rhino phoned me from Hong Kong and told me exactly what had happened and where you were. He was . . . very persuasive.'

She closed her eyes for a long moment. 'He had seen me having a coffee with . . . someone from Nemor Incorporated, and he threatened to tell you, and Natalie. I decided that my relationship with the two of you is much more important than my business relationships.'

'Gillian, what's the story with Nemor Incorporated?' Calum asked. 'What do they *really* want?'

'That,' she said, 'is a simple question with a very complicated answer, and I don't think I can give you that answer right now. They've been around for a hundred years or more. They used to be known as the Paradol Corporation, and before that they were something else with "Paradol" in the title. They have a lot of influence, but nobody really knows what they want.'

'How long *have* you been working for them?'

'*With* them,' she pointed out. 'There is a difference.'

'OK – *with* them.'

She still wouldn't meet his gaze. 'Since before your parents died,' she said softly. 'Let's leave it at that.'

Calum closed his eyes. Gillian wasn't going to tell him anything else – not now, anyway. He would work on her, subtly, over time, and he would get more details. And, after that, he and Nemor Incorporated would be meeting again – but on *his* terms.

epilogue

Calum, Tara, Gecko, Natalie and Rhino were all in Calum's apartment. Most of them were sitting on his sofa or easy chairs, but Natalie was over at his nine-screen computer system. She had headphones on. Instead of listening to music she was talking in a low voice into the attached microphone.

'Were the DNA samples viable?' Rhino asked, pulling Calum's attention away from Natalie. Rhino's hand was bandaged, and he kept rubbing it on the arm of his chair. 'Could you actually get anything usable?'

'Well,' Calum said carefully, 'yours was pretty crispy, and the one Gecko and Natalie brought back was hammered fairly flat, but between the two of them I think we can put together a good sample. I still haven't decided where to send them though. Same with the Almasti DNA. I've got to make the right choice, and I've got to be very careful that Nemor Incorporated don't somehow own or control whatever laboratory I decide on.' He hunched his shoulders, feeling a chill. 'I'd assumed they would leave us alone after the Almasti adventure, but that's not the case. They're watching us carefully, and we need to take precautions.'

He glanced sideways to where Natalie was sitting at his computer system. He hadn't mentioned the involvement of her mother yet. He wasn't sure he ever would.

'What *is* she doing?' Tara asked, following his gaze.

Gecko frowned. 'I believe she is talking with this United Nations biologist that she first spoke to in Hong Kong – the one who joined in the raid on Xi Lang's warehouse. His name is Evan Chan. Apparently he is very impressed with her dedication to endangered wildlife, and she is very impressed with his clean-cut good looks and his ponytail.'

Calum felt a little knot of jealousy coil in his stomach, and tried to quash it. Natalie could talk to whomever she wanted. Obviously she could.

'Typical,' Tara sniffed, which pretty much summed up Calum's real thoughts.

'You can talk,' Rhino pointed out reasonably. 'How many texts have you and this Tom Karavla exchanged today?'

'I don't know,' Tara said primly, but she was blushing. 'I haven't been counting.'

Gecko was shifting in his seat, and the expression on his face made him look as if he was feeling the same way that Calum was. Before he could say anything Rhino asked, 'So what happens to the giant centipedes now? Not that I wish them well or anything, but I know you have strong feelings about not letting things like these be exposed to the world or abused by anyone like Nemor Incorporated.'

'We know the location in Hainan Island,' Calum pointed out, 'because it was on Xi Lang's removable hard drive.

Assuming that he's now either in custody or on the run, we're the only people who know the spot, and I want to keep it that way. Hainan Island is covered in tropical rainforest. It's unlikely that anyone will just stumble across the centipedes, so they should be OK, living their lives, eating monkeys or whatever it is that they do.'

There was silence for a few moments. Tara broke it by saying, 'So what next? Are we working our way through a list, or what?'

Calum thought. It was a good question. The website hadn't come up with anything recently, but there were always the standard legends to investigate – the Loch Ness Monster, the Sasquatch, the Chupacabra. It was unlikely there was any basis in fact there, but it wouldn't hurt to take a look.

Although . . .

'Have any of you ever heard of the mokèlé-mbèmbé . . . ?' he asked.

Planning this, the second book in the Lost Worlds series, I knew I wanted it to be quite different to the first book while still following the same general plan – which sounds like a contradiction in terms, and probably is.

There had to be a 'cryptid', of course – a creature that biologists have either not discovered and catalogued yet or think became extinct a long time ago. I'd used a tribe of Neanderthal-like primitive humans in the first book, so I knew I wanted something as *in*human as possible here. Giant centipedes did the trick for me. I *was* going to use giant millipedes (I had a large millipede crawl over my hand, once, and it's a curiously pleasant tickling sensation), but I found out pretty quickly that millipedes are vegetarian while centipedes are carnivorous. Writing a book about kids trying to find a vegetarian that tickles you when it walks across you struck me as being essentially self-defeating. Where's the drama? So I went for centipedes. They wriggle from side to side when they run, which makes them creepier than millipedes, who travel in a straight line. And they can be poisonous.

Millipedes don't have a thousand legs, by the way, despite their name. They have between 36 and 750 legs. Centipedes, you will not be surprised to learn, don't have a hundred legs – they have between 20 and 300, more or less. Yes, that's right, there are some centipedes that have more legs than some millipedes. Taxonomy (the naming of living creatures) is a funny thing.

And before anyone decides to write to me pointing out an obvious mistake – yes, I know that arthropods can't grow as large as the ones in this book. This is because they don't have lungs and depend instead on oxygen transfusing through their bodies from holes along their sides, and there is a limit to how fast the oxygen can transfuse that limits their size. They can't *evolve* lungs because they have hard exoskeletons, and there's no way they could inflate and deflate them to get air in and out. I'm imagining, for the sake of art, that a giant centipede might have evolved a mechanism where the side-to-side wriggling as it runs could act as a crude set of bellows, pumping air in and then pumping it out again. Hey, it's my book; I can do what I like.

Why Hong Kong as a background? Well, again, in the first book I had the primitive humans living in a very crude, no-tech cave village in the wilds of Eastern Europe. For contrast, I wanted this book to feature a much more high-tech, crowded environment. I've spent a couple of weeks in Hong Kong in the past, and the place fascinates me. The Star Ferries journey from Kowloon to Hong Kong Island is possibly my favourite journey in the entire world. I've taken certain liberties with geography and names – Tungking Mansions is actually a dirtied-down version of a real building – Chungking Mansions – and I've relocated the Jade Market from a dingy covered square to actually being inside the Mansions.

Why Las Cruces as another background? I've spent quite a lot of time in America, over the past thirty years, and New Mexico also fascinates me – partly because of the geography and partly because of the Mexican influences on the architecture and the food. Especially the food. I do like food. I once flew in to El Paso Airport and drove to Las Cruces, on my way to the White Sands Missile Range, past desert and mountain ranges and miles and miles of cattle in pens, and had a really good time there. I wanted to recapture the environment in prose. Not that Calum gets to see much of Las Cruces, but at least *I* know what's outside his window.

Out of interest, I was intending to set the last few chapters on Hainan Island, where Rhino, Natalie and Gecko would have had to confront a whole *nest* of giant centipedes, but that seemed like overkill. I could do everything I needed to in Hong Kong – and, ultimately, the book is about the people in it, not the creatures. That's my theory, anyway.

So – here we are. Calum, Natalie, Gecko and Tara have changed and developed a little (Rhino not so much) and the plot has thickened in interestingly unpredictable ways. And we have two new potential characters to think about – Evan Chan and Tom Karavla. How will they change the relationships within the group of friends? Will they be there in the next book? Will there even *be* a next book? Only time will tell.

I'm off now to work on the next Young Sherlock Holmes book, and some other projects that I have been thinking about. Hopefully I'll be able to talk to you again in a few months' time. I'm looking forward to it already.

Andrew Lane

acknowledgements

I would like to express my thanks, as ever, to a trio of remarkable people: my agent, Robert Kirby; my editor, Polly Nolan; and my publicist, Sally Oliphant (now departed for foreign places that, hopefully, *don't* have cryptids anywhere in the vicinity). I would also like to thank Octavia Karavla, of the wonderful Octavia's Books in Cirencester, for allowing me to use her name. There are lots of lovely Croatians, and she is one of them. Two of the three Croatians in this book are *not* so nice. Thanks also to Linda Wilson and Liz Watson, for reading and criticizing an early draft of the book, and thanks to the gentlemen I will call 'Mark' and 'Duncan' for, between them, providing the inspiration for the character of Rhino Gillis.

the author

Andrew Lane is the author of the bestselling Young Sherlock Holmes books. These have been published around the world and are available in thirty-seven different languages. Not only is he a lifelong fan of Arthur Conan Doyle's great detective, he is also an expert on the books and is the only children's writer endorsed by the Sherlock Holmes Conan Doyle estate. *Lost Worlds* is inspired by another famous Conan Doyle novel, *The Lost World*. Andrew's main character, Calum Challenger, is the grandson of Conan Doyle's protagonist, Professor George Edward Challenger.

Andrew writes other things too, including adult thrillers (under a pseudonym), TV adaptations (including *Doctor Who*) and non-fiction books (about things as wide-ranging as James Bond and Wallace & Gromit). He lives in Dorset with his wife and son and a vast collection of Sherlock Holmes books, the first of which he found in a jumble sale over forty years ago.

READ THEM ALL!

'What a blast. Weird murders, creepy villains, fiendish puzzles, non-stop action – what more could you want?' **Charlie Higson**

LOST WORLDS

ANDREW LANE

IN THE BLINK OF AN EYE, CALUM'S LIFE CHANGED. IN THE CLICK OF A MOUSE, IT WILL CHANGE AGAIN . . .

Partially paralysed in the crash that killed his parents, teenager Calum Challenger lives alone, searching the net for proof that 'extinct' creatures exist. He believes that, if they do, their DNA could cure him.

When something that looks like a yeti is spotted in the Georgian mountains, Calum springs into action – but so does a corporation called Nemor. Calum wants to harvest the creature's DNA and then protect it. Nemor wants to harvest its DNA and then kill it.

From his high-tech apartment, Calum uses cutting-edge technology to direct a group of misfit friends on a deadly chase in the harshest of environments. As danger mounts, fear starts to spread: can the team really trust the boy on whom they are dependent for survival? And how can they save a creature already on the brink of extinction?

Access Calum's secret website, play the Lost Worlds
game and unlock confidential information

WWW.THELOSTWORLDS.CO.UK

Use the hacker codes below to reveal top-secret website content:

◎ **EXCLUSIVE DELETED SCENES
FROM LOST WORLDS:** HIDDEN1

◎ **NEW INFORMATION ABOUT A
GIANT SCORPION:** SCORPION2

◎ **CLASSIFIED ARLENE INSTRUCTION
MANUAL:** ARLENE1

◎ **NEWLY DISCOVERED DIARY ENTRY
FROM CALUM'S GREAT-GRANDFATHER –
PROFESSOR CHALLENGER:** DIARY1

◎ **LEAKED CLASSIFIED DOCUMENTS FROM
NEMOR INCORPORATED:** NEMOR1

◎ **DOWNLOADABLE DESKTOP AND
MOBILE WALLPAPER:** LOSTART1

Carry out a full search of www.TheLostWorlds.co.uk
to reveal the content

HIGHLY SENSITIVE INFORMATION
– DO NOT PASS THIS ON